To Lorraine

It is because of you
that I have formed such
joy and laughter along my
journey ..... This book is dedicated
to you ..... for giving me so
much hope, love, support, friendship
and laughter.

Enjoy & Happy
Holiday 2001
love, Cindy

dykes

with baggage

dykes

with baggage

the
lighter
side
of
lesbians
in
therapy

edited by
riggin waugh

alyson books
los angeles | new york

MANUFACTURED IN THE UNITED STATES OF AMERICA.

THIS TRADE PAPERBACK ORIGINAL IS PUBLISHED BY
ALYSON PUBLICATIONS,
P.O. BOX 4371, LOS ANGELES, CA 90078-4371.
DISTRIBUTION IN THE UNITED KINGDOM BY
TURNAROUND PUBLISHER SERVICES LTD.,
UNIT 3, OLYMPIA TRADING ESTATE, COBURG ROAD, WOOD GREEN,
LONDON N22 6TZ ENGLAND.

FIRST EDITION: NOVEMBER 2000

00 01 02 03 04 **a** 10 9 8 7 6 5 4 3 2 1

ISBN: 1-55583-568-6

For my therapist, Lynn Bonde,
See you on Tuesday.
Love,
Six-thirty

Contents

Introduction

Therapy. Who needs it? Well, apparently lesbians need quite a bit of it. I can count on one hand the number of dykes I know who have never been in therapy (nobody I've known in the biblical sense, that's for sure). And it sure wouldn't hurt a few of those therapy virgins to spend a year or two on the couch. Let's face it—lesbians corner the market on therapy. We thrive on it.

In general, one might not think of therapy as a suitable topic for a humor collection. I mean, there's all that denial and crying and processing and crying and self-discovery and crying and self-acceptance and crying. What's so funny about that?

I've wanted to compile this anthology for a while now. I had written a couple pieces on auditioning therapists, and I figured if I was writing about dykes and therapy, then lots of others were probably writing about this staple of lesbian life as well. Fortunately for this book, I was right.

Aside from the counseling center my mother dragged me to in the early 1970s—when the most pressing of teenage problems were pregnancy, drugs, running away, and skipping school—my sister found my first therapist for me. That therapist was a lesbian. I wasn't...yet. That's right: I started seeing a lesbian shrink before I became a lesbian. When I told a friend (whom I'd known since seventh grade) that my therapist was a lesbian, she shook her head and asked, "Don't you think you should find someone who has her own head screwed on straight?" Now *that's* an interesting way to put it. I came out about a year later. That was 16 years ago.

I remember the stigma attached to therapy back then (not unlike the stigma attached to antidepressants today). I didn't want anyone to know I was seeing a shrink—especially my mother, who thought seeking therapy was a real sign of weakness. And now, dear readers, *all* of you know the truth. In fact, wouldn't you agree that those who *aren't* in therapy are the real misfits? Of course, all the dykes who keep insisting they don't need therapy usually end up telling their problems to *me*. After listening sympathetically, my stock answers are "Get some therapy" and "They have drugs for that." But do they listen?

I stayed with my first therapist for about eight years. I've been to a handful of therapists since then, but stayed with none longer than a few months—until I found my current therapist, my therapist for life. But you can read about her later.

I had three criteria for including work in this book. One, it had to be funny. Two, it had to be about lesbians. And three, it had to be about therapy—not just lesbians who need therapy, but some kind of actual therapy. The response was overwhelming.

So, what have I got for you? I've got stories and cartoons about selecting, interviewing, falling for, and dumping therapists. I've got psychotherapy, couples counseling, group therapy, self-help, employment-centered therapy, dream therapy, nutrition counseling, relaxation therapy, therapy for road rage, high school therapy, and court-ordered therapy. I've got good lesbian therapists, bad lesbian therapists, male therapists, straight therapists, crazy therapists, shrinks in recliners, shrinks in dog collars, shrinks in polyester, matchmaking therapists, shamans, diet counselors, naked therapists, and dead therapists. I'm hoping I've got something for everyone.

Many people helped me in my efforts to bring this book to fruition. It was Scott Brassart of Alyson Publications who initially approached me about doing this anthology after hearing me read two of my own therapy pieces at the 1998 Lambda Literary Foundation's Behind Our Masks conference. Angela Brown, also of

Alyson Publications, worked with me with patience, enthusiasm, flexibility, diplomacy, and great humor.

Irene Zahava, the queen of anthologies, was most generous with her wealth of knowledge. My beloved, Meredith Pond—whose continuing presence in my heart and home guarantees my therapist a job for life—provided help, support, and minimal grumbling about my late hours spent with my computer. Toni Armstrong Jr., publisher of the late and much-missed *HOT WIRE: The Journal of Women's Music and Culture*; Roz Warren, a true diva in the world of humor anthology editors; and Brandie Erisman of Funny that Way: A Gay Girl's Guide to Humor (www.funnythatway.com) all were incredibly helpful in identifying lesbian writers and cartoonists to contribute to this collection.

I also must thank my sister Nancy Waugh, Anne Garrett, Charles Duke of Chuck & Dave's Books in Takoma Park, Md., Ursula Roma, Michael Dunham, Richard McCann, Kate Clinton, Jennie McKnight, Mary Beth O'Connor, and Bernard Welt for nonsexual favors. And last, but never least, I'd like to thank my own therapist, Lynn Bonde, for her inspiration, her insights, her goddamned ethics (which I almost always admire), and her sliding scale.

So, that said, please relax—take your shoes off, lie down on your own couch, and read this book. Then buy a copy for everyone you know who's ever been in therapy or needed it. Why not buy one for your own therapist? Go ahead. Enjoy.

Riggin Waugh
Fall 2000

On Becoming a Woman
C.C. Carter

I'm not sure when it happened, but it was around the time when people stopped calling me cute. I had stopped shopping in the Misses department because the cut of a size 14 didn't become the new shape of my now-fuller 14 woman's hips. I put that thing back on the rack and ventured into the Plus Size Unlimited area. There I shamefully searched through racks of clothes that years previous-ly I'd sworn would be only for women like my mother. "1X" the tag said, and from the look of the garment that meant they had added extra material—an extra yard to give reason for the plus extra price. And what was with the flowers and sequins placed around the col-lar? And where were the darts and tapered waist? And who said that all full-figured women wanted to be seen in colors so loud and beaming so bright that ships could mistake us for lighthouses? I cried as I paid the sales clerk.

At home I had long since given up full-length mirrors that revealed soft flesh that used to adorn Venus Williams thighs, Gabrielle's flat stomach, and perfect Halle Berry breasts. A scale that made me the envy of all of my friends was now a stopper to keep the closet door from swinging shut. Videos of *Buns of Steel*, *Abs of Metal*, and *Thighs of Stone*, with little anorexic cheerleaders who didn't need any more exercise than I needed another bowl of ice cream while watching them, had now become bookends for my new collection of self-esteem enhancers.

It wasn't that I didn't care what I looked like; it's just that what I looked like wasn't becoming to me. My idea of perfection had been me at a size 8 in spandex and three-inch "come fuck me" pumps; compliments like "You are such a cutie," and "Damn, did you see that?"; and hot, fast sex that lasted for four hours and yet still left me saying, "Wait a minute, you aren't done yet, are you?"

My lover was telling me that I was the cutest little thing that she ever saw—she lying on her back and me draped across her like a mink. These days I felt that my thighs and my once-petite frame must feel like some Navy tank pinning her to the mattress. I was afraid to have sex for the mere reason that if I went into the uncontrollable throes of orgasm, my thighs could give her whiplash or, worse, become a guillotine and snap her neck in two. Many nights I lost sleep because while asleep I couldn't control how heavy I'd lie on her. All I needed was to try to explain to the cops that her asphyxiation was not done out of malice or for the insurance money but was indeed an accidental suffocation, caused by me rolling over.

I was constantly reminded of a trimmer me by pictures wallpapering my bedroom and hallways. And God knows that I dreaded affairs, because that meant nothing to wear, which meant shopping in the fat women's section again. The final insult to injury was when my high-cut brief panties started fitting like thongs. And control-top and body-shaping panty hose was now a necessity to keep everything in place so as not to be mistaken for Jell-O in my back pockets. This was the case even though I wasn't wearing spandex anymore. I resorted to wearing oversize shirts and knits, covering up my not-so-petite body—hoping people wouldn't notice I had become unbecoming to them.

I decided to go to a food counselor, a therapist for overeaters. I walked into the room hoping to find and be able to talk to someone who remotely understood what I was feeling. Instead I was confronted by an anatomically correct Barbie knockoff, whom in a million years I couldn't look like if I tried. But I stayed anyway to hear what her prescription and diagnosis would be.

First there was the food modification plan. Yeah, right. If I wanted to give $100 a week to people who told me what to eat, how to eat it, and when to eat, I would still be living at home with my mother and she'd be a rich woman by now. Besides, I have a partner who can't cook and who doesn't need to lose weight. How do we work around that?

Next plan: Find a person whose body type you admire and study her. Look at what she eats, what activities she does, her environment at home and work. This would be simple if I could have Janet Jackson's home number and call her to ask if I could spend the night to follow her nutrition and fitness routines. "And by the way, Janet, did I tell you I am a dyke?…Just kidding…No, for real, I am."

Third: Try creative visualization. For a couple of days while walking or driving down the street, notice women who are the size you'd like to be. Imagine your face on their bodies. The better you see yourself, the easier it will be to become motivated to do something about your weight problem. This I tried. I figured, what could it hurt? I'd join Women's Workout World—nothing but women's bodies there. Somebody would have to have the body I want. Didn't work. Nobody had the body I wanted—parts of the body, but not in whole. I would put my head on my step instructor's body, because she had these breasts that shook and wiggled every time she would U-turn, then hop up and over. The only problem was, I was more engrossed in her breasts than in the class and kept tripping over my step. I imagined my face on the body of my Tighten and Tone instructor, except my face wasn't placed on top of her neck. I took showers after class even though I never broke a sweat…from exercising, that is.

This wasn't working, so I went back. Mostly because Barbie had this premeditated innocence of seduction that was addicting. My partner didn't care because—let her tell it—my food therapist was the best sex therapist there was. I guess I was kind of worked up by the time I got home. Girl watching does something to you.

So finally Barbie suggested that I give myself permission to eat. The way she saw it was that I was a closeted eater. I immediately thought, *How'd she know?* But when she kept talking about it in reference to food, I figured she didn't know. So anyway my new assignment was to forgive myself for not having the courage to stick to any diets and for eating all the food on my plate. And the only way I could cure myself was to give myself permission to eat. Therefore, I was to go home, sit in front of the refrigerator, and eat whatever I wanted, whenever I wanted. The only thing I can say for that assignment was that I became the garbage disposal my dog could never be. I'd sit in front of the refrigerator, calling it "cleaning it out," the whole time saying, "I give myself permission to be thin," the whole time eating Tuesday's leftover Chinese food, Wednesday's chicken, Thursday's pizza, Friday's fried fish, and on Saturday all the food left over from what I cooked on Monday. The whole time the scale is tipping over the 220 mark, and my lover is now getting more and more concerned with my mental health than my physical self.

One day my lover asked me if I had ever stopped to look at myself in the mirror or to listen to what people were actually saying about me. Yeah, right, like I wanted to get my feelings hurt all the time. "Girrrrl, how do you get all that ass in them jeans?" Or "Do you know you got a biiig ass?" My response would be, "You know, I knew it was there when I went to sleep, but sometime between last night and this morning when I got dressed in the mirror I forgot. But thank you for reminding me."

But OK, one day I took my lover's advice and stopped to listen; I still couldn't look at myself in the mirror. Suddenly I began to notice older, mature men glancing at me with smiles: "Sorry I was staring, but you're very pretty." Women stepped aside as I entered parties, and not for the reasons I thought (God, they had to open a space so large because my hips wore a sign, PROCEED WITH CAUTION: WIDE LOAD APPROACHING). Instead I heard things like, "Who is that?" as people asked their friends about me. Those women who braved a response would approach me and strike up conversations, usually ending with compliments.

People greeted me with, "Hey, sexy," "Hello, gorgeous." I'd look around wondering who they were talking to because I still dressed in a face-only mirror and always wore oversize clothes. Yet my lover secretly began replacing my oversize shirts and knits with tailored classic suits and dresses from the Voluptuous Store. She made me stop seeing Barbie and decided that old-fashioned cash was a cure for a lot of things. So she took me shopping in the All Women's and Plus Some departments—buying me 14 wonderfuls, 16 wows, and those 1X special sizes. We even found a lingerie store for me that has now become my secret—not Victoria's. And now I wear meant-to-be thongs, bikinis, lace teddies, and bras that don't need miracles, because I have developed two of my own.

At night she spoons me from behind—wrapping her arms around my fullness and caressing softness that she swears feels better than the onetime muscle that kept her head smashed like a rock—putting her face in the folds of my back and cupping breasts, whispering, "Damn, you feel so good." She turns me over and slowly loves the woman I've become, feeling the maturity in my hips, which have spread because I'm now in peak breeding time. She wraps her arms around a waist that can pinch more than an inch but still indents to form an hourglass, telling the time that it needed to make me this woman. I've called my mother to thank her for not letting this apple roll too far from the tree.

Barbie called to see why I was missing my appointments. I told her I was seeing another therapist, called "self-esteem," and that my lover had introduced me to the concept. I did lose 20 pounds, but I was holding at 200 and not depressed if I didn't lose any more. I lost those 20 without dieting, without visualizing myself as someone else, and without forgiveness or permission for sins I never committed except to myself. The way I figure it is that I was more concerned about how people would react to me and my new weight after having been an aerobics teacher and thin for more than 25 years. The pressure was coming from me needing to look like Barbie and resenting women who already fit the mode.

The scale has been thrown away, and full-length mirrors unveil a picture of the woman in me. New pictures drape my walls showing me as a girl who happened to be cute—transitioning into pictures that reveal the inner beauty of the woman in me. Lately I've had to count my blessings, and I smile—because my womanness definitely becomes me.

Kris Kovick

MY IDEA OF HAVING A MALE SHRINK.

Therapy Pride
Lorrie Sprecher

Before leaving for the Gay Pride parade I said to my friends, "Listen, I have something to tell you. We might see my shrink there." And I thought, it's not enough I have to come out every day to straight people, now I have to come out to my lesbian friends as someone who's in therapy.

But my friends admitted they had lesbian shrinks too; they'd just forgotten to be paranoid about running into them. Now we were all nervous, except for my lover, who wasn't seeing a lesbian shrink.

"So between four people," I said, "we have three lesbian shrinks." And I wondered what that meant statistically or per capita or whatever way you take seemingly useless information and make it into something meaningful.

I worried they might have their own booth—you know, the lesbian shrink booth where they stand around comparing notes about us. I didn't know what was worse, the fantasy in which they were as obsessed with us as we were with them or the one in which they weren't.

We marched with ACT UP, the AIDS Coalition To Unleash Power, and I forgot to feel completely freaked out for about ten minutes while I chanted, "They say don't fuck. We say fuck you." I heard someone call my name from the curb and saw my shrink. She was wearing a dog collar and a blue denim jacket that smelled cool—because it had been drizzling—when she hugged me. I didn't want to let go of her.

When I jumped back in line one of my friends said, "*That's* your therapist? Oh, my God, does she dress like that for your appointments?"

"Sometimes she wears leather pants," I admitted, as though I'd done something right because my shrink was cooler than anybody else's.

"My friends all have a crush on you," I said, next session after Pride Day.

"What?"

"I said you were extremely professional and they wouldn't actually like you. I don't want everyone crowding in on your therapeutic act. I want to be the center of your attention."

"You told them I was your therapist?"

"Sure," I said, "I'm not ashamed of you. Come out of the shrink closet."

She laughed. "If I were really acting like a shrink, I wouldn't be out dressed like that."

"Bullshit," I said. "Just because I'm your patient, I don't go around acting healthy on the off-chance I'll run into you."

"Did it make you uncomfortable to see me?" my shrink asked, because she's totally obsessed with assessing the impact of everything on the therapeutic setting. She's so conscientious.

"No," I said. "It was actually nice to see you."

"Even though I know so much about you?"

"Well, I didn't think you'd follow us around all day telling everyone how fucked up I am. Just think," I said, "not too long ago you would have been classified as too fucked up to be my therapist. We could have gone to shock treatment and same-sex aversion classes together."

"So how does it make you feel to have a lesbian for a therapist?"

"How does it make you feel to have a patient who isn't into penis envy?" I asked.

The Good Doctor
G.L. Morrison

The phone call was like a practical joke. One of those jokes you make a cliché out of. How often do I remember having said, "I've used up so much sick leave, I'll have to call in dead."

"Your appointment for next week is canceled," the voice on the phone said. And I remember being pissed off. This had happened three times before in the two years I'd been in therapy with the good doctor. Once she had the flu. Once a dying grandmother. Both were irrefutable, unprovable excuses. Although I'm sure she was telling the truth. After all, sometimes the dog really does eat your homework, doesn't it? The third time she canceled our appointment (she preferred the word *rescheduled*, while I liked the sound of *hung out to dry and left twisting in the wind*), another client was to blame.

"A client emergency," she said.

What sort of emergency? Was the woman on fire while we spoke? Dangling from the ledge of her office building? Suing her for malpractice, for implanted memories of alien abductions? Was she standing beside the phone with a lawyer on one hand and a legal injunction—"You cannot practice therapy"—in the other?

Whatever the emergency was, it was resolved enough by the following week to not interfere with my next appointment. Dr. Goodman wouldn't talk about it. Something about privacy, ethics, you wouldn't want me to tell your mumble, mumble. But I wasn't satisfied. It seemed like whatever emergency that was happening in my hour, I was somehow involved in: I had a right to know. This vague dissatisfaction haunted me for months. If I saw someone in the waiting room during my therapeutic comings and goings, I gave them the most vicious stare. Was she the one? Was he? How dare they?

I had the same feeling after the phone call. Not grief or shock or fear or some predictable human emotion. (Is any human emotion predictable? I don't think so. I'm not sure Dr. Goodman would have agreed. But she's not here to ask.) I felt only deep dissatisfaction. Someone had disrupted my routine. Permanently. "Your appointment for next week is canceled," the voice on the phone said. "Dr. Goodman is dead."

It had all the qualities of a practical joke.

But if it was a joke, everyone was in on it. Dr. Goodman's office partner, her lover, the funeral director. I was invited to the funeral. I'm not sure how that happened. Did someone go through her address book? (Weren't doctors' records supposed to be confidential?) Did they invite all her clients, or was I on some sort of A-list of crazies? Had someone thought it was good therapy, help us to grieve and reconcile her death? *Yup, she's really dead. I'd better find another doctor.* Maybe it was a mistake. Maybe my address got mixed in with some personal papers and whoever made the funeral arrangements didn't want any friend overlooked. It could have happened that way. Dr. Goodman didn't seem all that organized. What is more disorganized than dying?

Services were held in the chapel of the funeral home. The windows were painted to look like stained glass. The room had the look of a warehouse-turned-cathedral. Like a Catholic Wal-Mart. Was Dr. Goodman religious? I'd never thought to ask her. I suppose I wouldn't have been surprised if the service was conducted by a coven of naked witches who threw Dr. Goodman's body onto a funeral pyre during the eulogy. Spiritual practices in the lesbian community are very diverse. It's surprising how little I knew about the good doctor. A nude sabbat (or, in fact, anything much showier than this subdued gathering) would have surprised me, I admitted to myself. Dr. Goodman never appeared that diverse to me. What did I know about her? She was Mother Jones on the outside (grandmotherly feminist), Freud on the inside. She had an expression that said *I ask the questions here.*

But that wasn't the reason I didn't know much about her. I wasn't in therapy to hear about anybody but myself. I had made mental notes of whenever she nodded in agreement during a story I told. I would assume that she had found something we had in common. How many of the people at this service were her clients? Did she have something in common with all of them?

A somber usher escorted me to a folding chair. I watched the serious, black-suited young man deposit mourners on the left or right aisle. I wondered if there was some order, like at weddings. Cousins to the right. Business associates to the left. Are there usually ushers at funerals? I don't remember seeing any before. Not that I'm an aficionado of funerals. Was the brooding usher an employee of the funeral home? Did they also rent weeping mourners for the funerals of the friendless? Was he Dr. Goodman's son or a favorite nephew? The boy who mowed her lawn? Should I have offered him my condolences?

Or perhaps ushers are specific to therapist funerals, and they were organizing us by disorders: Don't mix the paranoid-schizophrenics with the eating disorders. Or perhaps he had appointed himself usher. Couldn't he have been an obsessive-compulsive client, organizing us in whatever way suited his uneasy mind, the same way that he might line up cans of soup in the cupboard, alphabetically, label turned out?

In the front row someone was weeping. I recognized her as the ex-lover. I had seen her, sometimes, when I was the last appointment and she was waiting impatiently to take the good doctor home. I remember when she became the ex. Not because Dr. Goodman talked about her personal life. She didn't. I remember when the picture on the desk disappeared. I could surmise a lot about Dr. Goodman by the pictures that appeared and disappeared from her desk. Different women. The same frame. Personally, I wouldn't have gone to her for couples counseling. She seemed to have little practical (successful) experience.

The current "Mrs. Goodman" also sat in the front row, dry-eyed—several chairs and little love between her and the sobbing ex. I scanned the audience for other women I might recognize from their pictures. Before I left I was sure to offer them both profuse condolences. The sad ex grabbed my coat sleeve. Her fingers pressed into my arm.

"Thank you," she said. She said it like a question. I didn't know the answer. I reached in my pocket, searching for a Kleenex, a napkin, something I could give her in lieu of an answer; something to appease her so I could get away. My hand fell on a slip of paper. It was a receipt. A receipt Dr. Goodman had written me, I don't remember when. *I should throw it away. I should throw it away.* I folded it carefully back into my pocket. I took her hand off my arm. I kissed her empty hand. She looked at me in relieved surprise.

I followed the stream of mostly black cars to the cemetery. Were they all rented or did clinically depressed people buy black cars? Clouds followed us at the same funereal speed. We stood around the hole. Someone was saying something, reciting poetry I think. He was unused to public speaking. I could barely hear him. He threw in a handful of dirt. The clouds broke. The rain came down so hard it hurt. Flowers bent under its weight. We ran for our cars.

Jane Caminos

As Liz awaited Meg's return, late again, from the office,
she began to suspect why her therapist was recommending anti-depressants.

Jung and the Restless
Meredith Pond

As we trudge up the asphalt driveway lined with wilting daffodils and drifts of cedar mulch, I start humming a Broadway tune, something from *Les Miserables*. You know, music to walk to the guillotine by. In my heart I'm kicking and screaming all the way. This is the clincher. The last nail hammered in that proverbial coffin of love, the end of the vampire within. No more making love all night and sleeping all day. I'm being dragged to couple's therapy two days after a root canal. I'll bet this isn't going to hurt a bit either.

My almost-ex girlfriend—let's call her Zee, because she's at the bottom of my alphabet soup right now—slithered home from her last therapy session and suggested couple's counseling, but she didn't offer many details. We weren't talking all that much back then—last week.

At the door Zee knows the drill. This session makes five times total for her. She knows the key is in the chickadee's belly next to the birdbath. I assume giving clients access to the house key is an exercise in trust, but if you ask me, it's downright dangerous. The French doors are ornate, maybe imported or from New Jersey, which if I remember correctly is the only state where a woman can still buy '60s-style sconces for her living room walls. But the door sticks and then squeals open like the jail cell at the Mayberry sheriff's office. You need to know this about me: I'm confessing right off the bat to my addiction to Nick at Nite. But that's not why Zee and I are breaking up.

She admits to an uncontrollable crush at work. The woman in question is a friend of ours (not), a younger woman, Zee's editor for a women's health newsletter. (Hey, delete *this*, frog fanny.) As you can tell, I am still in the throes of disbelief. Unless this therapist can stop the forward motion toward disaster, Zee and I are finished.

Inside there's an overhead light blaring even though it's way before sunset. Who's afraid of dykes in the dark? Zee opens the closet door (metaphor alert!) and hangs up her jean jacket. When I go to hang up mine, I'm eye to eye with the framed photo of a woman who looks like Susan B. Anthony attempting to crack a smile. And right next to her is a mirror of the same frame size and style. I still have that cowlick even though I just got a haircut, and I'm getting a zit on my chin. Who hangs pictures in an otherwise empty closet? I hope this woman doesn't spend too much time in here. Nothing like our hall closet, crammed with boots and games and mittens and parkas and old skis and the landlord's vacuum cleaner. But I suspect what is going on here. The therapist is throwing me a mental curve ball. Messing with my head in advance of the session. Maybe I'm too judgmental, too resistant to new ideas, unaccepting of change, a complete moron, or, call me crazy, I just never thought of hanging pictures in a closet. Or, hey, maybe I think too much. That is a monstrous possibility.

Zee is fishing through her backpack and pulls out her checkbook. She's paying because *she* is the reason we are here. She's the one who fell in love with somebody else. Now I understand those little lemmings a whole lot better. Everybody's running, running to that cliff, and it's kind of hard to stop and say, "Hey, we don't have to do this." It's a law of physics. An object in motion remains in motion. Cliff or not. Sure, they all might slow down and listen to you for a minute, but pretty soon the magnetic pull toward that cliff calls them like Scylla and Charybdis called those sailors in ancient Greece to jagged rocks and wave-crashing death.

Some people say I exaggerate. I wish they would shut up.

"Don't you pay her *after* the session?" I ask Zee.

"No, Madeline, I have to write it out now," she says, "before we start. And put it here, like this." She lines up the check with the upper-right-hand edge of the end table on her side of the love seat. "Exact-ly like this-s." She elongates her words, pulling them like bubble gum way out of her mouth.

The check lies there, and we both stare at it. It's Annie Hall's dead shark all over again. A wee bit anal herself, Zee seems to enjoy this little ritual, kind of like Mr. Rogers in the wrong neighborhood. I hope we don't have to change into ratty old sweaters.

I'm trying to quiet down, avoid obsessing, but I'm reading meaning into everything. The check on the "end" table. The "blue" lamp. I hope it's polyethylene retro chic, not, you know, a sign of depression.

So here we are parked like stuffed animals at either end of the love seat in total silence. No clock ticking. No background music. No white noise of any kind. Even though the couch is small, we are not touching. I listen hard for the sound of my breathing, but I hear nothing. I could be hyperventilating, and I wouldn't even know it. The silence is thick, pressurized. I think I'm on my way to a real anxiety attack. And I've never had one before. I put my hand over the SILENCE=DEATH button on my vest. My heart is racing. Everybody knows that silence makes queers nervous. That's why we never shut up.

I think I hear a washing machine. This is worse than a root canal, worse than the gynecologist. All probing and pushing and asking a lot of questions. Now it's my brain that's getting poked at. "I'm leaving." I blurt out to Zee.

"Mad, you promised." Zee is diplomatic but does not look up.

Her backpack is on her lap, a little desk in the middle of all this chaos. The couch is uncomfortable, prickly and itchy right through my chinos. I've decided not to call it a love seat anymore, especially now that I might be breaking out in hives. The hand that gripped the armrest moments ago is now itching like crazy. Like crazy. Oh, Patsy Cline, I'm feeling so lonely. Blue. Like the lamp. But not depressed. Not depressed. I am overcome by the psychic messages this therapist is sending in here like a hoard of winged monkeys. We are only a few minutes early, and already I'm getting hysterical. I'm trying to relax. Looking for a magazine, anything to look at. There's nothing anywhere. Nothing on the coffee table, nothing in the magazine rack, nothing anywhere. I am having an existential crisis.

"It's creepy in here," I say in my littlest voice.

No response. Zee is balancing her checkbook with the calm of a Buddhist monk with a Swiss bank account.

"This is…a garage," I say.

Zee lets out a big sigh. "It's completely remodeled."

"Indoor-outdoor carpeting," I whisper. "And there's no way in here. Where's the door?"

Zee points to a blue door across the room and up two or three steps. "There. From inside the house."

"Have you ever been in there?" I ask.

She rolls her eyes. "Of course not. June comes in that door and sits in *that* chair." Impatience is a big Zee virtue.

An empty straight-backed chair, oak framed, with a cane seat, is set out right in front of us. I hate those chairs. They are so uncomfortable. The legs poke through the corners of the cane loops and dig into the back of my thighs. I hate that. This woman is too tidy, and she likes uncomfortable chairs. What kind of a dyke is she?

"She told you she *is* a lesbian, right?"

"Yesss," Zee hisses as she resets her calculator and erases the penciled-in numbers in the check register. She gives me "the look," an icy sideways glance that says, *Get over it.*

"Hey, pardon me for asking. Please admit this place is a little weird," I say, holding up my hands in front of me like I'm about to catch a basketball. "I mean, gee, I wonder why I never thought about hanging pictures in the closet...or using AstroTurf for carpeting in a place where I charge $100 to come in."

"Maybe if you didn't have so much junk, it might make sense to you," Zee fires back.

"Whoa there. Uncalled for. OK, let's talk about closets. Two can play this game." I move over a little farther away from her.

"Your sarcasm is not cool," Zee barks.

I'm ready for this one. Deep breath. "Neither is cheating."

"I never had sex with that woman!" Zee shouts.

"Oh great, let's start quoting the president now." I win. "Hey, if you weren't a commie leftist dyke, you could join the Republicans."

Zee squirms and tries for a quick retort. She's just not fast on the draw, though. I'll report this to Ms. Therapist as soon as she comes in. I want to tell on my girlfriend. She is bad. I'm not the only one who is messy. I couldn't imagine making a mess like she has made. Of our lives. A total mess.

I'm not done yet. "I'll bet you think this couch is comfortable, too." My sarcastic tone, right. I can see her redden around the ears.

"What's wrong with the goddamn couch?"

"Nothing. Nothing at all." My arms tighten across my chest. "I love picky and itchy. Or is that itchy and scratchy. Really, I would not want to be anyplace else right now."

Zee takes in a breath to think a minute before she snaps back, but she stops herself and returns to her calculator. I know there's not that much to figure out. This is simple math. We are fucked, pure and simple, in all the wrong ways.

Here I am parked on this scratchy couch in an ex-garage staring at an empty straight-backed chair with a woman who I used to love more than soap, who seems less and less bubbly and more and more slippery and slimy every second. Maybe I'm supposed to make a wish and the therapist will appear, like my fairy godmother or the wicked witch of the east, and we'll throw her in the oven and eat her for supper, and my girlfriend and I will get to go to the Mautner Ball after all! And at midnight that other woman will turn into a rotting pumpkin!

It feels like we've been here for hours. OK, now I'm exaggerating. We were ten minutes early. The silence is spongy, damp, like the inside of a terrarium. Maybe the therapist keeps lesbians like little hermit crabs, moving them from one relationship to another like changing shells. *Excuse me, I'd like a little more space this time around.* The silence pulls at my secrets, scrubs at my surfaces to get to the real nitty-gritty grunge underneath. OK, let's face it, I'm not happy. And I'm not feeling too good about myself right now. And meditating on an empty chair is not helping. People say I read too much into things. So what if I'm thinking the chair, the empty chair, is a metaphor for the kind of person this therapist is—plain, uncomfortable, Spartan, no frills, very little padding. No arms. *Arrgh.* I do need a therapist. She'll probably ask what kind of chair I would be, if I were a chair. And my well-worn, forest green velvet overstuffed armchair with the ottoman is hardly a match for her ascetic, let's-stick-to-business perch.

Zee is frowning, preparing words of wisdom, I'm sure, when that blue door swings open and in swoops…June Cleaver? Am I in a time warp? Is this a joke? This woman looks like the Beaver's mother! Polka-dot shirtwaist dress, bangs, and all. Looking like she just jumped off the Tidy Bowl cyclone, she gives us one huge smile, grinning from ear to ear. Zee is in therapy on Nick at Nite! I'll bet this woman has a crinoline under that dress.

"You must be Mad," she says, breathless, as she extends her hand.

I grin like an idiot. "Yup, that's me." I'm good at handshakes. Definitive and polite.

She notices me staring. "After the session I'm going to a '50s party. I'm—guess who—the Beaver's mother. Just for fun. I hope the outfit won't be too distracting."

"It's convincing," I say. This is home turf for me. Maybe she watches *I Love Lucy* too.

She circles the chair before sitting down like a puppy dog settling into a perfect spot. I can see what her perfect spot is. She leans back a little until her spine touches the back of the chair; then she places both her hands on the tops of her thighs. Fingers touch and point right at us.

Leaning forward, taking a deep breath, she focuses one eye on each of us and says, "So how are we today?" A black hole opens in the middle of the love seat. I look over at Zee and notice her hands are on top of her thighs too, fingers pointing forward. Zee stares down intently as if the answers to the universe, or at least her current situation, are tattooed on her knuckles in tiny print.

I pipe up with the facts. "Well, we are still on the verge of not being a 'we' anymore."

June nods. "Describe what's been going on in the last few days, would you please?" Her voice is wispy, youthful, a little high-pitched and breathless, like Jackie Kennedy or Truman Capote. I'm guessing she's about 50. A good collection of laugh lines. She mouths her words with care as if I need to read her red lips too.

I begin the tale. Lover ignores warnings about how dyke at work seems to be madly in love with her. Lover admits to crush (on cheap stenographer). Ruins my birthday with announcement after I make love to her. And blither blither blah blah, can I have a tissue, please? All the time the familiar story rushes out of my mouth, I watch June and think how much she reminded me of Miss Owlette, a substitute in tenth-grade geometry who made the unfortunate decision to enhance her nerdy looks with excesses of red lipstick applied in a manic sort of way, overlapping the edges of her lips so she looked like someone who had just escaped from an orgy of strawberries. June's lipstick is applied well, it's the color. A wild red. A color I am wondering if I will ever feel in my heart again. So I finish the story of Zee's restlessness, her erratic absences, my rages, my moving out of our bedroom and into my office, her staying out later and later with that woman, and how Zee and I decided to stay just friends and how that idea is a failure because I still love her.

"But how do you really feel?" June asks.

"Like an idiot," I reply. "Just like radio therapy or *Divorce Court* on TV." I'm thinking of Miss Owlette again. We tortured her unmercifully in that class, so sure we were cooler than she was. She had the same tight ringlets as June. I wonder if June used spoolies to get that tight '50s curl and what store she went to find them. McCrory's?

"You didn't do anything wrong," June says. I can feel her trying to look at me, but I am looking at my own knuckles now. White as the whipped cream I will never slather on another woman again.

"I'm thinking I didn't do much right." I look up for a moment and then avert my eyes again.

"Sometimes the shadow side takes over," she explains as if we are there for a Psych 101 review. "Jung talks a lot about this in his writings. It's the dark side. The secrets we keep from each other." The rest of her words blur over me like a flock of tiny birds. I am floating in a neverland of turquoise and tigers, the Bay of Bengal. Anywhere but here. "Sometimes we do things or let things happen that we don't really mean to. We are all afraid of our dark side." She nods, agreeing with herself.

And I'm Darth Vader, lost in space with June Cleaver and the lover from hell who just got dragged, unrepentant, from a make-out fest with her new squeeze in the netherworld parking lot of a downtown Denny's.

"What I'm saying is," June shifts in her chair, moves closer. "Sometimes we do things, bad things, that hurt other people, and we just can't stop ourselves."

I understand her. "Like lemmings."

"Who? Lemons?" June seems off balance for a minute, then she catches up with me. "Ah." She nods. "Lemmings. Following the wrong idea to its ultimate, literal, pathetic, and unfulfilled ending."

"I'm sorry," Zee blurts out, leaping out of her silent slump. "I'm so sorry. I feel...so restless." She starts to cry into her cupped hands as if catching the tears might stop all this from getting any worse.

We are finished. The graffiti is on the wall in red. I am sailing over the cliff with the other little fuzzy rodent-lesbians, and June Cleaver is leading the way reciting Jung and trying to help us make peace with our shadows. *Sew them back on. Wendy. Wendy. Wendy. Help us, we can't fly anymore.* In case you are wondering, *darling*, I am not Peter Pan. But we are surely careening toward Never-Never Land. As my mother used to say, We're going to hell in a handbasket. Believe me, I can tell.

Zee finds her way to the tissue box and honks her brains out like a goose. What a noise. So endearing, just like a little kid. June stands, pivots, and the blue door swings again. "Time is up for today. Talk to each other. See you next week."

Later that night Zee and I talk about how this must be the way Neanderthals lived. I mean it's all about sex, isn't it? Dragging women off by the hair. Taking them hard in the bushes. Humping in the shadows in the back of that prehistoric cave or in a dark corner of the Bob's Big Boy parking lot. Because there's no place else to go if you're too cheap or too scared to be seen at a local motel. Because your real girlfriend, who you've been living with for five years, is home putting away your socks and your cocks and two years' worth of laundry detergent you bought together this morning on sale at your favorite discount store.

We laugh about how all the soap we bought together will last way into the new millennium, but we had no idea that our relationship would collapse long before that, going the way of 5¼-inch floppy disks and unprotected sex. Into oblivion, swallowed by another kind of lesbian bed death: one with ten too many fingers under the covers playing with your lover's clit.

We see June three more times, but the pull to the cliffs is too strong at this point, and we run and tumble over the edge into the canyon of doomed lesbian love until I meet another woman, reclaim my shadow, and start this all over again. But that's another story.

My Therapist—I Think I'll Keep Her
Riggin Waugh

I'm perusing the health insurance company catalog in search of a therapist, but the listings don't label which ones are lesbians. I call the insurance company and tell the nice man on the other end of the line what I'm looking for.

"Well," he says, "the directory doesn't identify the sexual orientation of counselors. However, specialties are listed under each name, and many specialize in gay and lesbian issues."

*Specialize in gay and lesbian issues...*What the fuck does that mean? I'm thinking somebody just wants a piece of the queer pie.

"Do you have any who specialize in gay/lesbian issues *and* anxiety disorders?" I ask.

He says there are ten.

"OK, how about gay/lesbian issues, anxiety, *and* hopelessness and despair?"

"Do you mean depression?"

"Oh, no," I insist, "I'm not depressed."

We narrow it down to three female psychotherapists within ten miles of my house. Over the telephone I ask each if she's a lesbian. None are, though I find it curious that two seem reluctant to admit they're not. I decide to stop fucking around, and I call a shrink who's not in the insurance company book. Of course, without health insurance kicking in, I'll have to fire my cleaning boys to afford it. But we do what we have to do. Perhaps the most attractive thing about this prospective therapist is that she comes highly recommended by two lesbian friends, neither of whom is a nutcase or an ex-lover of mine. Plus she has a sliding scale. Bingo.

Although this shrink generally sees clients at a counseling center in Washington for people affected by illness, loss, and grief, she also sees people one night a week at her home, which is in my neighborhood. She has an office in her basement. At our first session I ask this woman, who may become the keeper of my secrets as well as the key to my psyche, if she's a lesbian.

She asks if that's important to me.

I say it is.

She says she was married twice to men, she wouldn't do it again, and she identifies as lesbian. Besides, I feel comfortable talking to her. She passes the audition.

At a party the weekend after my first appointment I ask a friend if she knows my new therapist, because I know they've both volunteered with a project for lesbians with cancer. My friend says they dated a few times years ago. More brownie points for the shrink, because this friend is smart and funny and charming but not someone to whom I confide my deepest secrets. I don't need to know anything more about my new therapist's personal life. I don't even *want* to know more. This is *so* unlike me.

During the first few months, I train my therapist well. When I arrive for my 6:30 appointment she is sitting in her black leather therapist's chair. Like the nice man who does the radio ads for Motel 6—"We'll leave the light on for you"—she pretends she has not moved since my last session. At my request, we dispense with our given names. I call her "My Therapist"; she calls me "Six-Thirty." This seems to work for both of us. (The fact that she shares the same first name as my most recent ex-lover plays no part in this whatsoever.)

After several sessions I come home and rattle on to my lover about how perceptive my therapist is, how wonderful, how brilliant, after she has offered some particularly insightful...well, *insights*. My therapist sees patterns in my "issues" to which I have been totally oblivious.

"My therapist is so smart," I tell my lover.

"Is it that she's so smart—or that you're so easy to figure out?"

"I hate you. You know that, right?"

My lover laughs.

Six months into therapy, I'm leaving for the MichiGYN Womyn's Music Festival for the first time—which is a whole 'nother story, because I'm a big femme with a fondness for flush toilets and other creature comforts. But my lover goes every year, so I'm going too (as a worker bee, no less), because I couldn't think of a good excuse fast enough, except that I'm a big femme with a fondness for flush toilets....

My therapist and I discuss my anxiety over this trip. At the end of our session as I'm signing my check, she informs me that her breast cancer has returned after seven years and that she is having a double mastectomy in a couple months. Cancer killed both my parents and one of my best friends. Even though I think I know better, cancer means death to me. My therapist downplays the seriousness. Her HMO is authorizing only one night in the hospital for a mastectomy. My shrink says perhaps she will lie down in her driveway and let someone roll a lawnmower back and forth over her chest.

Noticing the tears in my eyes, she assures me the cancer will not kill her.

I blow my nose. "How could you do this to me?"

She knows I'm not really thinking about myself because, like all good therapists, she's somewhat psychic. Still, she apologizes for her carelessness. I am no longer anxious about Michigan.

The next morning I receive this E-mail:

```
Dear Six-Thirty,
Have a glorious time in Michigan. Learn to love sleeping
on the ground. I will not move until you come back. And
I will be fine. Really.
Your Therapist
```

While she is in the hospital (the insurance company ends up letting her stay two nights) I type up a complete list of my private video collection, from *All About Eve* to *Zorro, the Gay Blade*. I figure I can bring her movies during her recovery. Not only do I list their titles, but other pertinent information as well. For example:

❏ *Bound*—1996, color, 108 minutes (Jennifer Tilly, Gina
   Gershon)
❏ *The Children's Hour*—1961, color, 107 minutes (Audrey
   Hepburn, Shirley MacLaine)
❏ *Desert Hearts*—1986, color, 96 minutes (Helen Shaver,
   Patricia Charbonneau)

I have about 350 movies. My list is nearly ten pages long, single-spaced. What a time for me to become anal-retentive—when my shrink is out of commission. Soon after she comes home from the hospital she sends me an E-mail assuring me that she is healing well, should be back to her therapist duties within two weeks, is checking E-mail every few days, and is always available by phone. I ask her if I can bring her anything. I know she has lots of friends, and I don't want to step over any therapist–client lines, but I want to do something for her—anything. She says I can come visit. I take her a get-well card and a book and cassette tape and my list of movies. My therapist and I share a love of movies. Sometimes when I'm not up to talking about hard stuff I can get her talking about movies for at least five minutes. Especially once the nominations are announced for the Academy Awards—the queer Super Bowl.

This is the first time I've seen her living room—I've only seen her basement—or her in a bathrobe. She looks much better, healthier, than I expected, and I start to believe that she really will be OK. I stay maybe 15 minutes so as not to wear out my welcome. After our visit I receive another E-mail:

```
Dear Six-Thirty,
Your list is A TREASURE! I am struck by the number of
animated movies you have listed. Is this something we
should work on in therapy? Also, I am a little concerned
that your message was timed at something like 3:30 in the
morning...Are you getting enough sleep?
Your Therapist
```

I feel good. My shrink looks well. Her chemotherapy is finally over, and her bald head is beginning to sprout tiny fuzz. I ask if I can touch it. It is very soft. I notice a small tattoo of a rose on the base of her skull, which her hair always covered before—unless she got it in the weeks since her surgery.

"Wow, did that hurt?" I ask with admiration.

"Not at all."

It's a rub-on.

I give my shrink all my good news of the week. First I received some unexpected money, which will cover my graduate school tuition. Then, without even trying, I lined up a great part-time summer job. Then I signed a book contract to do an anthology on lesbians and therapy for *the* biggest gay/lesbian publisher in the world. And my lover and I made love this morning. Life is good.

"What about your conundrum?" my therapist asks.

"Excuse me?" I instinctively tighten my pelvic muscles—you

know, Kegel exercises, so I will never have to depend on Depends.
"What conundrum?"

"Your lover. Is she moving back in?"

It's a long story, but eight months after my lover first moved in,
she moved back out because she "needed more space." We didn't
break up. She didn't want space to date others, just space to go
through her shit—papers, books, her kids' art projects from the past
20 years. She wanted to "get organized." *My lover needed more space,
so I locked her outside.*

The day my lover brought the U-Haul to move out (a lesbian
joke gone awry) my therapist was on vacation. Realizing a little
self-help was in order, I left the house to pursue a bit of "acquisition
therapy"—otherwise known as shopping. But not just any shopping. For instance, you can't go to the grocery store for acquisition
therapy, unless you spend the whole 50 minutes in the bakery
department. Acquisition therapy is about buying stuff you don't
need that makes you feel better. My friend Rickey is an inspiration.
Once he called me from Miami after he'd been on a spree—I mean
session. Wearing Gianni Versace from head to toe, he proceeded to
give me an audio fashion show: And here's Rickey, coming down
the runway wearing a $600 pair of tight black jeans (liposuction
scheduled for the following Monday), a $1,600 yellow silk shirt, a
$580 black leather belt, a $3,000 black leather bomber jacket with
fur collar, and a $300 pair of red underwear with the Versace lion-
head logo in a strategic position. And on his feet, an $800 pair of
Salvatore Ferragamo shoes. Boy, was he hurting.

So on this day my own acquisition therapy is limited by my
meager bank account, but still I buy myself a spider pin made of
silver and amber, two novels, a blouse that's hand-washable (I'll
wear that once), and a harmonica just in case I ever want to learn
to play the blues. At each store I chat with the shopkeepers as if
my lover isn't moving out as we speak. (Then I stop by the house

of a friend with a hot tub, which has absolutely nothing to do with acquisition therapy, but self-help is self-help). Acquisition therapy is self-help at its best. Unfortunately, although it's more fun than psychotherapy, it costs a lot more.

So after the U-Haul drives away, my lover housesits for her friend Goddamn Pam for a year and a half. Now that gig is ending, and we're talking about living together again—talking about it again and again and again. And I'm talking about it just as much with my therapist.

"Oh, *that* conundrum." I relax my vaginal muscles. "We haven't decided yet."

My therapist lives across the street from a well-known lesbian photographer. On my way out after therapy I mention that on my way in I saw this woman sitting on her porch and we'd chatted a minute. Knowing how private a person I am, my therapist asks, "How was that for you—her knowing you see me?"

"No problem," I assure her. "No problem at all."

My therapist raises one eyebrow. I can tell she's impressed (but a bit surprised) by this new display of self-esteem. Maybe I *don't* need therapy anymore.

I put on my jacket and walk out the door. I stick my head back in. "My Therapist?"

"Yes, Six-Thirty?"

"I told her you and I are dating."

She smiles. "Ahhh. Something to talk about next week."

When my shrink talks about things I don't want to talk about, I keep looking at my watch. I let her know she's making my head hurt.

"Just tell me what to do," I say, getting frustrated with trying to figure things out myself. "I'm not paying for self-help here."

She laughs but offers no immediate solutions.

When I forget my watch I have to turn my head sharply to the left to see the clock on the wall. I suggest that she hang the clock on the wall behind her—above her right shoulder. But perhaps she thinks it's more important for *her* to see the clock. Therapists.

"Well, I think that's all the time we have for today." I say, pulling out my checkbook.

A year after my therapist's surgery I end up in the hospital myself. Fortunately, my lover *did* move back in, so when I pass out, she's there to catch my head before it hits the floor. I languish on our leopard-print sheets waiting for the paramedics. Never short on charm, I ask my lover to find some refreshments for the five nice young people surrounding our bed. I lose half the blood in my body, am rushed to the hospital in an ambulance, and receive four transfusions before having an emergency hysterectomy—I get spayed.

After I come home from the hospital my therapist offers to make a house call because I can't drive for a couple weeks. She says I can let her know, even up to the moment she's standing on my doorstep, if I don't feel well enough to do it. We have our session in my living room accompanied by my two dogs, Diesel and Scoutie. Mostly I'm concerned that my recovery is making me miss the first two weeks of my third semester. Supportive of my decision the year before to "retire" from the corporate world and go to graduate school full-time, my therapist quashed my fears that I would end up penniless and eating cat food out of a can.

This is one of many reasons why my shrink is up on a pedestal with my poetry mentor, Myra, and my friend Sue. In my eyes, the three of them can do no wrong. (Sue's lover, Judith, thinks she should be on the pedestal too, but Judith doesn't realize that Sue is up there precisely *because* she is Judith's lover. Please don't tell her. Besides, Judith and I are both Scorpios, and our innate badness precludes us from being pedestal material.)

On occasion I have forgotten to go to my therapy session. This usually happens when my life is either going really well or very hectic, or because we've changed the day, which we sometimes do if there's a literary reading at school or my therapist has a meeting or it's Rosh Hashanah. I'm convinced that all good lesbian therapists celebrate Rosh Hashanah, although I'm equally certain my shrink has no faults whatsoever to reflect upon or make amends for during the ten days between Rosh Hashanah and Yom Kippur. I apologize profusely when I forget an appointment. She always understands and never charges for missed sessions.

```
dear my therapist,
i am SO sorry i forgot about therapy tonight. we had a
visiting writer this week, which makes for much craziness
(but its own type of fun as well). that's craziness in
the very-busy sense, not craziness in the perhaps-one-
night-a-week-of-therapy-is-not-enough sense. of course,
as soon as i got your message (about 11 o'clock tonight),
it all sounded familiar. oh yeah, therapy. anyway, i am
sorry, sorry, sorry, and i look forward to seeing you
next tuesday.
xoxo,
six-thirty (except when
i'm five-thirty or
seven-thirty)
p.s. five-thirty, six-thirty, seven-thirty...do you think
i have multiple personality disorder? hahaha. oops,
sorry, not funny. (i lost a lot of blood.)
```

My shrink replies promptly:

```
Dear Six-Thirty,
Circumstantial shifts in our meeting time have no bear-
ing on your essential six-thirtyness. I am glad to know
that the reason was nothing drastic. I appreciate your
```

apology, but we should talk about its apparent abject-
ness.... I'll see you next Tuesday. I'll be here in my
chair (which I've never left, actually, except to go to
your house that one time....)
Your Therapist

Some of my excuses are better than others, but all are true. Once
I missed a session because I had thrown out my calendar and forgotten to copy down all my upcoming appointments before doing
so. My calendar was in my knapsack along with some brie cheese,
and I don't know how long that cheese had been in there or even
why, but the Saran Wrap had started to come off and the whole
thing was very squishy—but for some reason not stinky—and it got
on my calendar. (I threw out the knapsack too.)

My lover and I are now living happily ever after—together—and
I've been on Paxil, an antianxiety drug, for more than a year, after
months and months (OK, years) of relentless encouragement from
my therapist and my primary care doctor. My shrink asks me what
I want from therapy now that I'm doing so well.

"I'm not quitting therapy," I insist.

"I'm not trying to get rid of you," she assures me. "I only want to
discuss where we should go from here."

"You mean now that I'm no longer beating myself up and obsessing?" For years I have beat myself up for procrastinating, not exercising, not eating right, having no self-discipline. In other words,
I've been beating myself up for gluttony, pride, sloth (although idle-
ness sounds a bit less harsh), and yes, occasionally anger. Three and
a half out of seven deadly sins—this is not good. And I've obsessed
over my weight, my eyebrows (I think they're disappearing), and my
feelings of inadequacy, just to scratch the surface.

But mostly I've obsessed about dying. Aging doesn't worry me;

dying does. And aren't we all dying, when you think about it? Every day, we're that much closer. I don't feel that old, but once your parents are dead, you know you're next. Also, I'm now older than John Lennon, Martin Luther King Jr., and Jesus when they died, not that I have much in common with those three. Hell, at 42 I'm the same age *Elvis* was when he died. Maybe I *am* depressed.

But all that worrying and obsessing was before Paxil. While I still wish I were thinner, more disciplined, and tidier, when it comes right down to it, I just don't give a fuck anymore. And life is easier. In fact, I think they should just put Paxil in the water supply, along with fluoride. Here, have a glass of water.

So where do we go from here? Yes, I'm happier, and I use far fewer of my therapist's tax-deductible Kleenex these days. But I'm hardly problem-free. Let's just say I'm a work in progress. How could I leave my therapist now—my therapist who has been there for me when no one else was? So what do I want to work on in therapy now that life is good? Hell, I don't know, but I'm sure I'll think of something by Tuesday at six-thirty.

I would have followed her anywhere.

Therapy
Sara Cytron with Harriet Malinowitz

Thank God for therapy. By this point in my life I go to therapy so many times a week it's like I live my life in little 50-minute intervals. And I've been talking about my family with my therapist for so long that by now she has her own problems with these people! Last week I was talking about my mother, and she said, "Look, I don't want to hear a thing that woman has to say!"

This is my therapist in New York. But for a lot of years in my life, I lived in the Washington, D.C., area, and I had another therapist who I really loved, but I had to move to New York. She told me to stay in touch. So I wrote her a letter, and she wrote me back: "Dear Sara, Uh-hmm. Uh-huh, Uh-huh."

Actually, I ran into this therapist not too long ago—this therapist who I had loved so much. She came to see me when I was performing at a women's comedy conference, and I was thrilled. I hadn't seen her in seven years.

So she says to me, "Sara, how are you? How's Harriet? How's comedy?"

So I answered these questions. And then we came to that part of the conversation where you usually ask the other person about their life. But then I realized I never knew anything about her life to begin with.

So I said, "Ellen, what are you charging these days? You still get *Newsweek*? You ever get that door buzzer fixed? I bet you must have repotted that spider plant by now."

How many people here go to therapy? All right. Now how many of you know that you're your therapist's favorite client? Right? Everybody else they see 'cause they have to—to make money. But you! You! You're so fascinating! Your mind is so complex! Your life is such a lesbian soap opera! They'd really see you for free, for nothing, but they can't, due to professional ethics!

Crazy Is as Crazy Does
Kelli S. Dunham

Don't be jealous, but I was diagnosed with bipolar disorder about five years after I diagnosed myself as being queer. It certainly isn't fun to be queer and crazy, but at least it gives me something to talk about at parties—not everyone gets to belong to not one but two despised minority groups.

There is a receptionist who works at my psychiatrist's office who apparently thinks that Person With Bipolar Disorder is synonymous with "dumb as a row of corn." Perhaps she thinks she is helping when she insists on conducting the conversation in very LOUD tones…very…slowly…using only words that have one or fewer syllables. Of course, far from being reassuring, this makes me feel like conducting a conversation with her in VERY LOUD tones with only very simple four-letter words. Or possibly just countering with a lighthearted "HEY, YOU IGNORANT PUSS, DO YOU REALLY THINK I CAN'T UNDERSTAND WHAT YOU ARE SAYING? I'LL HAVE YOU KNOW I GRADUATED FROM NURSING SCHOOL WITH A 3.89 GRADE POINT AVERAGE, AND I WORK FULL-TIME AND I GO TO SCHOOL FULL-TIME AND PLUS I'M WRITING A BOOK AND WHAT THE HELL ARE YOU DOING WITH YOUR LIFE?"

I don't do this, of course, because this would only confirm her perceptions that people with mental illness are unreasonable.

Besides, receptionists in mental health offices are notoriously skittish, and I'm always a tad fearful that she might mace me.

Altercations with receptionists aside, I attribute a great deal of my success in dealing with bipolar disorder to my "happy team" (as my friend Maura somewhat flippantly calls them)—i.e., my psychiatrist and my therapist. They are both gifts of the HMO gods, who for whatever random reason decided to favor me with folks who actually take the "professional" part seriously in "mental health professional."

My psychiatrist, for example, is definitely in the top ten percentile of shrinks. She has a dry sense of humor, calls me Ms. Dunham, never keeps me waiting, and treats me exactly like a human being, in the manner I've become accustomed to in the days before I was diagnosed with bipolar disorder. When I am doing well, her primary function is to write my prescriptions and ask me how much I am sleeping (which is never enough in her estimation).

My therapist is straight, married, living in the suburbs, and, bless her gizzard, more disgruntled about my childhood than I am. She is both direct and kind, and she likes to use the furry characters from children's TV shows to make occasional therapeutic points. For example, we'll be talking about the issue of my overworking and have pretty much talked the issue to death. Suddenly she'll get the teeniest twinkle in her eye, gesture a bit with her hands, and say, "To quote the Muppets, 'Moderation good. Excess bad.'" So, yeah, to misquote the Muppets, "It's not easy being green…or bipolar and a dyke, for that matter."

But when my mother calls, talking about how Jesus is going to reward her in heaven for continuing to live with alcoholic husband number six, I think, *It could be worse.*

Queer and crazy is easier than straight and stupid any day.

Adventures in TherapyLand
Yvonne Zipter

I am no stranger to therapy. Believe it or not, I was once horribly neurotic. But after a year or two of therapy, off and on—why, now I'm delightfully neurotic. Or so I like to think. A dissenting opinion on the "delightful" part can be heard, I'm sure, from my girlfriend, family, and friends. But as I used to say to my mom, if I wasn't a little crazy, I'd go insane. It seems to me that normality, like any other good thing, can be carried too far. Look at Ward and June Cleaver—they were supposed to be as normal as anything. And they were as bland as mashed potatoes with no gravy.

The Cleavers may have been on the bland side, but Wally and Beaver—or so the presumption goes—no doubt grew up to be healthy, happy, well-adjusted adults. (Although, really, how well-adjusted *can* someone be whose lifelong appellation refers to a large-toothed, soggy rodent?) Most of us, however, did not grow up in such a blissfully bland household. My own family, for instance, was less like the Cleavers and more like *The Beverly Hillbillies* meets *Knots Landing*, with a little of *The Addams Family* thrown in for color—and without all that messy money to muddy things up.

Yes, it's true: I too am the product of the ever-popular dysfunctional family. Time-tested, father-approved. Incest, the emotionally absent father, physical abuse—these are just some of the things offered to the lucky graduate of the nuclear family—that commodity so highly prized by the "Moral" Majority. (Don't make me hurl!)

Is it any wonder some of us need a little help unscrambling our brains? And then add to the "normal" stuff of growing up in a dysfunctional family the confusion of being gay or lesbian in a homophobic society—well, doctor, when does my 50 minutes begin?

Finding a good and/or compatible therapist, however, is not always so easy. And a bad therapist (or a bad match) can be worse than no therapist at all. Fortunately, my first time (yes, way back when I was a therapy virgin), I got very lucky—without breaking any therapist/client boundaries, that is. Actually, I may have been too lucky. I mean that I don't know if, like a baby dyke—oops, Freudian slip—if, like a baby *duck,* I was at the imprinting stage or what, but I've never been able to waddle off and find another therapist with whom I work as well as the first one.

Having emerged from a household in which the father figure (i.e., my stepfather) didn't believe in therapy—as if we were talking about the tooth fairy or Santa Claus—but believed instead that one should pull oneself up by one's own bootstraps (a gravity-defying feat in actual practice), it seems doubtful that I would ever have sought therapy out. As it happened, I ended up in therapy kind of by accident. Here's how it came to pass: One day in Milwaukee I went to the student health center at my university, complaining of a sore throat. While there I noticed the name of a new psychologist posted among the undistinguished names of all the other staff. The name was that of my former psych statistics T.A., on whom, it just so happens, I had had a wicked crush. I stopped in to see her under the pretext of congratulating her on having completed her Ph.D. By way of conversation, she asked me how I was doing. I, by way of an answer, burst into tears. And the rest, as they say, is therapeutic history.

Actually, I got at least two things from being in therapy with Dr. K. that bear mentioning. The first was that I learned to put things in perspective. To illustrate, I offer the following statement from

Dr. K.: "Now let me get this right—you have no friends, no pets, no TV or stereo, you're broke, you live in a tiny studio apartment downwind from the tannery and have to put buckets out all over the room when it rains—and you wonder why you're *depressed*?" Oh. Now I get it.

The other thing I got from Dr. K. was this wonderful diagnostic assessment: "You wouldn't be happy if they hung you with a new rope," which has provided me with years of entertainment, trying to figure out what the hell that *meant*. But whatever it means, I'm sure she was right: Dr. K. was perfect. A little transference going on? What? Who, me? Naw. OK, so I never got over the fact that she didn't follow me when I left Milwaukee—that doesn't mean I was experiencing any *transference*.

But the fact is, I never did find such a good therapist/client match again. Then again, maybe I did and just didn't know it. Comedian Margaret Smith does a joke about therapy in which she ponders how you know whether you really have a good therapist. "Does your therapist have a balloon business on the side?" she asks the crowd anxiously. Well, none of my therapists had a helium tank sitting in the corner or anything, but that doesn't mean I didn't still sometimes feel like I was at some sort of carnival—the carnival of souls, I think.

Take Dr. S., for instance, who practiced out of her home, an unassuming, typical sort of structure on a typical sort of tree-lined street. At least she said it was her house. I never actually saw more than the sun porch, where her office was, although I did some-times hear male voices coming from the other end of the hallway, presumably those of her husband and son. I have to admit, though, that even her office wasn't terribly office-like, with plants and art-work everywhere and a series of couches and chairs arranged into a "conversation pit." Still, that's the sort of thing therapists do: cre-ate a homey atmosphere to put you at ease—as if you could be comfortable in any type of setting in which you describe to a perfect stranger how sleeping with your ex-girlfriend's old softball mitt that she left behind is somehow comforting. There was one session, though, that did offer up pretty strong evidence that there were in fact living quarters in the part of the place I never saw.

It was the time I arrived for my session desperately needing to use the facilities, just a few steps beyond the glass-paned door of her office. No problem: I simply had to share the space with her five-year-old daughter, who happened to be taking a bath on the other side of the drawn shower curtain—drawn for whose privacy, I'm not sure. Do you know how hard it is to pee with a total stranger not more than four feet away from you, sitting quietly and nakedly nearby? As if that wasn't bad enough, I then discovered that there was no more toilet paper on the roll. While contemplating what social etiquette might dictate about this dilemma, Dr. S. slipped her hand into the room with a new roll. I was less than at ease for our session.

Another time, as I worried about what effect my breast biopsy scar might have on my dating life, Dr. S. graciously offered to assess my scar and to let me take a look at her own. And before I could say "Pop goes the suture," her breast was right there, in front of my disbelieving eyes. I was so taken aback I have no recollection of what sort of blouse she had on or her undoing any kind of bra—it all happened so fast. Like an accident. Her bare breasts, however, are forever burned into my memory. I know she meant well, but a provincial gal like myself just isn't used to authority figures disrobing in her presence. In fact, not since Clifford and I were behind the garages at the projects, when I was about eight, had I played "I'll show you mine if you'll show me yours." I shudder to think what might have transpired if my concern had been with an episiotomy.

One of my most recent therapy experiences involved no literal baring of the breasts, but I had a funny feeling of exposure nonetheless. The sessions in question were with Dr. j., which I'll spell with a small "j" so you don't confuse her with the basketball player, like I know you would otherwise. Anyway, Dr. j.'s sparsely furnished office—three leather director-type chairs, a small crate of children's toys, and two small end tables, one bearing a telephone (next to what was clearly the doctor's chair) and the other bearing a box of tissues (between what were clearly the client's chairs)—was also equipped with one of those two-way mirrors. On the other side of the mirror was another therapist who would occasionally sit and phone in questions for Dr. j. to ask the client—i.e., me. I felt like I was in one of those old movies about Greek mythology—you know, where the Gods would sit up in the clouds and move the mere mortals below as though they were chess pieces? And even though I knew the "cloud" in this case was only a piece of glass and that probably no one back there was named Zeus, I kept expecting to be turned into a swan or to have babies come bursting out of my forehead or something.

The other "tool" that Dr. j. used was a video camera, with which she recorded all of our sessions. This, she said, was to help her remember all that transpired. "Oh, sure," my girlfriend responded skeptically when I told her of this arrangement. And then she moaned, "You're going to end up on *Hard Copy!*" More likely *America's Funniest Neurotics*, I suspect. Between the mirror, the video camera, and Dr. j.'s eagerly receptive face, I had a hard time, as you might imagine, deciding exactly where I should be looking. Naturally, though, I generally looked directly at the radiator on the right side of the room.

I have also had, I admit, a therapist whom I went to see only once—a sort of therapeutic one-night stand, I guess. There was just no chemistry, you know? Like a duet between Melissa Etheridge and Wayne Newton, maybe. Given that we'd only been together for 50 minutes, I didn't think I had any moral obligations beyond leaving a message that I wouldn't be keeping my next appointment—or any others, for that matter. That, I thought, was the end of it. However, I made the valuable discovery that quitting your therapist is like breaking up with someone: Leaving a message just won't do. She called me back, apparently feeling the need to process, to understand why it was that I didn't want to see her anymore after just one "date." And the woman wasn't even a lesbian, for heaven's sake. The only good point about this is that at least we didn't have any property to divvy up.

Adding up these different experiences, though, I'd have to say that I did come away, in the end, with new insights. Like did you ever realize, for instance, how when the client before you comes out you look discreetly away, even though you're dying to know what this person looks like and what the hell *her* problem is that she needs a *therapist*? And did you ever notice that whichever chair you sit in at your first session is the chair you use for the entire rest of the time you continue to see that therapist? Of course, couples counseling can throw a different dynamic into the whole chair thing. When my lover Kathy and I went, we decided after a session or two that one seat in particular seemed to be the "hot seat"—that is, whoever sat there was more closely and nerve-wrackingly scrutinized by the therapist. Thereafter, upon entering the room, we would race for the non–hot seat, elbowing each other aside in that friendly, mature sort of way that characterizes our relationship. The therapist, I think, lost all hope at that point.

These insights aside, what I've just recounted is the therapy version of serial monogamy: limited forays, one after another, into the wacky, fun-filled world of psychological counseling. But in some parts of the lesbian community the most stable relationships you'll find are those between a lesbian and her therapist. Therapists have taken on, in fact, an almost higher-being quality in the lesbian community. So great is our belief in therapy that we lesbians not only go individually but also, as I alluded, as couples—and, in many cases, as ex-couples, and even sometimes *before* we're a couple. I feel that it is only fair to confess that I have participated, however briefly, in all three types of these couples counselings.

Couples counseling, you may be thinking, is not so weird—married people frequently seek such counseling. Relationships are stressful, people grow and change, become disillusioned with one another. Couples counseling, you think, makes some sense. But *ex-couples* counseling?

Well, it's a widely known fact that lesbians frequently stay friends with their ex-lovers. Unfortunately, sometimes they just can't figure out real well how to do that. Some of the same crap that bugged the hell out of you when you were together can still bug you when you're not. For instance, when she says "I'll call you later," "later" might mean in two hours...or in two weeks. And then there are whole new arenas to explore, like "How could you leave me for *her?*"And: "When you give me a hug now, does that just mean you want to hug, or does it mean you want to, um, you know?" So even though you've *both* (yeah, right) decided that you just want to be friends, there's still a fair amount that needs to be sorted out. Why bother sorting, you say? If you're split up, you're split up—that's it. Well, that's not the way lesbians figure it—and that's just one of the many things that make us so special.

Also, there are two other considerations with this ex-lovers counseling thing. One is, if both of you are going to continue to hang out in the same circles—and chances are that you will, the lesbian community being the inspiration for Disneyland's "Small World" exhibit—you need to learn how to be in the same room with each other without picking up a meat cleaver or keening sorrowfully at the moon. Such actions can be disturbing to those around you—not to mention to each other. The second consideration that enters in these days—something most people thought they'd never be hearing lesbians say—is, What about the children?

That is, lesbians who have kids together and have decided to continue to coparent even though they no longer cohabit must, like many a divorced hetero couple, learn how to pretend to be grown-ups during the ritual passing back and forth of the children on weekends. This is where your friendly local therapist comes in.

So you might be willing to buy the ex-couples counseling, but what about counseling for couples who aren't even a couple yet? Well, all I can say is that, as ex-Girl Scouts, many of us lesbians try to be prepared for anything. In our case, Kathy and I had unwittingly fallen (one of us less unwittingly than the other, I'd have to say in all honesty) onto the bobsled course of monogamy and were trying to figure out a way off—or at least a way to slow down the momentum. Hell, who were we trying to kid? We were already buying groceries together and might as well have been keeping the other apartment as a summer home—if it hadn't been for the fact that it was roach-infested and disgusting. Nevertheless, we were trying to be responsible about getting involved, so we decided to allay our fears about that involvement by seeing a therapist.

Unfortunately, we only made it to one session. The problem was, sitting there in front of the therapist, Kathy suddenly got couch fright. Or at any rate, she seemed to have lost the power of speech. I felt like a ventriloquist, telling the therapist what Kathy felt, what Kathy wanted, and what Kathy would say if she were capable of speech, while Kathy nodded her head dumbly in confirmation, a look in her eyes like Baby Jessica in the well. To this day, I'm sure that therapist worries that Kathy had fallen under the spell of a domineering older woman. Well, she'd be half right, anyway: I do sort of have an enchanting personality…. In the end, we jettisoned therapy altogether and stumbled blindly into a relationship like every other red-blooded American lesbian.

Of course, the stumbling part was pretty much our own fault—there must have been a self-help book out there somewhere that addressed our dilemma. There are self-help books for everything, aren't there? *Healing the Three Stooges Fan Within; Now That You Know: A Guide to Running Screaming From the Room; The Big Hair Syndrome; No More Barbie Bashing: Confronting the Feminist Censor Within; A Nintendo Duck-Hunting Plan for Your Inner Child; Opening the Door to a New Fuller Brush Man; Healing With Chiclets; Learning to Say Whoa: Putting the Brakes on Your Monogamous Bobsled Slide.* If we had only taken a trip to our local feminist bookstore, I'm sure we would have found something there to enlighten us. Self-help books may be generally hot right now, but lesbians are among the biggest buyers, I'm sure. If we don't help ourselves, who will? And we've been doing it for years....

As evidence of our avid readership of self-help books, just look at the illustrious career of codependency. Why, before lesbians discovered codependency, it was nothing, a nobody. And now look at it: poster child of neurotic behaviors, malady to the stars. We were healing spiritually—New Age religion, crystals, the whole ball of feathers—before most heteros too. And then there's The Child Within—almost nobody even knew theirs was missing until lesbians started looking all over the place for their own. Frankly, I don't quite get this one: Most lesbians I know pretty much have their child right there on the outside where everybody can see it. Who else do you think is buying all those softballs, train sets, Pee Wee Herman dolls, electric hockey games, and *Brady Bunch* memorabilia?

Like self-help books, another area of lesbian self-improvement mania that I haven't explored is 12-step programs. Consequently, I know little about them, except what I pick up through the buzz in the community. So here's my impression of the 12-step groups frequented by lesbians, based on those little snippets:

1. The 12-step programs are like the Rosicrucians, the Masons, the Nihilists (of turn-of-the-century Russia), or some other exotic

secret organization: No one outside the group is supposed to know who else is in the group, and, for safety's sake, only first names are used.

2. The 12-step programs in the community are like big dating services. This made no sense to me in light of another thing I had heard about the program: Participants are encouraged not to date at all for their first year in AA (so they could concentrate on getting/staying sober). Still, this was definitely the impression I had. For instance, couples were always turning up who had met each other...under mysterious circumstances—circumstances that they later confessed were AA meetings.

I have recently discovered that this last impression is indeed correct. A friend told me that at one of the groups she was attending, every time a new person would come in, the others would turn and look at this new person with the gleam of possibility in each of their eyes—and a little drool on their lips. When my friend realized they were spending far more time processing the ever-shifting tides of coupledom in the group than they were on what *she* thought the topic was supposed to be—staying sober—she left the group. Ah, those lesbians—you can lead them to water, but you still can't get them to talk about drinking! I imagine, of course, that surely not all lesbian AA groups are like that, and yet.... When you put a group of attractive women together, all in one room, sharing their most intimate thoughts and problems, bonds are bound to form.

As for myself and why I've never learned the secret handshake of a 12-step group, well, it actually makes a certain amount of sense: I'm not an adult child of alcoholics, and I'm not an abuser of either alcohol or drugs. You might think this is because I don't have a particularly addictive personality. True, but it also has something to do with what was so aptly phrased on a California bumper sticker many years ago: "Reality is for people who can't handle drugs." In other words, I always felt like I had sort of a tenuous hold on reality at best, and I didn't want to risk doing anything to mess that up. In the long run I guess this has turned out for the best. But there was a time when such a drug-free stance was definitely not cool. So what's changed, in some places, I guess. (Which is why those wrestling with an addiction problem are even more admirable.)

But even if there were a 12-step program for overwriters anonymous or adult children of couch potatoes, I'm not sure I'd go. I don't mean to imply that these programs don't help a lot of people. On the contrary, I've seen evidence that they do. I'm just not very good at group confession. Personally, I like to embarrass the hell out of myself one person at a time—like with you right now, reading this book.

It is this same embarrassment factor that has caused me to be hesitant about going to a lesbian therapist, someone who hangs out in the same community that I do, who knows some of the same people I do. I know they're sworn to secrecy and all, but I still think it would be awkward to see one's therapist socially. I'd be thinking to myself, *Why is she smiling like that? Is that an "Oh, poor thing" smile? Or an "I can't believe the things I know about you that all these other people don't" smile?* It's bad enough, at parties and concerts, to run into your ex-lovers, who know way too much about you—stuff that could be astoundingly embarrassing—but at least with your ex-lovers, you know plenty of potentially mortifying stuff about them too. This creates a nice system of checks and balances that helps keep people morally upright. Generally one does not have such reciprocal knowledge of one's therapist. I have weighed these cons of having a lesbian therapist against the pros—having someone who understands lesbian culture without having to consult her copy of *The Well of Loneliness*—and so far, I have decided to throw my lot in with the hetero women who show me their breasts and videotape me for posterity. But that's just me.

Therapy, of course, is a different experience for everyone, though my experience, perhaps, has been more different than most! I'm seeing a new one on Monday. And I'm bringing along some balloons, just in case I spot that helium tank.

Cato Sheehy

Five Bottles in a Six-Pack:
Excerpts From a One-Woman Show
Renita Martin

it is a lot a muthahfuckahs up in the crazy house that make yo ass look sane. you know, in jail or the crack house, you can get the feeling that you in the same boat as everybody you know. but in the crazy house you bound to find that one somebody mo fucked up than anything you ever seen.

like my last therapist. she had issues with her father, her husband wouldn't get no job, and she got two sisters and a brother who don't speak to her. now ask me how i know all this and huh ass sposed to be my therapist.

she had to keep her dog with her at all times 'cause the dog got separation anxiety when she was away. now that would be fine. but the dog got nervous around other people and would git the shits in the middle of every session.

then you got them niggahz who ain't as crazy as they act. the last time i was locked up they had this ole white chick sitting in a wheelchair in the middle of the hallway. you got to walk past her to pee, talk on the phone, eat and shit. she obviously done been aroun, musta been a teacher or a actor or somethin 'cause she callin all these names: the Shubert Theatre, the Huntington, Greta Garbo, Paul Newman, Leon, France…

but i notice (i'm the only spot up in the joint) that every time i pass by, the bitch go to yellin some black shit. the first time i thought it was coincidence, i walk by, she say, "harlem." then i walk back by, she say, "ray charles." so, i'm thinkin, this bitch ain't as crazy as they think, she identifying with somethin.

so every time i walk by i'm diggin some sounds of blackness comin from this old white lady: "Roxbury, West Africa, Jesse Jackson, Paul Robeson, Sammy Davis Jr., Ruby Dee...." i'm gettin off 'cause me, this black dyke, is vibing wit this li'l old white lady. i'm floating! til i'm on my way to the bathroom and she yell "jesse helms!" i pushed that wheelchair—white lady and all—so hard i know that bitch is still rollin.

i don't hafta buy drugs on the street no mo. i'm a legalized dope addict now. but the pharmaceutical companies is thuggish. long as i been buyin on the street, the price don't change that much unless it's a drought. i go to the drug store, they tell me the shit cost $60. the next time i go, the shit cost $164.16.

they say i'm crazy, i gotta have it. and to tell you the truth, if i miss a hit, i get the shakes, break out in a fever—be jerking like a heroin addict. but they won't give me no crazy check.

the first time they took me to the disability office i didn't even know where i was, and they still wouldn't give me no check. somebody told me you got to act even crazier than you is to get your check.

so the next time, i come in the office like this here—"here, chick, chick, chick, here, chickadee."

they say, "sit down, Miss Martin."

i acted like i didn't even know my name, "here, chick, chick, chick."

they said, "sorry, Miss Martin, you're not eligible for a check."

then some in me just snapped! i said, "who ain't eligible? which one a us ain't eligible?...that's all right." pointed to the empty chair next to me, "it's all right if y'all don't wanna give me my check, but please give this man right here his check. he need it bad."

i gits my check, now.

Shrink Shopping
Jaime M. Grant

Therapist #1

Outer Office: White wicker chairs. New Age music on scratchy radio. Women's monthly events calendars in lumpy stack. Lavender Lesbian Network flyers pinned to resources board. Nervous, nail-bitten girl I'd never meet anywhere else in chair across from me.

Inner Office: Large Buddha-like lesbian ensconced in big leather chair, opposite. Favorite colors: purples and reds. Favorite fabrics: billowy rayons and gauzy cottons. Appliqué jacket.

Answers the question "What is your therapeutic style?" with "Jungian." Answers the question "What are your opinions on S/M sexuality?" with "Let me make a referral…."

Therapist #2

Outer Office: Cherry mission-like furniture. NPR on Bose radio. Big gold-framed Georgia O'Keeffe poppies hanging over us like shouting cunts. Glitzy magazines in wrought-iron magazine rack. Reserved, carefully arranged professional men and women sitting in waiting area.

Inner Office: Impeccably dressed, avowedly feminist woman in Morris chair, opposite. Favorite colors: black, gray, anything subdued. Favorite fabrics: Wool, cotton, the classics.

Answers the question "What is your therapeutic style?" with "What kind of style are you looking for?" Answers the question

"Are you a lesbian?" with "And what would it mean to you if I were?" Answers the question "What are your opinions on S/M sexuality?" with "Let me make a referral...."

Therapist #3

Outer Office: Two simple chairs crammed into small waiting area with stacks of old *People* magazines on tiny table in between. No one ever in other chair (except, occasionally, a lover who needs to be dragged in for couples work). Classical music on simple radio.

Inner Office: Improbably straight lady who wears shamrocks in her ears on St. Patrick's Day, big frou-frou snowmen on her busy sweaters at Christmas. Pictures of the kids crammed onto book-shelf full of resources on recovering from rape, toxic families, various and sundry addictions.

Answers the question "What is your therapeutic style?" with "Whatever works." Answers the question "What are your opinions on S/M sexuality?" with "S what? We can work with whatever you're into, dear."

THIS IS CALLED "TRANSFERENCE" AND IT'S PERFECTLY NORMAL TO SEE YOUR THERAPIST THIS WAY.

Dueling Zombies
Gina Ranalli

B*itch.*

The word buzzed around in my head like a pissed-off yellow jacket, fighting furiously to escape the web of my mind and sting the living shit out of the woman before me. I tried to think coherently, but the only clear thought was that one word: *bitcchhh.*

The rat zombie (also known as Evelyn Rattazzi, the dean of my high school) stared at me from behind her desk, her beady little rat eyes looking slightly larger than they really were, due to the ugly purple-framed glasses that kept sliding down her nose. She was even giving me what I suspected was her best attempt at a human smile.

"I know you're angry, Teresa," the rat zombie said. "But I ask you, what choice did you leave me, hmm? And I honestly believe you'll find it beneficial. You might even enjoy it." She paused, the tiny black pellet eyes watching closely for my reaction. When she realized I wasn't going to give her the satisfaction, she added, "And your parents weren't the slightest bit upset about it either. Your mother said she thought it was a wonderful idea."

"I'm sure she did," I mumbled.

The rat zombie's smile slipped a notch. "Your appointment with Dr. Goldberg is scheduled for 12:30 tomorrow. I suggest you make the best of it. Failure to show up will land you yet another suspension, and we don't want that, do we, Teresa?"

I slumped lower in my chair and issued a loud sigh.

"You're on the edge, Teresa. Right on the edge of *not graduating in June*."

Still I refused to respond. Her gaze left my eyes, settling instead on my nose and the onyx stud that pierced my right nostril. Her own nose crinkled in distaste, and she quickly looked up again. "Now, about the T-shirt. Obviously you know you can't continue the day wearing it. Do you have anything to wear over it?"

"I don't see what's wrong with it," I told her honestly. "I think it's funny."

I could tell she was close to losing it. Getting her to that point was becoming easier with every visit, it seemed. I fought against my own smile and decided to try to nudge her a little further by "absently" twirling and tugging at my nose ring. When she only glared, I ventured, "C'mon. You *really* don't think this shirt is amusing?"

For approximately the last six months I'd been designing my own T-shirts, which basically meant drawing and/or writing on them. As a completely out 17-year-old dyke, I'd been feeling the need to express myself to the world, and I found my T-shirts gave me a tremendous sense of satisfaction. Oddly, though, they seemed to infuriate everyone else in the tiny, zombie-infested suburb of Medford, where I lived.

On the white shirt I was currently wearing I'd used a black Sharpie and drawn two stick-figure girls, one standing and wearing a broad grin while the other one was kneeling, her face in the standing girl's crotch. Above them, in thick block letters, I'd printed FAHRFROMFALWELL. I thought it was cute, but as usual, I'd sustained the usual harassment from most of the zombie students. Some of them were downright hostile, but they weren't nearly as belligerent as they had been the previous week when, in an especially rankled mood, I'd come to school wearing a T-shirt on which

I'd boldly written I'M NOT GAY BUT YOUR MOTHER IS in red acrylic paint. Spoofing what I considered to be lame advertising slogans and sayings had always been particularly fulfilling to me, even if it meant possibly offending a fellow dyke—and there were none in my town, so I figured I was pretty safe.

The rat zombie looked like she'd just taken a nice big bite out of a lemon wedge. "If you have nothing to put on over that atrocity, Teresa, I'm going to have to send you home. Just like I told you last week. And the week before that. And the week before *that*."

"I feel it's my right as an American citizen to—"

"*Enough!*" She slammed her fist on the desk, knocking over a framed photo of who I assumed were her cutie-pie grandzombies. "You know the drill, young lady. March yourself across the hall and ask Mrs. Klein to find you something out of the lost-and-found box for now."

"But the crap in that box must be a decade old!" I protested, sitting up.

"Oh, really? Well, guess what? *Tough!*" She resumed smiling sweetly. "I don't want to see you in here again, Teresa. Consider yourself warned."

Right, I thought to myself. *We both know damn well we'll be sitting in these very chairs again tomorrow.*

I rose and exited the office, defeated yet again. I had absolutely no intention of wearing anything "borrowed" out of the ancient box of moldy lost-and-found items in the secretary's dungeon. But on the other hand, I couldn't afford another suspension either, and so reluctantly I made my way upstairs to my locker and spent the entire day sweltering in my zipped-up Goodwill army jacket. The snickering that followed me everywhere I went wasn't that bad, really. At least it reminded me that *I* wasn't a zombie.

There is a plot afoot, and it has been in place probably since the beginning of time. The plot is simple: The zombie's mission in limbo is to convert nonzombies into zombies by any means necessary, including sending nonzombies to rural public schools where they will endure any number of vile tortures. Even the strongest of nonzombies have been known to crack under the horrors of the dreaded suburban high school, what with its zombie-cheerleaders and zombie-jocks, its zombie-teachers and zombie-clubs, zombie-newspapers, and maybe worst of all, its zombie-yearbook.

These things are bad, granted. I have encountered them all, and they are nothing to be flippant about. I thought I had suffered through what surely had to be the worst of what the old zombies giddily call "the best days of your life." After all, I'd been alone (several times, even) in a closed office with the rat zombie, sometimes for as long as *15 minutes*, and I had emerged intact, a feat few, if any, had accomplished before me. Without fear of sounding too arrogant or smug, I could honestly say that I was among the strongest of the nonzombies to *ever* walk the cursed corridors of Medford High School. I had fared well and had every confidence that I would continue to do so.

Until that fateful next day.

Waiting in the office belonging to the school nurse, a.k.a. the Baby Jane zombie (or B.J. for short), I must admit that I became more than a little nervous. B.J. was an old, bird-like zombie with lavender hair who sat behind her desk staring at me and twirling a tongue depressor in her clawed hands as if she were pondering how to use it as a weapon. She was dressed in her usual white polyester uniform, complete with white rubber-soled shoes, white nylons, and a starched white hat that had probably gone out of style back when athlete's foot was considered a fatally dangerous disease.

Never taking her watery blue eyes from my face, she softly sang the lyrics of that time-honored Glen Campbell classic, "Rhinestone Cowboy," over and over.

She scared the living shit out of me.

I decided the best course of action was to avert my eyes as much as possible, so I buried my nose in a paperback while I waited for the shrink zombie to finish her current session of brainwashing.

I couldn't understand why the shrink zombie's office was located inside B.J. zombie's office, but it certainly explained why I'd never noticed it before. I avoided B.J. with even more fervor than I employed in avoiding panty hose, churches, and the Spice Girls.

As I pretended to read I began wondering how the hell I was going to get out of this new pickle I found myself in. Therapy was definitely not something I felt I needed, and I understood that it was just another way, maybe even a last resort, for the zombies to try to break me—get me to conform and become one of them. I had no idea of what to expect from this shrink zombie, but instinct told me to keep my mouth shut, eyes open, and guard up.

I was still considering these words of wisdom when the shrink zombie's office door opened in front of me and a boy emerged, looking both humiliated and defeated. The kid was only about 14 or so, obviously a freshman, with enough metal in his mouth to pick up Mexican radio stations. It was clear he'd been crying, his puffy, red eyes meeting mine for the briefest of seconds before darting shamefully away.

It was then that I got my first glimpse of the shrink zombie. She stood in the doorway of her office, holding the door open and smiling a saccharine smile at the poor sap who was leaving.

"See you next week, Brian," she said cheerfully to the kid's back just before he slipped out the door and into the school's main corridor.

She stared after him for a moment before turning her attention to me. "Hi. Are you Teresa?"

I nodded, sizing her up. She was tall and thin, her legs appearing frail beneath the hem of a plain beige dress.

"I'm Dr. Goldberg," she said and offered me a dry, skeleton hand. "I'm sorry I'm running so behind today. I'll be with you in just a few minutes, OK?" She gave me the same smile she'd given the boy and then disappeared into her office, closing the door behind her.

I didn't realize I'd been holding my breath until I released it in a long, loud sigh.

The Baby Jane zombie yelled something about a star-spangled rodeo, causing me to let out a little squeal of terror and drop my paperback on the floor. When I looked at her, she was still staring at me and wearing the kind of grin usually reserved only for serial killers and evil clowns.

Mumbling an expletive, I snatched up my book and eyed her nervously. I quickly decided that if the B.J. zombie even *appeared* to be rising up out of her chair, I'd have no choice but to bounce Kurt Vonnegut off her forehead and then hope my beat-up old Converse sneakers would have enough gas in them to fly me safely to Jupiter.

Fortunately it didn't come to that, because the shrink zombie suddenly opened her door and motioned for me to come inside. I stood, grateful to be getting away from the terrifying zombie that masqueraded as a sweet old school nurse but still uncertain and wary of what lay ahead.

As I closed the door behind me I realized that I hadn't stepped into an office after all; I'd entered what must have at one time been a storage closet. There was barely enough room for the shrink zombie's desk, chair, filing cabinet, and a second chair that hid behind the door and couldn't be seen until the door was closed.

Sitting down, I immediately knew it wouldn't take long for me to feel claustrophobic in the tiny space. I was less than three feet from the shrink zombie.

"Why don't we start off by you telling me a little bit about your-self?" she asked, leaning forward, her hands folded neatly on top of her desk.

I cleared my throat. "What do you want to know?"

"Anything you feel comfortable telling me." She gave me what I assumed was supposed to be a reassuring smile, and that was when I noticed that not only was her dress beige but so was she. Her short, sensible hair was beige. As was her skin, nail polish, shoes, and eye shadow. For a startled second it even appeared as if she had beige eyes, but upon closer inspection I saw that they were just brown. A *very light* brown.

"Well," I began. "I feel comfortable telling you that I don't need therapy."

The beige zombie nodded.

"I have no idea why I'm here. It's ridiculous."

She nodded again.

I frowned. "I'm the least screwed-up person I know, actually."

Still, no reaction.

"Therapy is bullshit," I told her. "I don't believe in it, so natural-ly it won't do me a damn bit of good. This is a waste of time."

I paused, waiting for her to tell me I had a shitty attitude, which was something most zombies enjoyed informing me of on a regu-lar basis.

When it became apparent that I wasn't going to get a rise out of her with my usual method, I told her, "You know, I have no idea how old I was when I finally stopped wearing diapers."

This seemed to pique her interest. Her beige eyebrows rose, and she sat back, placing her folded hands on her beige belly. "Does that bother you?" she asked.

"Isn't it important to know that kind of thing?"

"Is it important to you?"

I shrugged. "I thought you'd want to know all about my toilet training. Isn't that what we're supposed to discuss first?"

"We can discuss anything you'd like, but I'm sure there are other things you'd prefer to talk about, aren't there?"

"I can't think of a subject more intriguing than toilet training," I told her, trying to keep my expression serious.

"But you already said you're not sure how your toilet training went, so what exactly would you like to discuss about it?" Her face was equally serious.

I had to admit, she had a point. I'd basically backed myself into a wall on the toilet training subject, and I didn't see how I could take it any further. Sitting up again, I glanced around the tiny room searching for inspiration.

The beige zombie's office was neat to the point of being sterile, which was alarming enough in itself, but then my eyes fell on a coffee mug she had sitting by a yellow legal pad. Not only was the mug beige, but it was also decorated with the smiling face of a famous radio personality who went by the name of Dr. Laura. I'd heard her once and became convinced that she was the Reigning Queen of All Zombies. Apparently she was a doctor of some kind, but within about five minutes of listening to her I could tell she had to be one of the most evil zombies walking the earth, and I'd quickly snapped off the radio, fearing for my sanity. I knew what she looked like because her smiling face adorned the sides of buses everywhere.

"Would you like to tell me about your T-shirts?" the beige zombie asked suddenly. I looked at her; if she'd noticed my anxiety at the sight of her mug, she gave no indication.

"As in, why do I wear them?"

"Sure, that would be a good place to start," she replied, reaching for the yellow pad and a pen.

"It's just an effective way of getting back at the jerks who perpetrate injustices against me. I even make up things about the kids who pushed me around back in grade school. It's a pretty harmless way to mend some of my damaged self-esteem, don't you think?"

"You felt out of place in grade school?"

"I *was* out of place. I've *always* been out of place. Look at me! Do I look like I fit in with all the other people walking around Stepford?"

"You mean Medford?"

"Whatever. The point is, how many spiky-haired, nose-ringed dykes do *you* see attending the pep rallies and hanging out down at the mini-mall?"

By now she was writing so fast I expected to see sparks flying up from her pad. "So, you would say you were angry even as a small child?"

"You'd be angry too if everyone was always throwing things at you and pushing you."

"Other kids literally pushed you? What did you do when that happened?"

"You mean, in general?"

She looked up from her scribbling. "Sure."

"When they pushed me, generally, I fell down." As the beige zombie fixed me with a blank stare, I smiled and added, "I think our first session is going great, don't you? I feel like we're really bonding and making lots of progress."

As I continued to grin I noticed her eyes narrow a fraction, and she began to lightly tap her pen against the paper. A long moment of silence passed.

Finally, she said, "Teresa, for this to work, we both have to take it seriously. I know your feelings about being here. Mrs. Rattazzi filled me in on your history, and I understand that you're feeling hostile about the entire situation. But honestly, I think it's better for both of us if you just try to cooperate and make the best of it. I know that it's awkward at first, but I can assure you it will get easier." She paused and smiled, still tap, tap, tapping. "What do you say? Are we a team?"

My jaw dropped. I could only stare at her, genuinely speechless, and wondering if I'd just heard her correctly. Had she really just asked if we were a *team*? I considered asking her if she had enjoyed her daily dose of LSD for lunch or was she actually just that stupid? But I closed my mouth, bit my tongue, and let it slide. I figured she couldn't help it; she was infected with the zombie bug, after all. *Way* infected. The mug on her desk was enough to prove that.

And then she repeated it. "Teresa? Are we a team?"

I couldn't believe it. I opened my mouth to tell her that I'd use a cactus for a tampon before I'd ever be on a team with her, but suddenly there was a short rap on the door and it flew open fast, slamming into my knees. I yelped and wasn't particularly surprised to see the rat zombie poking her head into the room.

"*Oh, my goodness!*" she exclaimed, as if it were *her* kneecaps that had just been cracked. "Teresa, I'm so sorry! I thought you had left already." She glanced at the beige zombie. "I'm sorry, Ruth. Margaret said she was gone." With that, she abruptly closed the door and disappeared.

Margaret, I knew, was the evil, singing nurse.

The beige zombie regarded me apologetically as I rubbed my knees and we both listened to the unmistakable sound of Baby Jane's witch-like cackles.

Then, finally, she said two truly magical words: "Time's up."

I had to go back again the following Thursday. The rat zombie had insisted I see the beige zombie not once but *twice* a week. They were determined to break me, mold me, make me conform. And the harder they tried, the more I resisted. But the rat zombie continued to menace me with threats of not graduating and spending another year in that zombie-ravaged hellhole, threats my zombie-parents backed up wholeheartedly.

And so I went.

I soon discovered that the beige zombie didn't always dress completely in beige. Sometimes she dressed completely in powder blue. Or pale yellow. Or baby-bonnet pink. But still, she was always beige. That's how I saw her, and I became convinced that beige was truly the color of her aura. Maybe it's the aura color of all zombies. I wouldn't be surprised.

When she came out of her office and saw me waiting for her, her eyes widened considerably.

"Dr. Goldberg." I gave her a neutral nod of greeting, stood up, and gestured to her office. "Shall we?"

"Teresa…your hair…"

"Yeah, yeah, yeah," I said as I brushed by her and waited at the threshold of the torture chamber. When I'd seen her two days before, my hair had been short, spiky, and dyed an inky black. Now I had none. "I shaved my head. Big friggin' deal. Let's get this shit over with, OK, teammate?"

A few minutes later I was once again marveling at the beige zombie's capacity for stupidity. She had just asked me how I felt about being a lesbian. I shrugged and mumbled, "How do *you* feel about being a member of the Stepford gestapo?"

"I beg your pardon? I'm sorry, I didn't hear you."

"I prefer to be called a dyke, actually."

The beige zombie cleared her throat and wrote something on her pad. "You don't find that derogatory?"

I smirked, knowing how uncomfortable a "bad" word like *dyke* made her. "I find many things derogatory, but that isn't one of them. I'm not comfortable being called a lesbian. I think it sounds too clinical, but that's just me."

The tapping-of-the-pen ritual began. "OK, then. Why don't you tell me how you feel about being…uh…gay?"

"I think being *a dyke* is the best thing in the whole world I could ever be. The only thing that would be better than being *a dyke* would be being a disgustingly *rich dyke*."

"I see." She seemed uncertain of how to respond to that, but finally asked, "And you don't currently have a…significant other?"

I couldn't help smiling at that. "Not currently, no."

"But you have? I mean, in the past?"

"You're getting kind of personal. What's your point, Doctor?"

"Have you ever had a boyfriend?"

Instantly bristling, I replied, "No."

"You've never had relations with a boy?"

"Not the kind of relations you're talking about."

"Well, I'm not sure I understand."

I stared at her coldly, waiting.

Continuing to rap her pen, she said, "Forgive my ignorance, Teresa, but then how do you know for sure that you're a lesbian?"

After counting to ten three times, the urge to reach over and bitch-slap her finally subsided, but I still didn't trust myself to speak yet.

"Teresa?"

"I'm sorry. I was just wondering exactly how long gay people are going to be asked to forgive ignorance. Personally, I'm sick as shit of all the forgiving we're supposed to do."

"I apologize, I didn't mean to—"

"Have *you* ever screwed a chick, Dr. Goldberg?"

Her cheeks immediately flushed bright pink. "Wha…*excuse me?*"

"Because if you've never *had relations* with a woman, then how do you know you're straight?"

She gaped at me, dumbfounded and looking like she might hyperventilate at any moment.

"Age-old argument, I know," I told her. "But none of you breeders have ever been able to answer it to my satisfaction."

"I…you…I…" She continued to sputter for several seconds until she finally tossed her pad and pen onto her desk and asked if I would excuse her for a minute. Then she rose and exited the office without waiting for my reply.

The next thing I knew I was back in the rat zombie's office getting my ass chewed out for being disrespectful.

"She's trying to *help* you, Teresa," the rat zombie bellowed. "And you go and call her a *breeder*?" She glared at me through her Coke-bottle glasses. "What the hell is a breeder anyway?"

Ignoring the question, I said, "I just thought—"

"*Don't think!*" she screeched, punctuating each word by pounding her fist against the desktop. "*Don't think, don't think, don't think!*"

I scratched my newly bald head and said nothing, though the irony of being told not to think in school did not escape me.

"When you see Dr. Goldberg again, you are going to apologize for your rudeness and then you will continue with your sessions without causing her any more grief. Is that understood?"

Long seconds passed before I said, "Do I get to tell my side of this or what?"

"*Is that understood?*"

A mini-staredown ensued, but eventually I dropped my eyes and nodded, knowing it was pointless to try to reason with a zombie.

"Good. You're excused."

"Now, what I want you to do," the beige zombie said as she handed me a blank sheet of white paper and a pen, "is just draw me a picture of how you see yourself. It doesn't have to be anything fancy, but since you're an artist of sorts, I thought it would be something that would appeal to you."

It had been just over two weeks since she had ratted me out to the rat zombie, and though I'd never apologized as I'd been ordered to do, she'd never mentioned the incident. That fact only reinforced my theory that the beige zombie was a total quack with no inkling of how to conduct therapy because, to the best of my knowledge, good therapists do not choose to ignore unpleasantness.

I looked down at the empty page she had handed me. "Huh?"

"It'll be fun." She smiled at me as she rose from her chair. "I have a tiny errand to run, so you give it some thought and then draw whatever comes into your mind, however you see yourself. OK, then, bye-bye."

She squeezed past me and disappeared out the door, closing it behind her.

Left alone, I briefly entertained fantasies of booby-trapping one of her desk drawers or staging a mock suicide like the kid in my favorite movie, *Harold and Maude*. Something that would make her shit Twinkies. But ultimately I decided that after the initial amusement I would be nailed to a cross and the zombies would get the last laugh. No fun there.

Scrunching down in my seat, I stared hard at the wall, wondering what the hell I was supposed to draw. Myself burning alive at the stake seemed fitting but inappropriate somehow. I sat up again and, leaning on the desk, hastily drew a circle the size of a half-dollar in the center of the page, intending to draw a head. Then I changed my mind and colored the circle in, just to be doing something.

"This is bullshit," I told the Zombie Queen as she sneered at me from her place on the beige zombie's mug. "But you wouldn't think so, would you? Then again, you probably think Rush Limbaugh is sexy and intelligent, right?"

Realizing I was talking to a mug, I turned my attention back to the task at hand. I looked down at my solid black circle and still didn't have a clue as to how to proceed. "Screw it," I muttered and drew another wider circle around the first circle. And then I drew another one and then yet *another* one. Eventually I had what resembled a bull's-eye.

I studied my creation, pondering it. Next I put down about ten lightning bolts, some surrounding the circles while others crossed directly through them. My mind wandered to the biology exam I had coming up in a few periods as I hummed and mindlessly continued coloring in my page of doodling.

Lost in thought, I jumped in surprise when the door clicked open and the beige zombie reappeared, still wearing her thin smile. "I'm sorry about that, Teresa," she said, once again squeezing past me to her chair. "Did you draw a picture?"

I slid the page across the desk to her. "That was an easy enough assignment. Isn't picture drawing something you shrinks have little kids do? As in, like, four-year-olds who can't quite form a complete sentence and tell you their *true* feelings?"

The beige zombie either didn't grasp the gibe or she chose to ignore it. Examining the halfhearted drawing, she said, "Well, this isn't quite what I had in mind, but I'm sure we can make use of it."

"That's swell," I said, trying to match her enthusiastic tone.

She put the drawing aside and then began with her usual barrage of questions about my week—what had transpired in my classes, if anything, how I was getting along with my parents, etc., etc., etc.

However, after several minutes of our customary volleying, she surprised me by bringing up a subject she had never brought up before. "Do you remember when you first started having sexual feelings?"

I blinked in amazement. "Sexual feelings?"

"Is this something you're uncomfortable with?"

"No," I paused, curious of where she was leading with such a question but also leery. "I can't pinpoint when the feelings started exactly, but I can remember when I first started *doing* something about them."

She snatched her notepad off the desk, her pen poised for action. "And when was that?"

I hesitated, thinking, and then abruptly began giggling. "I was in the fifth grade when I had my first lover."

Looking up from her writing, she eyed me skeptically.

"It was a sweet little brown teddy bear that my grandmother had given me for my birthday that year." I struggled not to laugh, but was rapidly losing the battle. "I used to sleep with it every night, and for some reason, one night I just wanted to sleep with it between my legs. And *then*, even though I had no idea what I was doing or even *why* I was doing it, I just started rocking against old Teddy. Pretty soon I slipped it up under my nightgown and went to town. I couldn't believe something could feel so good! From that night on, for probably a whole year, Teddy was my loyal bed buddy."

Biting my tongue to prevent myself from bursting into laughter, I stopped my narrative and noted that the beige zombie was once again tapping her pen and looking completely unamused. I had no clue why I was spewing on the way I was, but nevertheless, when I felt like I could speak without laughing, I forged on with my story.

"You should have seen the teddy bear by the time that year was up! All the fur was worn off its face, especially around the nose area. That thing really took a beating! Anyway, I eventually started feeling all the shit kids feel about masturbation. You know, guilt and shame, like you're the only one in the entire world who's such a big perv. It got so I couldn't stand it anymore, so I brought the thing back to my grandmother's house and told her to hang on to it for me. I said I'd like to have it there for when I visit. It's still there to this day."

The beige zombie had ceased all writing and was staring at me as if I'd just tweaked her nose.

I stared back. "Well, you asked!"

She placed her notepad on the desk, consulted her watch, and announced, "I'm sorry, Teresa. That's all the time we have today."

As I was just about to slip out the door, she said my name. I turned back to look at her.

"One quick question," she said. "Was your teddy bear a boy or a girl?"

"*What?*" Then, before she could say anything, I snapped, "A *girl*, OK?"

Then I slammed the door and mumbled, "And she was a hell of a dominatrix."

I spent the next few days stewing over the fact that I'd run out of ideas for my T-shirts. I'd toiled for several agonizing hours trying to think of some witty way to further express my endless cynicism before I finally gave up, reluctantly admitting that perhaps that particular well had run dry.

Knowing I would have to come up with some other medium for my creativity, but not yet having even the slightest clue as to what that would be, left me aggravated and depressed.

And that was still my mood when it came time for my next session with the beige zombie.

As I sat waiting outside her office, not even the Baby Jane zombie could frighten me, though she was trying like hell. She sat at her desk staring at me as usual, but she had a new form of mental torture: constantly snapping the wrists of the latex gloves she'd taken to wearing while simultaneously singing her new favorite song, "Suspicious Minds." Pretty unnerving on the whole, but I had to admit that she did a pretty mean Elvis impersonation.

When the beige zombie finally opened her door and told me she was ready for me, I stood up, looked the Baby Jane zombie directly in the eye, and said, "Hey, latex lover, if you'd like, I'd be happy to donate my hour to you. Honestly, I think you could use it more than me."

"Come on, Teresa," the beige zombie said, giving my sleeve a gentle tug.

Before I was pulled into the office I was able to catch the Baby Jane zombie grinning while she yelled, "Because I love you too much, baby!"

Closing the door, I said, "And you guys force *me* to be here?"

"Sit down, Teresa. I have some exciting news to share with you."

I sat, sensing that something weird was going on. The beige zombie seemed entirely too happy, and not just her bogus happy either. She seemed *genuinely* happy. "What?" I asked dubiously.

The beige zombie pulled out the drawing I had done the week before and held it out for my inspection.

Looking from the doodle to her face, I repeated, "*What*?" She put the picture down and folded her hands together. "I think we're on the verge of a breakthrough, Teresa."

I frowned, pointing at the bull's-eye. "Because of *that*? What kind of a breakthrough?"

"The kind of breakthrough that will leave you feeling a million times better about yourself."

"Oh? I can't wait to hear this."

"Do you know what this is?" She tapped the center of the bull's-eye. "Do you know what it represents?"

Taking a stab at it, I guessed, "I think I'm the center of the universe?"

Beaming brightly, she laughed and replied, "No, silly, this is your vagina."

I gaped at her. "My *what*?"

"The center symbolizes your vagina, while the circles around it symbolize all the walls you've built up around your feelings about sex." She pointed to the lightning bolts. "And do you know what these symbolize?"

I shook my head. "I'm not sure I want to know."

She laughed again. "It's actually quite obvious. I can't believe I didn't see it right away."

After a dramatic pause, she proudly announced, "These symbolize *penises*!"

When I finally found my voice, I asked, "Are you trying to make me puke or something?"

"This entire drawing you did clearly shows that you aren't truly a lesbian. The fact that you gave away your female teddy bear says the same thing. You're just insecure about your heterosexuality. Now our job is to find out why."

Suddenly I felt my heart slam against my rib cage, and the palms of my trembling hands grew moist. I spoke barely above a whisper. "Please tell me this is your idea of proving that you have a sense of humor."

"We still have a lot of work ahead of us, Teresa," the beige zombie continued excitedly. "The first step is to figure out why it is that you find men threatening."

"Oh, my God, you really *are* serious."

"Of course! Your confusion and fear are results of the desires you can neither control nor deny."

"*What?*" Without warning, my calm demeanor snapped. I snatched the picture from the desk and yelled, "You're wrong! The center circle represents my *asshole* and the lightning bolts represent what all you *zombies* are trying to do to my *asshole*! The outer circles represent the way my *asshole* grows larger every time I'm forced to bend over and receive *one of your lightning bolts*! How's that for Freudian?" I savagely began shredding the drawing and flinging the pieces in the direction of the beige zombie. "Or perhaps the picture isn't about me at all. Maybe it's about *you*! And if that's the case…well, we don't really need to go into all the unpleasant implications of *that*, do we?"

I let the last pieces of the destroyed picture flutter to floor and glared at her. She was no longer smiling. In fact, she looked a bit like Elmer Fudd when he's so pissed that he's turning purple and about to blow the brains out of that wascally wabbit.

When she finally spoke, it was very slow and deliberate. "I think you need a time-out, young lady."

"Oh, yeah?" I snorted. "Well, I think you need to bite me."

Her eyes widened considerably, and I'd swear the temperature in that tiny room dropped about 25 degrees. I braced myself, though I wasn't sure for what.

"*Get out!*" the beige zombie suddenly hissed, sounding frighteningly like the possessed kid in *The Exorcist*. "I'm finished with you. You are beyond help. I give up!"

I didn't make a move. I could only stare in disbelief.

"*Get the fuck out!*" she screamed loud enough to be heard all over the school.

That got me moving. I jumped up and shot out of there before she could put me in a headlock and start gnawing on my skull to eat my brains, which, of course, is the true motive of all zombies. I didn't even dare a single glance back.

I was going to be expelled. I could see it in the rat zombie's eyes as she looked at me from across her desk. She'd surprised me with her calmness; I'd expected the usual yelling, the pounding of the desk, the threats. But none of that had come. She had yet to raise her voice, and her expression was one of dull apathy.

"Do you realize that you nearly had Dr. Goldberg in tears?" she asked.

Unable to come up with an adequate defense, I remained silent, focusing hard on a spot on the wall.

"She considered resigning," the rat zombie went on. "A lot of kids would have been deprived of a good therapist had that happened."

I pressed my lips tightly together, forcing myself to stay quiet.

The rat zombie sighed heavily and looked down at an open folder, *my* folder. I noticed with a twinge of pride that it seemed to be pretty damn thick. She rifled through several sheets of paper and said, "I see you've applied to several exceptional universities."

I looked at her and nodded, wondering why the hell I was allowing my own torture.

"Your grades have always been outstanding, Teresa. I've never denied that. Your SAT scores certainly prove that you're far ahead of your peers and—"

"Why don't you just say it?" I snapped. "I know you're enjoying dragging this on and on, but come on already! If you're gonna boot my ass, just do it!"

She eyed me from over the rim of her glasses. Ignoring my outburst, she said, "I understand you intend to get a degree in graphic arts."

I groaned and slumped down in the chair, as I'd done a million times before.

The rat zombie closed the folder and said, "OK, Teresa, you win."

My eyes narrowed. "Huh?"

"Dr. Goldberg gave up, and so do I. I can't expel you for your behavior, and despite all my threats to the contrary, there's no way in hell I want to see your face in this office again next year."

Slowly, I sat up, suspecting some kind of cruel joke.

"Obviously you'll no longer have to see the school therapist." She cocked her head slightly to the side and raised an eyebrow. "What are you waiting for? You're dismissed."

Swallowing hard, I remained seated and mute.

"Go!" she barked. "I'm sick to *death* of your face!"

Finally realizing she was serious, I tossed her a curt "thanks" and then got the hell out of there before she could change her mind.

I'd won.

The thought stayed with me for the rest of the day, and I moved from class to class with a certain smug glee I'd never known before. For now, I'd actually won.

Sometime during the day I decided that the beige zombie really deserved a token of my thanks for releasing me from the hell of her grip. I struggled to come up with a gift that would be appropriate, something to drive home the depth of my gratitude—a special gift I might deliver on a special day. Graduation Day, perhaps.

Walking down a shady suburban street, my combat-booted footfalls echoing pleasantly back to me, I entertained thoughts of piercing my tongue in celebration. Or maybe my eyebrow. I figured it would look pretty cool with the newly bleached stubble I had growing on top of my head. I damn well deserved *something* anyway.

I was happily considering the possibilities when I finally reached my destination: a small yellow bungalow with navy trim and a bed of tulips in the front yard. Passing through the gate of the white picket fence, I followed the flagstone walkway up to the front door and pressed the bell. Momentarily, the door opened, and I was face to face with pale blue eyes the exact same shade as the netted hair above them.

"Hey, Grandma." I grinned. "I've come for the bear."

My therapist said I shouldn't see you anymore because our relationship is a classic case of codependency. Why don't we go see her together and show her how independent we are?

What Do You Say to a Naked Therapist?
Lesléa Newman

First I go straight (so to speak) into denial: This cannot be happening. Then I judge myself for going into denial: Good one, Glory. Just pretend what you see right in front of your face isn't even there. Well, why not? It got me through my entire childhood, didn't it? Next I try to channel Pollyanna and look on the bright side: At least this will give me something to talk about during my next therapy session. Finally the cold, harsh voice of reality sets in: What are you, crazy? You can't talk to your therapist about seeing your therapist naked. Then she'll know.

Know what? Know that you (say "I," says my therapist's voice, which lives rent-free in my brain). OK, OK, know that I saw her buck naked in the locker room of the YMCA. Yes, it's true. And I'm so shocked, so horrified, and so fascinated that it takes me a full minute to realize that I'm buck naked too. As are the dozen or so other women in the locker room, but I don't even see them. It's like that costume ball scene in *Romeo and Juliet* where the two star-crossed lovers lock eyes and everyone else just fades away.

Here's a trick question for you: Which would be worse: seeing your therapist naked or having your therapist see you naked? Well, of course, your therapist sees you naked, in a manner of speaking, every day, or in my case every Wednesday at 3:15. Not literally (like right now) but figuratively, with all those ugly emotions hanging out all over the place. I've told her that it isn't fair, I show her everything—

my weak side, my vulnerable side, my angry side, hell, even my sleazy side. And now what do I get to see? My therapist's backside.

It could be worse, right? She could be facing me. (I hope she doesn't have eyes in the back of her head like my mother.) Or she could have picked the locker right next to mine instead of one clear across the room. I can't believe she has all those freckles on her back. And what's that on the left cheek of her cellulite-free ass—a mole, a birthmark, a hickey, God forbid?

What if she turns around? I really will kill myself. And why is my girlfriend taking so long to bring me a new towel? Why I had to drop my towel into the whirlpool today of all fucking days I will never know. *Hurry up, Jan*, I want to scream, but if I scream my therapist will hear me. And then what? Would she turn around and say hello to me? She's not supposed to. I'm the one who calls the shots—outside her office, anyway. We spent three whole sessions ($225, thank you very much) figuring that one out. Because I've felt so powerless my whole life around personal space and limits and boundaries (don't get me started), my therapist and I agreed that I would decide if I wanted to say hello to her or not out on the street (and I do mean street—singular—because we live in one of those towns that if you blinked while driving through you'd miss). And if I do decide to say hi to my therapist, she is allowed to say hi back. But if I don't say hello, she's supposed to respect my privacy. Of course, the first time that happened I had to spend the whole next session wailing about what it felt like to be ignored by her and whimpering that I didn't think she cared about me. It took another two sessions ($150) to untangle that mess.

As I stand here calculating how many sessions it takes me to pay for my therapist's membership to the Y and plot ways to kill Jan for taking so long to bring me my towel, a thought occurs to me that gives me goose bumps on top of the goose bumps I already have from standing here naked and shivering: What if my therapist has already seen me and is pretending she hasn't? What if she's waiting for me to make the first move? She's had her back to me this whole time, hasn't she? She's got to be doing that on purpose.

I know I should look away, but I just can't. I'm like someone at the scene of a terrible accident, repulsed and mesmerized at the same time. My therapist is bending over to put some cream on her legs. Even from here I can see she's using the expensive kind, the kind I only use when I can cop a free sample at Lord & Taylor. I've helped myself to so many freebies that Jan is sure the cops are going to bust down our door one day and arrest me. I've told her over and over not to worry; that's what those testers are for. And besides, I can't afford to actually buy the expensive stuff they sell at Lord & Taylor. I spend my money on therapy.

Finally Jan arrives with my towel. (How long has she been gone—ten seconds, ten minutes, ten years?) I snatch that piece of light blue terry cloth like it's a lifesaver and wrap it around my body (is it always this small? I mean the towel, not my body). Then I indicate to Jan with a wordless tilt of my head just who is on the other side of the room.

"Is your neck out?" Jan, ever the perceptive one, asks.

"Shh," I say, not wanting to draw attention to myself for once in my life. I motion for Jan to bend closer. "That's my therapist," I say, now pointing with a shift of my eyes.

"Oh, my God!" Jan is equally horrified, and all of a sudden I can't look. "Is she dressed yet?" I ask under my breath.

"She's in her underwear," Jan replies.

"What kind is it?"

"Uh…black."

"What kind of black? Bikini, brief, thong?" Oh, please God, don't let it be a thong. I almost fall to my knees and utter a silent prayer, for how could I possibly go back to therapy and sit there week after week knowing my therapist was wearing Monica

Lewinsky-ish lingerie under her outfit?

"Why don't you just get dressed?" Jan whispers, "so we can get the hell out of here?"

"I'm waiting for her to leave," I whisper back. "What does she have on now?"

Jan shakes her head but indulges me. "She's got on a green blouse, and she's putting on a pair of black pants. Are you happy now?"

I'm so happy I could scream. She's dressed! She's leaving! In a minute it will all be over. But as I step into my clothes, I realize it isn't over. It's just beginning. I'm going to have to bring this up in therapy. Aren't I? Maybe I can just forget it. Pretend it never happened. *Like half your childhood*, I hear my therapist's voice remind me. Her voice, with its trace of Midwestern twang, sounds so close and so real I look up, half expecting to see her standing next to me, handing me my other sock. But it's Jan holding out my argyle. My therapist is gone.

The following Wednesday I'm a total mess, wondering exactly what it is I'm going to say to my therapist. Wednesday's my day off, so I have lots of time to obsess about it. And I don't even realize until I'm sitting inside her waiting room ten minutes early (once an obsessive-compulsive, always an obsessive-compulsive) that I'm wearing the exact same outfit I was wearing that day at the Y. What can this possibly mean? I know it has to mean something. All right, I admit it, I'm one of those people who actually writes down what I wear to therapy so I don't wear the same outfit two weeks in a row (please tell me there are other people out there who do this sort of thing). But that doesn't stop me from making other fashion faux pas. The first time I arrived at my therapist's office, she asked me if I was nervous. "Of course not," I said, as if plunking down $60 (she hadn't gone up yet) to tell a perfect stranger the most intimate details of my life was no big deal. At the end of the session she informed me my shirt was on inside out and backward. "I just thought you might want to know," she said. Another time I showed up at her office with two different colored socks on. I'm surprised I've never shown up stark naked.

Naked. I can't get the image of my naked therapist out of my mind. All those freckles. The tiniest bit of flab at her waistline. The varicose vein behind her left knee. I almost canceled my session today, but I couldn't decide, and by the time I made up my mind it was too late. Most therapists have a 24-hour cancellation policy. My therapist has a 48-hour cancellation policy. When I protested—another therapy session wasted on how I felt about her, rather than talking about my real problems—she informed me that her policy wasn't for clients like me (I'm a good client, I thought, sitting up straight in my seat like a dog that's just been patted on the head). No, her policy is for those pesky little clients who constantly stand her up. So, I argued, and rather brilliantly I thought, if the policy is for her other clients, why does it have to apply to me as well?

"I can't make exceptions, Gloria," she said, shaking her head slightly as if she wished she could, but it just wouldn't be fair. I wondered at that moment if she gave the same party line to everyone or if I really am one of her better clients. Then I felt despair descend as I was forced to face a truth too painful to bear: My therapist actually does see other people. I can't stand this fact. I would rather Jan see other people—ten, 20, 100 other people—I wouldn't care. But my therapist—how dare she see other clients? If she really loved me, she would learn to live on $75 a week.

The door opens, and my therapist tells me to come in. I enter her office and take my place on the brown corduroy couch as she perches on her green recliner. Are these colors supposed to be soothing? Today my therapist is wearing a rust-colored chenille sweater that costs at least a session and a half, and a brown suede skirt. *Are you wearing your black thong underwear?* I want to shriek. But I say nothing. I wait to see if my outfit registers with her. It doesn't seem to. But she's a therapist. She's trained in the fine art of banishing all emotions from her face. I often think my therapist would make a great newscaster. "Ten thousand puppies died today in a freak accident," she could read off a TelePrompTer without batting an eye. Once I asked her why she was so unemotional. "Why do you think I'm unemotional?" was her reply. Another time I asked her why I was paying her so much goddamn money to basically nod her head and say "uh-huh" every once in a while, and she said she was supposed to be like a mirror reflecting myself back to me. So if I was really smart, I'd talk to myself in the mirror for an hour every Wednesday afternoon, put 75 bucks in a jar, and at the end of the year take Jan to Honolulu for a second honeymoon.

"So what's going on?" my therapist breaks the silence.

"I don't know. Nothing much." Oh, great, Glory. What's that supposed to mean? I fidget in my chair. My therapist waits. So I start in with the usual crap. My depressed mother blah blah blah, my workaholic father yadda yadda yadda, my sadistic cousin who used to lock me in my parents' bedroom closet to see how long it took for me to lose it and pee in my pants. Then I tell her some stuff that's going on with Jan and throw in a dream or two. My therapist loves dreams. She always leans slightly forward in her chair when I start telling her one.

Suddenly I have an idea. "Why do you always sit in that chair?" I ask, putting a great deal of emphasis on the *why*.

"Would you prefer to sit here?" she asks, though I notice she doesn't make any kind of move to get up. She'd probably rather fight than switch.

"No, I just wondered *why*, that's all." I dangle the word *why*, as in YMCA in front of her, but she doesn't bite. "*Why* do you think I exercise at the *Y*?" I ask her.

She gives me a funny look but goes along, letting me just for a moment be the alpha dog of the session. "To relax," she says. "To get rid of tension. To de-stress."

De-stress. I love it. Is that a therapist's word or what? "Correct," I say, as if this is some kind of test. "So *why*, if this is the case…" I pause dramatically, as if I'm Marcia Clark in front of Judge Ito, "why would someone who knows this about me show up completely unexpectedly at the Y, in the locker room, totally naked, and freak me out?"

I realize I'm yelling by the way my therapist has shrunk back in her chair. I've always suspected she's more of a wimp than she lets on, and perhaps I'm right. I don't recall ever yelling at her before.

"Did your ex violate your agreement?" my therapist asks gently.

"No," I say. My therapist knows my ex is not allowed within county limits. I, on the other hand, cannot set foot in her new place of residence: the entire state of New York.

"Hmm." I see my therapist wracking her brain. She probably doesn't know this, but when she's really thinking hard—in other words, when I'm really getting my money's worth—two tiny creases appear on her forehead right above her left eyebrow.

I can't take it anymore, and I yell, "You! It was you! You know you were at the Y last Friday."

"What makes you say that?" she asks, and I think this answering-a-question-by-asking-another-question thing has gone a bit too far.

"I saw you," I say. "It was around 6 o'clock. You were putting cream on your legs."

"Friday night…" my therapist ruminates, staying perfectly calm. "Would it upset you if you saw me at the Y?" she asks, remaining noncommittal.

"Would it upset me if I saw you at the Y?" I echo her words. Who's the mirror now, I wonder. And if I'm reflecting my therapist's words back to her, shouldn't she be paying me? But at the moment, that's beside the point. My therapist has not exactly confessed, nor has she exactly denied. Is this some sort of test? Is she trying to recreate a scene similar to my entire childhood, when no one would tell me what was going on and I felt completely crazy? Are they allowed to do that?

I don't know what to say. Have I been obsessing all week over nothing? (It wouldn't be the first time.) But, no, wait a minute. It was her. I'm sure of it. Yes, I did only see her from the back, but I'd recognize that mousy brown pageboy anywhere. Wouldn't I? After all, I have been sitting across from the woman week after week after week for the last four years. I know what she looks like. Don't I? A thought occurs to me, and suddenly I know how we can get to the bottom of this. What if I asked her to drop her drawers? Then if that scar or pimple or bugbite is there on her left cheek, I'll know it was her. Hey, if they could inspect Michael Jackson's you-know-what, they can check out my therapist, can't they? But Jocko was accused of child abuse. And I'm accusing my therapist of...of what exactly? Working out? Yes, working out at my gym. How dare she? Doesn't she know therapists have no right to go anywhere after work except straight home, do not pass go, do not collect $200? (They don't need the money.) I really think all therapists should be banished to Planet of the Shrinks after work so the rest of us can relax and not have to worry about bumping into them anytime, anywhere. Clothed or naked.

My therapist glances at the clock on the little table beside her, and I know our time is almost up. Soon she'll give me the high sign, the two-minute warning.

"Are you lying?" I ask her, even though this question doesn't make any sense. She hasn't told me whether she was at the Y or not, so how could she be lying to me?

"Why would I lie to you?" she asks back. Or does she say, why *should* I lie to you? If I can't trust my eyes, what makes me think I can trust my ears? Maybe my therapist wants to drive me crazy so I'll keep coming back and she'll continue to be able to afford hand-woven sweaters, leather skirts, and expensive body cream.

"Glory," my therapist tries to bring me back to the present. (Good luck!) "This is important work. Are you accusing me of lying?"

Bad client, bad client! I mentally slap my wrist. Should I deny it? Or speak up? "I…I guess so," I say, trying to sound unsure, since I don't know what she wants me to say.

"That's wonderful." My therapist beams. "You finally trust me enough to accuse me of doing something wrong. You're beginning to know I'm not perfect."

Hooray! I feel like shouting—not. *This* is an accomplishment?

"Our time is almost up," she says, and then reaches down into her pocketbook, which lies on the floor next to her left leg like an old dog to extract her appointment book. I don't know why she does this, because we always meet on Wednesdays at 3:15. It's really my signal to pay her, but it would be crass for my therapist to say, "Hand over the dough, Gloria," so she pretends to browse through her Week-at-a-Glance and mark down our next meeting while I write out her check. I write her name out in slow motion, trying to stall for time, just like when I was a kid trying to put off going to bed. *Mommy, I need a drink of water. Mommy, read me another story. Just five more minutes, Mommy. Please.*

At last the inevitable arrives. 4:05, the end of our 50-minute session. Do you know that there are exactly 168 hours in a week, which means I only have 167 hours and ten minutes to go until I see my therapist again? Unless of course I see her at the Y. Was it her or not? I want her to tell me.

"Listen," I say, standing up to (reluctantly) hand her the check. "Would it kill you to tell me if it was you at the Y or not?"

"Would it kill you not to know?" she asks. Oh, she is so predictable, my therapist. So infuriatingly, maddeningly predictable.

What if I said yes? Yes, it would kill me. Would she tell me then?

"I'll see you next Wednesday." My therapist has that look on her face—a cross between I-really-care-about-you-a-lot and your-time's-up-loser-so-get-the-fuck-out-of-my-office.

"Bye," I say, closing the door behind me. I walk down the street, find my car, and get in. But I don't start the engine right away. First I have to think. Was it my therapist or wasn't it my therapist? Clearly she's not going to tell me, so I get to decide. The way I see it, either I'm totally freaked out because I saw my therapist naked at the Y or I'm totally freaked out because I didn't see my therapist naked at the Y. Either way, I'm completely fucked up. Thank God I'm in therapy.

The Car of the Year Hits the Road
Mary Beth Hatem

I write poems.
I read them out
loud. This one, for instance, I read to
my new would-be flame soon after
our very first date.
I think she'll be impressed.
I read:

People ask me about my car,
MB, you have such a nice car. Why
buy a Honda Accord and not tend
to its most basic needs? You have
the Car of the Year and
you treat it like junk. Dents are why
you pay insurance.

Dents to you, I say, but there's more.
My lover Pat scraped a patch
off the right front door. A performing
artist, she always moved fast.
It was one of the first things
I noticed about her. I called
her Charlie after Charlie Chaplin;
she hated it, but once she sent roses to my
hotel and signed the card "Charlie" not "love, Charlie"—

we were too new. A crisis at first since
I worked with a very important
Charlie, and worried he had a crush on me.

I took a drink of water, barely pausing.
I went on, less certain:

So about the car. She seemed sorry,
but as time wore on not sorry enough.
She wrote a check for the deductible I carry around.

At first I thought she didn't owe anything—
It was just one of those things,
it was also about whether
to make the claim at all and if not,
did she owe more since
fixing it would cost more than the deductible and I knew
she couldn't afford it (she gave such lavish presents).
It was about us.
And what if I
didn't fix the car at all, taking my
chances? Did she owe me
anything—for what?
Would there be a cure later for rust?

Does it seem fair that I had to think
about this? She zoomed off easy enough.
Couldn't she take care of the mess she had made?
Still these problems seemed uniquely mine.
To her, it was clear.
The car needs fixing: Fix the car.

She began to have doubts. Was
it my net worth or ours
that was eroding?

It was also about insurance
and the false protection it offers
and still we go around feeling
safe and secure.

Not even water now.
Just a pause.

Let me tell you about the driver's side.
You'll see a mean scratch, longer
this time—a wrinkled ridge,
slowly more prominent, a face
that is aging and becoming more and more itself.

I was late for work, a day
like every day at a job I
mostly hated but didn't know yet,
screeching into the employee garage
too small for cars. Every day, danger on
tight ramps—just one more
ounce of flesh—they even wanted
our cars to look alike. Or
maybe I am missing the meaning:
it could have been that we
were all being punished for driving
our toxic, greedy cars even
though the subway was so close you could see it.

I was especially guilty.
A Honda was good,
but why an Accord when the whole
world knew the Civic
a perfectly good car and
also because I drove through
the trees in Rock Creek Park
every day hardly caring
if other routes were quicker.
Forgive me; I must apologize.
I see I digress.

How could I just blithely,
routinely fix this new hurt when
my story was that I was too
busy to do anything? I had
the most important job in the
world. It was all on me
to get that sun up and
then get it back down.
Who had time to think weighty
thoughts on net worth?

To have neglected my car—
it was the same theme, no
washes, no oil change, hardly
stopping for fuel except when
in peril—all part of my commitment
to work that claimed
every scrap of attention
ever mine to give. I think

this might have bothered Pat.

It began to bother me too, but I get ahead
of myself. I haven't
even mentioned the accident.

More water, and then,
bravely forward:

Things were seriously wrong just
then; my driving suffered. I knew
I should be doing something
but what? One day on 13th Street
where it bottles up before Georgia
I hit a man, he was in his car, and
a man hit me, also in his car.

A brilliant sunny day it was.
We all said the same thing—that the
sunshine on the year's first great day
called us from our office towers.
There had been some problems up
ahead and so our three cars met—all
the same color, you would probably say silver
rather than gray since we were two Accords
and a BMW but then mine hadn't been washed
unless maybe Pat washed it once. One driver said
our color car was the hardest to see.

What I got out of the crash,
in addition to whatever lasting

effect it has on my rates, was six
long months of transmission
woes. Finger-pointing all around—
a faulty part perhaps, poor technique by
the mechanic, a failure of judgment in
towing the car to nearby Ford
instead of Honda mechanics.
Anyway, the gears lurched:
I had a bucking bronco.
Everyone involved agreed I needed a
new transmission and that it didn't seem fair.
But the problem was mine.

Well, I drew the line. Busy
at work still but this was too much.
So I went to arbitration and what
happened was they held the car hostage.
I was tethered first to Pat, and
it seemed we were unraveling—we
never seemed to get it right, when exactly
to leave the house, where exactly
to meet at the subway. Worse,
I was quiet in the morning, liked
NPR and this was her only
favorite time to talk.

Lucky for me, my friend Gordon
had a spare car. He and Cindy managed
mostly on just one. They seemed happy,
and lived near the subway.
The car was rustic and had an odor

so pungent that my artist friend Tom
who bummed rides decided he
would rather walk, thank you.
Truth be told, Gordon's car—also gray
if any color other than rust—proved
more comfortable to me, and this
bothered me, that it felt more
comfortable than my own car even
though it was a Subaru, steered
like a truck and hurt my
foot when I shifted gears, which was
a lot because they were working on
Rock Creek Park and now I had to
drive through town, where
no matter how late or early even,
it was starting and stopping which was
good for reading the paper and would
have been good for NPR if the Subaru had
had a radio but bad for my foot which
I didn't tell you I hurt and so the whole
time I didn't really have a car, my
foot ached and couldn't much walk.

The transmission problem I must
say did some good.
Work loosened its hold; there
were mechanics, supervisors, lawyers to
talk to and all during business hours
although, looking back, if
I had used some leave,
I might have forced action a month

or two quicker. Or maybe it was the dents,
and they all thought I didn't care that
much about the car one way or
the other.

Which brings me to now.
I have become religious about internal
combustion and lubrication, even air
pressure and timing. The car is well
cared for and, although it is not
quite paid for, it's mine—
all mine. I love every single
thing except that
the ride is so smooth
sometimes you get where you
are going before you are
quite ready.

It took me a minute
to remember my listener.
I looked her way, and
tried to read her face.
She had listened intently,
hearing more more than I
had meant to say. In
her down-turned eyes that
night I found an
urgent message and I took it.
Not right away, but soon after.
That girl, long gone,
I barely remember, but

her legacy lives on. It's
a short drive I make on Mondays.
Jane is my new girl,
and I never miss a single session.
Sure, I bring my checkbook,
but I think just maybe
I've found my true audience.

Squirrel Day Afternoon
Judith K. Witherow

The first thing I do upon waking each morning is raise the window blinds next to my bed. This gives the earth and me first sight at how we're both doing. As a Native American, I always rely on my observation of nature. It is the one absolute in my life.

Because of various health problems, sometimes my only option is to stay in bed. Not being able to walk outside whenever I want creates a depression like no other hardship ever has.

There's always been a need inside of me to get next to all of nature's elements. It's the therapy of choice to aid in whatever form of recovery is needed. When this became harder to achieve, I brought bits of nature within eye's reach to create what I've named my Comfort Corner.

From the black walnut and maple tree hang metal suet feeders for the northern flickers and other woodpeckers. Mesh bags filled with thistle seeds swing freely from their branches to attract martins and goldfinches. A bluebird house placed on the trunk of the maple tree so far entices only sparrows.

My bedroom is on the bottom floor. With privacy in mind I asked my longtime partner, Sue, and my youngest son to build a privacy fence to shield me from our loathsome neighbor's view. When the work was completed I started decorating the fence. My daughter-in-law, a tattoo artist who did my own three tattoos, painted a mural, which included Native American symbols for Sue and my three boys, and various animals—a groundhog, a rat, and a squirrel.

In a moment of misplaced brain cells I placed a squirrel feeder on the fence. It held dried cobs of corn. What a joke! It's not like the squirrels don't take over and eat more than their share of everything. One of them has a missing tail. Probably from a run-in with a neighborhood cat. This winter, for the first time, three hawks have come by to hunt for food. I love it when they visit. They act like they own everything. For some time I'd been wishing for a hawk, and one day I looked out and there one sat. It didn't even ruffle a feather while I took numerous pictures of it to show my family.

A large, round thermometer shows the temperature year-round. My rain catcher measures the amount of whatever is falling out of the sky: rain, sleet, or snow. I want this information. I need this information. The gadgets are nice, but the most accurate notification comes from observing the habits of the wildlife. When they start to feed heavily you know there will be a weather change. This is particularly helpful during the winter season.

Countless hours are spent watching the action that takes place in my private habitat, my Comfort Corner. It soothes and salves whatever mental or physical hurt requires attention. It has been my one constant—that is, my one constant until the unthinkable happened. The unthinkable made its presence known in the form of a plague of squirrels. I know. I was the one who placed the corn out there to attract them. Attract, yes. Invade, no.

When I looked out the window that afternoon I thought, *There goes my eyesight deteriorating again.* I put my glasses on to prove whether it was another symptom of the multiple sclerosis or systemic lupus. No! The dreaded shapes were exactly what I thought them to be—"Squirrels A Plenty." They were the size of my killer dachshund, Marcus. *Perhaps* they were a little smaller than that, but I'm on steroids, which can cause a number of distortions.

One varmint was up in the corner bird feeder. It was scaring the birds away, but worst of all it had invaded my Comfort Corner. I took a number of pictures to prove to my partner what I had witnessed. The time used for picture taking also gave me time to think up a new plan. The squirrels weren't leaving. If they weren't leaving, they were mine. Safety and the potential of rodent bites nibbled at the back of my brain. All right, I'd use a butcher knife. No, wait. I'd use my red cane and the small wastebasket next to my bed. I'd knock them into the little basket and finish them off with my cane. Little basket? No good. The big trash can in the kitchen would be much safer. Okay. The red cane and the big trash can.

This is the kind of incident where it would be helpful if I could walk a little better. It would also be useful to have more physical strength. My mental strength was in overdrive, so that might equal out the other two.

Opening the laundry room door quietly was going to be a problem. The noise might make them run as soon as they heard me coming. I was saying prayers faster than a street-corner preacher, asking for a miracle that my approach wouldn't be heard. The next hurdle would be opening the privacy fence gate. It was one heavy, creaking gate. With the aid of the cane I made it out to the gate. A sudden burst of strength helped lift and open this gate that had never opened without a lot of trouble. Steroids.

We all spotted each other at the same moment. The squirrels hauled hairy ass along the top riser of the fence. So much for plan A. About halfway through the kitchen, the realization of what had almost occurred sunk in. Yeah, I know. Steroids. Every story about cornered animals and people being bit hit me like a physical punch. *Judith? What the hell were you thinking about? Certainly not your health. Would you like a series of rabies shots to add to the rest of your problems?* No indeed! I think I'll move on to plan B.

Plan B consisted of buying a "few" Have-A-Heart animal traps.

In less than three weeks I had trapped and relocated 52 squirrels to better neighborhoods. Not exactly neighborhoods where people lived. These 'hoods consisted of populations of their own kind. I made sure that we took them across so many main roads that there wasn't the slightest possibility of them finding their mind-mauling way home.

My grown sons were prouder of me than I could ever have imagined. All three of them asked me why I didn't use my pistol, since the yard was so overrun.

As the one who is supposed to set good examples, I told them, "You know you can't fire a gun inside the town limits. Also, at the angle the feeder is at, the bullet would have gone through the bastard's house next door." *My gun? I could've used my gun! Damn steroids.*

I'm still amazed at how much in awe my sons remain of my bravery. It enhanced their image of me as the toughest woman they know. When you raise three sons it doesn't hurt to have them see how capable and forceful women are.

Because my sons were so proud, they bought me a paint-ball gun—a beauty when filled with different colored balls—for Christmas. At the family holiday gathering, the boys instructed me to keep my ammo in the refrigerator because the paint balls would be more accurate when cold. They also asked (begged) me not to shoot at them because they were wearing their dress clothes. *Sigh.* When the time is right they will never see the ball with their color—and name—whizzing in their direction.

Two years have passed, and I've started to see the mental marauders running along the top of the privacy fence again. Just when you think that you can relax, hell thaws out, and that which plagued you returns. Fine. This time I'm legally armed and oh so ready.

Recently while looking out the window, I saw a large squirrel sitting on one of the posts, nonchalantly eating a fistful of berries from the firethorn bush. The weather was cold, but that didn't deter me from opening the window and raising the screen.

Plan C was quickly put into action. I retrieved my jars of colored paint balls from the refrigerator. It was time to lock and load. While I'm making preparations I'm thinking that the squirrel will surely be gone. No such varmint-munching luck. Sanity or squirrels? Squirrels! I take careful aim and slowly squeeze the trigger. *Bam!* *Bam* is right. Just as I shot, the squirrel leaned over, and the bright orange paint ball sailed over its head. The beast had set me up!

I might have missed the squirrel, but I was right on target with the pale gray siding of the dreaded house next door. Gawd bless it. Now what? From the trajectory, you could tell the exact location where the shot was fired. I watched as orange paint slowly oozed down the side of the house. Any way I looked at it, orange and gray were not going to blend. That woman-hating man detested me as much as I did him. He was not going to let this pass. I would say "pass unnoticed," but that would just be me starting to mentally lose it big time.

Sometimes—not often, but sometimes—nature cuts you a break. As I sat watching the paint reach the halfway mark on the house, it started to rain. Yes! It rained softly at first, but as the hours wore on the rain got heavier. Every time I looked out, more of the water-color paint was gone. Like a demented cheerleader, I rooted the bad weather on. Before darkness shut out my view and the neighbor came home, the paint had washed away.

I wish I could say that a lesson was learned. I could, but it wouldn't be the one most folks would guess. The lesson I've learned is to shoot lower if the opportunity arises and to pick a target larger than a squirrel. Better yet, make it a woman-hating target—one that doubles that hatred when two women-loving women live next door. Now *that's* therapy.

Affirmations in Action
Ellen Orleans

A few months back, steeped in despair over a recent breakup, I noticed that I wasn't sleeping well, wasn't eating well, wasn't feeling any enthusiasm for life. Fortunately I was able to recognize the true nature of my listlessness: symptoms of depression.

The next week I plopped down on my therapist's couch and announced, "I'm clinically depressed."

"Let's not toss around psychological jargon," she replied. "What are you feeling?"

"I'm not hungry. Can't sleep. My self-esteem is shot. What's the purpose in living since we all die anyway?"

"Hmm," she said. "Sounds like you're depressed."

I glared in her direction.

"So what do you want to do about it?" she asked.

"I want to *wallow* in it," I said, acknowledging that the depression had not dulled my sarcasm.

Of course, I didn't *really* want to wallow in it. But how could I get out of it? My brother was always proclaiming the virtues of affirmations, and I figured I could handle listening to an affirmation tape as long as I kept busy doing something else, like driving or washing dishes.

So I took myself to the neighborhood New Age store, Healing and Feeling, and asked the clerk if they carried any tapes of loving affirmations for depressed people wallowing through the aftermath of a breakup.

"Over there," she said, pointing to the back of the store. Figuring there'd be maybe a dozen affirmation tapes, I was bowled over to see a whole wall full of them. Louise Hay had two shelves just to herself: *Healing Your Body, Healing Your Mind, Teaching Your Dog to Heal.* I eyed other titles as well: *Affirmations for the Joyous Heart, Six Weeks to Inner Peace, Guided Meditations for the Spiritually Inept, Jane Fonda's Seven-Chakra Workout.* Nothing seemed right. Besides, at $14.95 each, they were rather pricey.

Then I spotted the discount bin. Rummaging through, I found a pile of tapes by T.J. Hay, Louise's lesser-known lesbian sister.

Now I'm getting somewhere, I thought, reading the titles: *Getting Clear, Being Queer; The Inner Journey to Coming Out; Affirmations for the Radiant Clitoris.* I finally chose *Letting Loose of Your Lesbian Ex-Lover.* At $2.99, I knew I'd gotten a deal.

I trotted home and popped the cassette into the tape player.

"Hello," a warm and kind voice said, "I'm T.J. Hay, and together we're going to let loose of your lesbian ex-lover."

I looked at the tape player. "Right," I said.

"Find yourself a comfortable, safe space. Sit down and relax."

"Forget it," I told T.J., "I'm putting away my laundry."

"That's good," the tape said. "Now take a deep breath. And another."

"Whose idea was this?" I muttered, gathering my underwear off the drying rack and putting it in the drawer.

"Fine," the tape said. "Now repeat after me, I *love* myself."

OK, I told myself, *this was my idea, and I can do this.* So I repeated after T.J., "I *love* myself."

"I am a good person."

I am basically good, I thought, rolling up a pair of socks. "I am a good person."

"My life is rich, and I am blessed."

Don't push it, T.J., I thought. But I *said*, "My life is rich, and I am blessed."

"I have a loving and forgiving heart."

"I have a loving and forgiving heart," I grumbled, rolling up more socks.

"I love and forgive my ex-girlfriend."

"I love and forgive my ex-girlfriend," I said, choking on my words.

"Except for that incident last winter."

"Except for that incident last winter...." Hey, how'd she know about that?

"I'm still pretty ticked off about that."

Damn right. "I am still ticked off about that."

"In fact, just thinking about it makes me pretty angry."

"*Very* angry." I told the cassette deck.

"In fact, I feel like picking up a soft object and throwing it across the room."

My hand reached out for the alarm clock.

"A soft object," the tape said. "Like a pillow."

I grabbed Ruby, a stuffed red dinosaur that my ex-lover had given me.

"Don't throw that cute dinosaur," the voice said.

"Fine, I'll throw a pair of rolled-up socks."

"How about a sock?" the voice said.

"I'm ahead of you," I told the tape.

"Well then, throw that object."

I heaved the blue-and-white socks across the room. My cat flew off the bed and ran for the closet, knocking over the drying rack in the process. Clothes spilled to the floor.

"I am really angry," the tape said.

"I am really angry," I said, throwing another pair, pink this time. The socks hit my change dish, and coins flew all over.

"Damn, am I pissed off," the tape said.

"Damn, am I pissed off!" I yelled, flinging yet another pair, these teal.

"I can't believe you bought trendy teal socks," the tape said. "Don't you know they'll be out of style in six months?"

"Shut up!" I screamed, hurling a pair of heavy woolen camping socks directly at the tape player, knocking it over.

"That's good!" the voice said from the floor where the player had landed. "Vent that anger! Beat on a pillow! Let's hear a primal scream!"

"Arrgh!" I yelled, shredding a pillow with my bare hands, feathers flying wildly about.

Suddenly it was quiet. I looked around me. Clothes were strewn everywhere. Nickels and dimes covered the rug. Posters, hit by socks, hung askew. Feathers continued to float down slowly.

I looked at the tape player. Side one was over. I flipped the tape and read the title of side two: *Cleaning up the Emotional Mess of a Breakup*. I put it in and pressed PLAY.

Lesbian Intellectuals Anonymous
Diane F. Germain

Good evening, and welcome to the Thursday night meeting of Lesbian Intellectuals Anonymous. My name is Diane, and I'm a Lesbian Intellectual.

I've been an intellectual since I was quite young—as long as I can remember, actually. But I didn't see it as a problem 'til I hit bottom. Oh sure, people were always making off-handed comments that I could have paid much more attention to, like "Your problem is you *think* too much," or "Diane, do you have to analyze everything?" Well, obviously they didn't realize that I *did* have to analyze everything as if my life depended on it.

People got tense with me because I had to know everything: "Then what did she say? What did *you* say? What did her face look like when she said that? Were her hands gesticulating or just in her pockets? How did you *feel* when she said that? How do you think *she* felt? Did she say? Did it remind you of your father? Tell me more." (I couldn't get enough.) "*Tell me faster.*" I was called intense; sure, I was intense—wasn't everybody intense? No? *Well*, they must be deadheads or druggies or something. If they aren't intense, they don't know what the fuck is going on in the world.

I was intense, all right.

But then I began to lose more and more of my old friends, one by one. I turned to reading to ease my pain, distract myself, and take up the extra time I had on my hands. Early on, Mary Daly's

Gyn/Ecology book convinced me to give up any medical care or therapy. Claudia Black's children-of-alcoholics book *It Will Never Happen to Me* convinced me to give up relationships. Sonia Johnson's book convinced me to give up religion, and Andrea Dworkin's book convinced me to give up sex. *So what?* I thought. *Now I have more time to read.*

I began hanging around libraries, anxious for a chance to fondle the books in a public place where I might get caught at any moment. I stuffed them in my jean jacket, thrilled to feel their heavy weight and stiff bindings against my body. As I walked around, faint gusts of warm glue and musty paper filled my mind with concupiscent fantasies. Just as long as I stayed away from the electronic detectors, I was more or less safe, even when I paraded around under the pinched nose of the head librarian. I knew she was trying to catch me at something but she never did. I was too clever for her. I was high with power and superiority. My books shielded me from mere human touch.

I began to get up earlier and earlier in the morning to watch a few hours of PBS before I went to work. Starting at 5 A.M., I was fascinated by *Aerobic Calculus, Computer Chronicles*, and *The Joy of Geothermal Physics*. I learned how to fix a toilet, a light switch, and a leaking nuclei. I became an expert on insect sexual practices, gourmet sea gardening, Ukrainian economics. Yet it never seemed enough. The more I learned, the more empty I felt. I was a great student but never a teacher.

I tried to teach! I wanted everyone to be an intellectual. I'd often buy my friends and even strangers sets of gift books. I'd step up to the counter and loudly say, "Yes, B. Dalton, the books are on me." But all too soon they got tired of me telling them what to read. I bought a Lhasa Apso, but she ran away after the first week. My boss caught me reading *The Wall Street Journal* in the toilet one time too many. He fired me. That same day I ran my car into a telephone pole while straining to read the bumper stickers pasted on a truck.

I was beginning to play Trivial Pursuit all by myself, pretending I was four or more players. I needed more and more card sets, Baby Boomer, Genus I and II, Silver Screen, the Gay and Lesbian version, the naughty *Heterosexual* version even. Then I knew I was in deep trouble.

So I came here to get some help. I know I can't do it alone.

I admitted I was powerless over books and ideas—my life had become...*literal.*

I came to believe a mind smarter than mine could restore me to blissful ignorance.

I made a decision to return my books to the library and pay my overdue charges, which by then were more than $100.

I made a fearless search and moral inventory of the *Encyclopedia Britannica.*

I admitted to my dog and several inarticulate animals in my neighborhood the exact nature of my intelligence quotient.

I was entirely ready to have the great professor in the sky remove all these high marks of my intelligence.

I humbly asked her to remove the A+ grades from all my report cards since kindergarten.

I made a list, oh yes I did, I made a list of all persons I was smarter than (and it was a *long* list, let me tell you). But I became willing to make witty statements to them all. I made direct biting satirical comments to such people whenever possible, even when to do so would insult them or question the nature of their parentage.

And I continued to take a personal inventory of each and every misspelled or mispronounced word of people around me, which I promptly announced publicly.

Yes, friends, I was unafraid in the glow of enlightenment.

And so, I sought through meditation and musing and thinking to improve my knowledge of everything I could understand, praying (only when I had a moment free of ideations and conceptions) for more knowledge and will and power to carry even more ideology in my left brain.

Having had a spiritual awakening as a result of modifying these steps, I try to carry this message to individuals all over the country, and to practice effete snobbism in all of my meetings.

Finally, I have made a solemn determination to turn my life over to Mary Daly, since I understand her so well.

Kris Kovick

I THOUGHT WHEN I GOT MY
LEATHER JACKET I WOULDN'T
NEED THERAPY ANYMORE.

The Y Files
Shari J. Berman

Dust bunnies were clinging to the sleeve of my blazer as I picked myself up off the floor. That was a sign, if there ever was one, of how low I'd sunk both figuratively and literally. The baby monitor was now behind the end table instead of on top of it. I walked back into my office and sat down at my desk.

Didn't I have a Miracle Brush somewhere? I settled for Scotch tape and began to pull the dust off of my sleeve and toss lint-covered strips into the wastebasket. Why was there so much dust under the end table? I contemplated calling the cleaning service, but then I thought about Sara M. Sara was a patient of mine who was still having nightmares after a skinhead had taken a cleaning job at her gay radio station so he could plant a bomb from the inside. She had barely escaped with her life. I took a deep breath to cast away the thought. I guess a little dust wouldn't kill me! A violent sneeze overtook me at that moment. Well, at least it wouldn't kill me all at once.

It was surprising that the space under the end table could get so dusty in six months. For years I had been sharing an office on a lower floor with a dentist and a podiatrist. My patients used to walk in chuckling over seeing a copy of *The Advocate* next to a copy of *Highlights* on the end table. Interesting chain of events, actually. I believe that my practice was completely out of the closet before I was.

My sleeve was reasonably tidy now, so I began combing out the cobwebs of my mind. How was I so sure about this new plan? Why was I so hell-bent on getting Gretchen and Lyndsay together? Every inch of this scheme was gray to black on the ethics scale, but I felt compelled to give it a shot. Why did I want them to meet?

Well, it was because I knew they'd be perfect for each other, but I couldn't very well use personality traits and privileged information that had come to me in sessions to send them on a blind date. Lyndsay, after all, was someone I just knew as a patient. Years earlier, Gretchen and I had traveled in similar circles socially, but she is currently a patient. Anyhow, I was fairly certain that her compulsively orderly world would be rocked by the idea of going out with someone she'd never met. No, this was the only solution. If my grandmother were still alive, she'd be calling me "Dr. Yenta" right about now.

The baby monitor would be on so that I could easily overhear their conversation in the waiting room. What was I doing with a baby monitor? Well, that had to do with the latest evolution of my client base. I've been practicing as a psychologist since the late '70s. I know it sounds like a one-liner from a Catskills nightclub act, but I believe that "practicing psychology" is an accurate term, because none of us ever gets it right.

I gradually became the mental health purveyor of choice to Chicago's gay and lesbian community. In the late '70s and early '80s, more men came through my office than women. I used to say, "Queens have means, and dykes have bikes."

It was beyond stereotypes. Lucy, a woman I saw regularly at a local women's bar, always asked me if I could adjust my fees for her. I'd mumble and say maybe we could work something out, but she'd invariably change her mind when she was sober and facing her grueling work week as a short-order cook on Monday. What got me was that, at the time, Lucy tooled around on top of a huge, brandnew, cherry-red hog that I imagined would have set me back several months of salary. Although I wasn't rolling in it, I was pretty sure that helping people reframe their feelings, even 20 years ago, was going for a few pennies more than slinging hash. Mental health was not a big priority for Lucy, and I just grinned and fielded the same poor-pitiful-me lines from her whenever we ran into one another at the bar.

A decade passed, and my new observation became "Queens have means, and dykes have tykes." That's when the baby monitor found its way to my waiting room. HMOs also made it possible for more women to have their mental health fees covered. Sadly, I lost some men to reckless youth in the era of a plague. My friends and patients Don and Joe were among them. They were very much in love with each other, but cruising was the name of the game, and the concept of exactly how high the stakes were came to them all too late.

Statistically—and all psychologists worship statistics—my practice was now heading into the millennium as 60% lesbian, 25% gay, and 15% an even split of heterosexual men and women. I often wondered about those straight referrals, but the people usually came in bubbling about how their gay friend or their lesbian cousin had told them I was the best. Unlike many lay people, I do know when my ego is being stroked, but when someone accidentally believes I really know what I'm doing, I'm loath to set them straight…especially when they're straight to begin with. Perhaps my unwillingness to correct straight people is internalized homophobia; or maybe I enjoy leaving them in the dark so I can smugly revel in my lesbian superiority. Either way, I really should make an appointment with my own counselor, sooner rather than later.

I penned a note explaining my "emergency" and addressed it to both Gretchen and Lyndsay. I glanced at the clock on my desk. T minus ten minutes and counting…I'd have time to grab a quick cup of tea, leave the note in the waiting room, and powder my nose before Gretchen was due to arrive. I went about the tasks at hand.

Somehow I completed my various chores with six minutes to spare. I sat back down and ruminated further. I called and left a message for Catherine, my therapist. Thank heaven she didn't talk in her sleep. I was trying to remember when I had started down this path of random acts of unprofessional kindness. It must have been Allison. She came to me in a state of depression after losing her job. She could no longer afford day care for her three-year-old, so she was being a full-time mother. In other words, she actually did have a stressful full-time job, but wasn't earning any money.

Allison was a car mechanic, and her feelers for new positions had met with actionable sexual discrimination, but she didn't have the desire or the strength to fight the world. I knew a woman in the community whose family owned a well-known garage on the west side. I talked up an upcoming lesbian picnic to both of them and made sure they were introduced. Allison has been working there ever since.

Catherine had reminded me in our sessions that the gray area I kept finding myself in was not that different from where the rest of the world lived. There wasn't too much out there that really spoke to the human experience that was easily divided into black and white. That comforted me for a nanosecond, but I knew that I was getting much too personally involved with my patients' problems. I had been more objective and standoffish when I was younger.

Allison may have been my debut as a busybody, but Bailey was my first voyeuristic foray into the love lives of others. She had called to make an appointment, and between her showgirl name and her bedroom voice, not to mention the announcement that she had a problem of "a sexual nature," I was mesmerized. The timing had been amazing. I was leading a group therapy session on lesbian bed death, and in the spirit of "physician, heal thyself," Marcy and I were going through a period of sexual inactivity. That was when I started seeing Catherine. My new patient at the time, Bailey, was actually trying to curb her sexual appetites. I was overempathizing with her, nonetheless. I also staved off feelings of attraction for her, which I'd never really had for a patient before. Catherine held me up and kept me from moving erratically and sending my life askew in domino fashion. She would have a field day with my latest caper. I looked at the clock again. Gretchen was due any minute.

During the first few seconds of monitoring, I was treated to a concert of seat adjustment noises, followed by sighing and throat clearing. I was starting to worry when I finally heard the rustling of her reading my note. To avoid being obvious, I pressed my portable phone to my ear and stood up. I began to talk into the dead instrument as I opened the door to the waiting room. "Has the doctor been in to see her? Uh-huh. Could I ask you to hold on for one minute? Thanks," I said to the receiver.

"Did you get my note, Gretchen?"

She nodded.

"Sorry. Just give me a few minutes here."

"No problem," Gretchen said with a smile.

"I'm sorry. When will I be able to speak with her directly?" I asked, continuing my staged dialogue and closing the door to my office. Safely back in my space, I put the nonactive phone back in its cradle and took a deep breath.

Gretchen was stopping by to pick up a copy of an article I'd written, and my note told her not only that I was in the middle of an emergency but also that I had to change the cartridge on my printer. I was counting on Lyndsay to be early. Our session wasn't supposed to be for another 15 minutes, but she was always there way before the bell rang, so to speak.

I sat at my desk and listened to Gretchen turn magazine pages. Surely only a few minutes had passed, but I was relieved to hear the office door open. Gretchen gave Lyndsay a minute to sit down. "There's a note," she finally said. I could hear her hand the paper to Lyndsay. "Sounded like one of Dr. Felton's patients was hospitalized or something. She stepped out here a few minutes ago."

"That's too bad. So is she running an hour behind?"

"Oh, uh, no, I'm here to pick up an article from her."

Lyndsay laughed. "Sorry, I didn't mean to mistake you for one of us nuts."

I heard Gretchen laugh too. "Actually, I'm a Friday nut, but I'm here on a Tuesday because she offered to lend me some material for an article I'm writing…. I'm a freelance journalist."

"It's kind of an obsessive-compulsive thing that I worry about time even when it doesn't make any difference. I don't have to be at work for another six hours."

There were a few minutes of silence. I was pacing back and forth hoping for a bit more chemistry.

Gretchen reopened with, "Interesting spelling for your name."

"How do you know how to spell my name? Oh."

I could only surmise that Gretchen had pointed to my note.

"So you start work at 10 P.M.?"

"Not always, but I do tonight. I'm an emergency room nurse. And the spelling of my first name is from an old Scottish family name on my mother's side."

"Really? I'll have to look it up. I have a big coffee-table book on Scottish clans that I got as a present. It has all of the tartans and things."

"No kidding."

"It's kind of cool. I remember being in Campbell Castle when I was traveling around Scotland, and they had a sample of the tartan. It looked like a pattern on a skirt I wore in junior high. I'd never thought about Glen Campbell and the soup heirs and all those people being related. It was pretty interesting."

"If you find the Lyndsays in your book, I'd love to see it."

Bingo! Take the bait, Gretchen. Lyndsay rarely travels this far out on a limb.

"Of course…but I can't very well show my books to a stranger. Could I buy you dinner before your shift?"

I held my breath. I thought Lyndsay might have been doing the same thing.

"That would be nice," Lyndsay finally managed.

"Great. I'll come back and pick you up when your session finishes."

"OK."

I jumped up and down and did a silent cheer. I pulled out the folder with the copy of the article I'd made two days earlier for Gretchen and headed toward the door. It was three minutes to 4, so I wasn't even technically late for Lyndsay's session.

"Sorry to keep you waiting," I said, handing the folder to Gretchen. "Maybe we can discuss it on the phone after you've had a chance to read it."

Gretchen took it from me, stood, and gave me a quick hug. When we disengaged, she offered me an enigmatic smile. "Thanks, Jude," Gretchen said. The look in her eyes told me she was so on to me. Well, of course. What was the likelihood of between 3:30 and 4 P.M. on Tuesday being the only time I could give her that article? I motioned Lyndsay into my office.

Lyndsay's spirits were high, and the session went by quickly. Lyndsay was working on being more spontaneous. She told me about what had happened in the waiting room. I feigned surprise and, with as little judgment as possible, matter-of-factly validated her willingness to take a chance on having dinner with a kind stranger.

When I walked her back into the lobby, Gretchen was sitting there with flowers. Nice touch! I bit my tongue to keep from grinning ear to ear.

I went back into my office and listened to Lyndsay gush over the bouquet. I made a note to myself to remember to put the baby monitor back on the end table and turn it off. I switched on my computer and entered the whole thing as a case history in my Y

Files. That folder was growing by the week.

I then retrieved my voice-mail. There was a message from Catherine giving me a couple of time slot options for my next appointment. Catherine sounded a bit down to me. Rumor had it that she'd broken up with her lover recently. Unlike my practice, hers was mostly straight, with a couple of exceptions...me, for example.

I listened to the next message. It was from a new patient, Gloria, a lawyer who had recently moved to Chicago from the Bay Area. Hmm...I was getting the strongest feeling that the calls in sequence like that were no coincidence. I just knew that Gloria would be perfect for Catherine. That was the end of the messages, I reset the phone to ring directly.

I tried to hold myself in check, but I could feel the plotting wheels turning again. If only I could get Catherine and Gloria to the same place at the same time. Uh-oh. Why couldn't I just sit back and enjoy what I accomplished with Lyndsay and Gretchen?

I needed professional help. Would I be able to see Catherine as my therapist when she was looking like my next project? Where was my peer group? Were there any 12-step programs for yenta psychologists? Would that be under Y or P in the phone book?

The phone rang. It was Ruth. We made an appointment for Thursday. Poor Ruth—she'd been with Noreen for five years, and Noreen had just up and left her for another woman. Ruth...she would be just perfect for that young woman Jean, who works with Marcy...Turn it off, Jude! I took a deep, deep breath. I could stop. Yes, I could stop matchmaking cold, I thought. But then where would all these lonely women be?

OK, I just have to be more clever. My setups must be foolproof. What about an accomplice? Could I talk Marcy into helping me? Marcy is so straitlaced, but maybe she'd understand the cause. These women need my help. What was that expression...so many women, so little time? I'd heard that before, but I was just beginning to understand what it meant for me. "Matchmaker, Matchmaker" from *Fiddler on the Roof* played on in my head.

I laid my head on my desk. I attempted to empty my mind of these conflicting thoughts. When I straightened up a few minutes later, I saw that I had bumped the keyboard and typed a series of Y's on the screen. It had to be an omen! Even my computer agreed that a yenta's work was never done. So, which did I work on first, Catherine and Gloria or Ruth and Jean? Ah…decisions, decisions.

Jane Caminos

Case History of a Warrior Princess
Julia Willis

I was preparing to leave my office for the day, watering my plants and shutting down my laptop, when three ferocious knocks loud as cannon blasts shook the outer office door, making me jump like I'd been shot. I considered calling security, but my instincts told me truly dangerous people didn't bother to announce their presence. So I squared my shoulders, walked briskly to the door—and opened it.

Before me stood a tall, dark woman wearing a fierce expression, carrying a sword on her back and dressed in a strange, skimpy costume made of copper-colored metal and brown leather.

"Are you the healer?" she blurted out, her jaw set and her fists clenched.

Despite her imposing presence, I felt I had nothing to fear from this woman, who was obviously seeking my help. Yet I froze, momentarily tongue-tied.

"Are you the healer?" she asked again.

"Well," I replied, "while I do see the therapeutic process as a healing journey, I'm not sure I'd specifically refer to myself as—"

She frowned impatiently.

"Yes," I admitted, "I am. I am the healer."

"The Amazons sent me," she said, as if that would explain everything, and brushed past me into the waiting room. Her darting eyes took in every detail as she moved swiftly to the door of my inner office and glanced inside. "You are alone," she stated flatly. "Good."

I confess I found her take-charge attitude a bit off-putting, and it had been a long day. "Look," I said, "it's late. Why don't we schedule you a session for tomorrow? I have a cancellation at 11…."

"No." She turned her steely gaze on me. "Now."

Her insistence forced me to question my initial judgment. *Was* I being too trusting? *Had* I something to fear? Again it flashed in my mind to notify the guard on duty—but, I asked myself, where had he been when she entered the building? It was after hours. Wasn't the main entrance locked?

"Excuse me for asking," I said, "but how did you get up here so late? Wasn't there a guard downstairs?"

"Oh, him. Yeah," she recalled. "He—he'll be all right," she said sheepishly.

It suddenly seemed prudent not to attempt to reschedule. "Fine," I said, throwing up my hands, "let's do this," and I indicated the inner office. "In there."

She fairly bounded through the doorway, and I followed, closing the door behind us. Wandering over to my desk, she picked up a carved faux ivory letter opener, running her finger along the edge. "Dull blade," she said too casually. "So what do we do?"

"Sit down, please," I said, pointing to the couch.

She strode over to the couch, plunked herself down, and adjusted her leather wristbands. "OK. Now what?"

"Now," I said, leaning against my desk, "we talk."

For the first time I saw fear in her eyes. To cover it, she gave a sniff of disdain. "Talk? About what?"

"Oh," I said, taking a seat in my chair beside the couch, "whatever it is that's bothering you."

"Yeah?" she said dubiously. I was not the sort of healer she'd expected.

I nodded, folding my hands in my lap, sensing any wrong

move—a reach for my notebook, a call to tell my partner not to hold dinner—might cause her to bolt. And I was becoming more than a little intrigued by the urgency of her plight, coupled with the hesitation in her manner. "Whenever you're ready," I prompted.

She gave a jerky nod and proceeded to exhibit a host of nervous tics: She squeezed her facial muscles and shook her head, ran her hand through her dark mane of hair and rubbed her neck, sighed, stared at the floor, and tapped her boots on the carpet. Finally she rose and paced to the door, whirling around to shout in desperation, "Isn't there some other way? There must be."

"I'm afraid not," I said simply.

A low animal growl emanated from her throat as she reached over her shoulder and pulled out a sword with a blade as thick as my arm. I gasped, but she was too absorbed in her own thoughts to care as she came back to the couch, took a small stone from a pouch on her belt, and sat down, examining the sword blade carefully. "All right," she said slowly, "we'll talk."

But we didn't. For ten long minutes I sat watching her as she sharpened her sword, methodically scraping the stone down the edge of the blade with a steady motion. It should've sounded like fingernails on a blackboard to my ears, and it did; yet her actions gave me insight into who this woman was, that it should be so hard for her to open up. Clearly she was accustomed to letting her sword do her talking for her.

But finally I felt there was little more to be accomplished by this delay tactic, revealing as it might be. "Whenever you're ready?" I said, and the scraping stopped.

Looking straight ahead, her lips in a thin line, she replied testily, "I'm workin' on it," and resumed her sharpening with renewed vigor.

Another few minutes passed. This time she stopped of her own accord, sat staring for a moment, then pocketed the stone and slipped her sword into its scabbard. Sighing, she leaned her elbows on her knees. "You know, it might help," she suggested, "if we had a campfire."

"I'm afraid that would set off the sprinkler system," I said, pointing at the ceiling. Following my finger, she grunted in disgust. Soon she was staring at the floor and tapping her boots again.

Outside the sun was setting. I stood up and switched on the desk lamp, reaching for my notebook and pen. If taking a structured approach scared her away, so be it, for we were getting nowhere fast. As I resumed my seat she gave me a sidelong glance and smiled at the sight of my writing tools.

"Are *you* a bard too?" she asked shyly.

"As well as a healer, you mean?" Perhaps talking about me would get us started.

"No." She took a deep breath. "I mean—Gabrielle is a bard. A poet. She has a great gift."

"I see. And who is Gabrielle?" I knew this had to be someone important to the woman. The very mention of that name widened her eyes and softened the corners of her mouth.

She took another deep breath and said, "She's—she's my friend," infusing the word *friend* with such meaning that no further explanation was warranted. Now I understood why the Amazons had sent her to me. Not necessarily how or for what, but certainly why.

"And would you like to tell me about Gabrielle?" I asked gently.

Her eyes took on a faraway look. "She's—everything to me. My family, my source, my heart."

"Hmm," I said. "And how does that make you feel?"

"Feel?" she asked, turning her hands over and gazing into the open palms. "Every day I thank the gods she came into my life. She's taught me how to love. I mean really love someone. Do you understand?"

"You're in love with her," I replied.

She shot me a look of surprise mixed with admiration. "Yes," she said, "I am." She got up and paced to the bookshelves. "So," she continued without turning around, "what can I do about it?"

"Well," I asked, "how does she feel about you?"

She yanked a thick reference book at random from a shelf, grasping it with both hands and clutching it to her breastplate. "She says she loves me," she mumbled in reply, her chin upon her chest. "She says it all the time."

"Then what's the problem?"

"The problem," she said with a hollow laugh, "the problem is she doesn't—we haven't—I can't—there's no—" She dropped the book, and it hit the carpet with a resounding thud.

"You're not sure she loves you in quite the same way you love her?"

"Exactly," she said, relieved, but poking the book nervously with the toe of her boot.

"And why would you assume that?"

"Because—" She hesitated. "Well, because she doesn't—we haven't—I can't—"

I interrupted. "Could it be," I ventured, my intuitive antennae up, "you don't feel worthy of her love?"

She frowned and bit her lip to stop its slight quiver. Then, as her pain turned to anger, one hard, swift kick sent the heavy volume at her feet soaring across the room, shattering the window behind my desk.

"I hope that doesn't hurt anyone," I said, a good deal more calmly than I felt, referring to the book that was now hurtling several stories to the ground.

"Oh," she said, hurrying to the gaping hole in the glass to check. "It's all right," she added a moment later. "It hit one of those carts that goes without horses. It smashed the blue fire on top."

"A police cruiser?" I guessed.

Shrugging, she returned to the couch.

"You are very strong," I said, "and very impulsive. That can be a dangerous combination."

"I know," she agreed, sitting back down. "It's lethal." Looking me straight in the eye, she said, "I've done terrible things in my life."

"I can believe it," I said, before her eyes made it abundantly clear she was not to be interrupted again. "Sorry. Go on."

"Terrible things," she repeated, and I just nodded.

At last the words spilled out in a rush as she told me of her years as a cruel warlord (her expression, not mine). The plundering, the pillaging, the slaughter of innocents—she painted a relentlessly callous, heartless picture of herself, and I took notes. Eventually, what I'd have to categorize as a conversion experience had led her to examine the terrible truth of her evil past and make a concerted effort to turn her life around.

"That must have been very difficult for you," I remarked, when she paused for breath.

"Yes," she said, "but not to change would've been harder."

"Often change comes about as an inevitable consequence of our actions."

"Then you believe that we, not the Fates, control our destinies," she said.

"In your case, certainly," I said. "Your own resolve and determination have motivated you to become who you are today."

"But it's not just that," she insisted. "I could never have done it alone. I needed help, guidance, patience—I needed Gabrielle." As she gave me more background on their relationship, I gathered Gabrielle had come along at the precise moment when the warrior woman was feeling especially lost and vulnerable. This younger woman's youthful enthusiasm and encouragement had been instrumental in effecting a more permanent change, affording this former warlord a fresh perspective on how she might now live to accomplish good and vanquish evil.

Still, in spite of Gabrielle's obviously deep and abiding affection, the woman had grave doubts concerning the nature of her love. "*She* came after *me*," she said, a deep furrow in her brow, "leaving her village and her family to travel with me and share my life. We've been through everything together—the waking, the sleeping, the bathing, the fishing, the fighting, the killing. The bond between us transcends even death, yet there's this line she won't cross." She scratched her knee, frowning. "I knew she was innocent when I met her, but she couldn't be *that* unaware of what's between us, could she?"

"You tell me," I said, gently prodding.

"*No!*" she shouted out of frustration. "Well," she went on, contradicting herself, "maybe she could...."

"Is it possible she's sending you mixed messages?" I asked. She looked puzzled. "She's saying one thing and doing another?"

"Yes! That's it!" she said, raising her voice again. "Mixed messages. She never speaks of men and marriage and settling down the way she used to. She's jealous of anyone who threatens to come between us. She watches me and strokes my head when she thinks I'm sleeping. And she knows how I feel about her."

"Does she?"

"Of course she does," she barked impatiently, staring over my head at the cool blue lava lamp resting on top of my lateral file cabinet.

"How would she know that?"

"How? The way I look at her, the way I act with her, my touch..."

"And you're not holding back, you're being totally honest with her about your feelings?"

"Yeah," she said uncertainly.

"Then why," I asked directly, "are you here?"

Without warning she grabbed a sharp, round object off her belt and launched it in my direction. I ducked as it flew by, shattered the lava lamp, caromed off a picture frame hanging on the opposite wall, and returned to her upraised hand. Her piercing blue eyes had turned colder than ice. I held my breath until her arm dropped to her side.

"Well, I know one thing," she said, in a voice ominously low. "I'm not here to be questioned like an oracle."

"But if I am to heal you," I replied, swallowing hard, "I must find out what you need."

With a sneer she hooked the deadly Frisbee back on her belt, but I could see that unless we arrived at a breakthrough soon, the next thing she'd be taking aim at would be my head.

I cleared my throat and gave it my best shot. "You consider Gabrielle the source of your redemption. You're afraid that without her you could revert to old ways, old patterns of behavior.…" *Old habits of killing people who displease you,* I thought but didn't dare say. "It's no wonder you fear her rejection."

"What do you mean?" Again her look was murderous.

"That it's understandable you'd be hesitant to make the first move—"

Her jaw dropped.

I finished quickly. "But you see, that may be just what she's waiting for. For you. To make the first move."

"For me?" she cried in astonishment. "Me? Don't you get it? Don't you understand anything?"

I prepared to duck—or die.

"I'm waiting for *her*. For *her* to come to *me*." As if she'd taken a blow from a heavy club, she sank to her knees. "Talk about your Greek tragedy," she said sadly, shaking her head. "I thought I knew all there was to know about seduction and conquest. Anyone I ever wanted was mine. Anyone," she repeated, with the sure gaze to back up her claim. "The act was for sport, it was for pleasure, it was for power, and once—maybe twice—it was even for love. Or what I thought was love. But this—this is not about conquest, it's about...surrender." She eased herself into a half-lotus position on the carpet. "It's out of my hands. Do you know how much that scares me?"

"I can imagine," I said. "But what is it you're waiting for? Exactly what is it you want from Gabrielle?"

Resting her temple against the flat of her hand, she exhaled noisily. "I want—" She began to describe the scene unfolding in her mind. "I want to hear her say my name. I want to turn and find her spreading my blanket by the fire. 'Come here,' she'll say, and I'll obey. 'I know what you want,' she'll say, 'I want that too'."

She sat up straight and focused. "I want her to touch my shoulder, here, and guide me onto the blanket. She'll take off my armor, and slowly she'll undress me, and all the while she'll be talking to me, telling me a story of how love once brought fire and water together, and because love was there fire warmed the water without boiling it away, and water softened the flames without quenching them, and each made the other stronger and better and more beautiful.

"But," she continued, "I won't be listening to her story. I'll be watching her mouth as she tells it and her eyes as they wash over my skin and her hands as they smooth my blanket and she gently lays me down. I want to lie very still as she undresses beside me, and when she lowers herself onto me I want to look into her face and know she's there because she desires me with all her heart.

"I want to feel the down of her cheek against my neck when she rests between long, deep kisses. I want to hear her moans as she presses into me, our breasts enfolded, our legs intertwined, our—" She looked up suddenly, her hand reaching for the hilt of her sword. Something had spoiled her reverie. "What's that?" she asked.

I listened. "Sirens," I said. "Something's going on out front."

Laying aside my notebook and going to the broken window, I looked out. Under the streetlight I could see three backup cruisers converging. "Cops," I said. The word meant nothing to her. "Soldiers, basically," I explained. "They've discovered the damage to their blue fire."

"Ah," she said, satisfied by my answer.

"They're pointing to this building. Sooner or later they'll spot the window, and they'll be coming up."

"There's time," she said, unconcerned. "Sit down. Let me finish."

I opened my mouth to protest.

"Sit."

I sat.

"Where was I?" she asked.

I consulted my notes. "Intertwined?"

"Right," she nodded, curiously soothed by this tale and the sound of her own voice. "Intertwined. I want to yield to her, defenseless against the power of her passion. I want to shiver in my own sweat and soak the blanket through. I want my cries to shatter the heavens as she takes me and rocks me till I explode with a force the gods will feel on Mount Olympus! And then," she said, quietly drawing up her knees and hugging them to her chest, "I want to lie looking up at the sky, memorizing every curve and fork in every branch of every tree towering over us, while her hands and tongue do the same with every curve and limb of mine." She stopped. Outside a rhythmic banging had begun. The police, apparently unable to rouse the guard, were using a makeshift battering ram to smash the front doors.

"And then what?" I asked.

"Then?" She smiled. "Then I'll take Gabrielle in my arms and give her more pleasure than any mortal woman has ever known." With that, she stretched, her arms high above her head and her legs extended till her boots banged the coffee table. "So, healer—will I ever *get* what I want, do you think?"

"Maybe. I guess that's up to Gabrielle."

She smiled again, a bit more ruefully. "Yes, it is. It has to be, to be right."

"And how long can you wait?"

Tilting her jaw, she gave me a crooked little grin. "Do you know why I came to you? I actually hoped you might take away this awful yearning, this desire, so I wouldn't have to wait any longer, so I could stop pretending it wasn't there, so I could face the day she might be taken from me or leave me or tell me we could never be more than…friends." Tainting the word with irony, she paused, shaking her head. "But that's not what I needed at all. It's my desire that's made me good, and human, and whole again. The fear of my desire—that's what was unbearable."

She looked herself over and slapped at her thigh. "Good work, healer. What was the question? How long can I wait? For a love like this? Forever." And with that she hopped to her feet and held out her hand to me. "You were right," she admitted, lifting me out of my chair and locking her forearm with mine, "talking is good. Talking helps."

"Well, I'm glad I could be of service to you," I said.

Just then the elevator bell rang, the doors opened onto my floor, and a dozen heavy boots clumped down the hall.

"I can pay you for what's been damaged," she said, reaching for the pouch on her belt, "and for your time."

"Oh, forget that," I said. "But we need to get our story straight."

"You're very kind," she said, and kissed me gently on the mouth. "Thanks."

I was startled by her kiss. I was startled even more by the sound of splintering wood. The police were breaking down the office doors on this side of the building, and they'd soon get to mine. "I'll go out to them," I said. "It's you they'll want. Wait here."

"Can't," she said, bolting to the window, "gotta go."

I watched, transfixed, as she yanked down a curtain, split it in half and knotted it together, hooked one end around a desk leg, and wound the other around her fist as she leaped onto the windowsill.

"Oh, no, careful—" I said hoarsely.

"Don't worry," she assured me, "I'm a lucky woman. I'm in love." And with a shrill, yelping cry she flung herself out the window. The curtain went taut, then limp as a second later she crashed through another window on the floor below and made her escape.

I had just enough time to stuff the curtain in a drawer and shove my notebook down my shirt before the men in blue broke down my outer door and rushed in, guns drawn.

"Freeze! What's going on here?" they demanded to know.

"Accident," I said, pointing apologetically at the window. "Slipped on a broken lava lamp," I explained, my hands over my head. "Dropped my book. Really," I insisted as they cuffed me and dragged me to the elevator.

"Have any of you gentlemen ever been in love?" I asked politely, when they tossed me in the back of an undented cruiser and, blue fires blazing, took me downtown.

Less Fucked Up
Sara Cytron with Harriet Malinowitz

Me and my friends, we all go to therapy. Now, my friends who have kids—the one thing they wish more than anything else is that their kids will turn out to be less fucked up than they are.

It's like our parents hoping we'd be more economically secure than they were. Like my mother used to say, "I was so poor. If I wanted a toy, I had to sew buttons on a dish towel just to make a doll. You don't know how fortunate you are to have everything you have."

My friends will say to their kids, "I was so fucked up! Just to be functional I had to go to group on Tuesdays, individual on Thursdays, 12-step on Mondays, Wednesdays, and Fridays. You don't know how fortunate you are just to call a couple of hotlines on the weekend!"

Beyond the Pleasure Principle
Lorrie Sprecher

A friend and I were saying what it's like having gorgeous shrinks, how it makes the transference easier. And we joked about people we knew who actually talked to their shrinks, actually *discussed*, for God's sake, feeling sexually attracted to them. It was the stupidest thing we'd ever heard. We couldn't imagine it.

So the next week, my shrink, Ms. Perfect-Timing, asks if the reason I'm uncomfortable talking about my sexual history, which she is writing the fuck down on her yellow shrink notepad, is because I have sexual feelings for her. But it's OK, she says.

Is she out of her fucking mind?

I was so creeped out I climbed all the way up into my chair and finally stood on top of it. I said, "Do you think this is making me more comfortable?"

She wanted to talk about the issue of sexual feelings in the room, for her, during therapy, in general. "It's an 'issue'?" I asked. I hoped I'd somehow misheard and she'd said "tissue," that sexuality had formed a tissue, like dust, all over the room. Something totally impersonal.

"Issue," she repeated, "let's deal with it."

I said, "I'm sorry, you've obviously mistaken me for someone with self-esteem. I'm not going to ask you out."

"Why can't you tell me how you feel about me? I tell you how I feel about you all the time."

"Not all the time," I said.

She said, "But I ask all my patients this same question, and you're the only one who says I'm making you uncomfortable."

"You ask *all* your patients if they're sexually attracted to you?" I asked. *Wow,* I thought. *I'd hate to think I pay someone with a narcissism complex for therapy.*

"Why does it freak you out to explore the feelings you have for your therapist?"

Is she serious? I thought. *Why would I want to do that?* "I love when you refer to yourself in the third person," I said, "as though that somehow makes it easier. Like you've left the room and given me this nonthreatening hologram of your body."

She sighed. "Our time's up, I've gotten nothing of your sexual history, but at least I get to be three-dimensional."

"Thank you for the creepiest conversation I think I've ever had in my life," I said. "Why do shrinks always think you want to fuck them?"

She laughed. "I don't know that we always think that."

"Goodbye, Ms. Center-of-My-Universe. See you next week."

I wondered if I'd end up needing another therapist to help me deal with this one.

Serial Therapy (or What to Do When Your Therapist Is Seeing Someone Else)
G.L. Morrison

This is a true story. The names have been (barely) changed to protect the neurotic. My early fumblings in therapy are similar to fumbling along the terrain of young lesbianhood. You look back on each attempt with nostalgia-glazed eyes and mutter wistfully, "What the hell happened there anyway?"

My first therapeutic fumble was with an elementary school counselor who thought my behavior and loudly professed opinions worthy of investigation—opinions such as "No one gets to be 7 and still a virgin," which I shouted during a heated recess debate on virginity: Is it a class distinction or a mean-spirited lie?

In the typical openness of the 1960s, what we talked about in all those sessions (with all those hand puppets) is what not to talk about at recess. (This was reinforced by the therapy I got at home.) And I learned a valuable lesson—therapy is a good way to get out of a math test.

I used this technique a lot in high school, excusing myself to the guidance counselor with urgent teen angst. An angst that oddly coincided with homework I'd forgotten to do. I made so many trips to the guidance counselor it taxed my brain to invent new angst.

Sometimes I'd tell her my friends' problems. Counselors don't believe you really have friends. Anytime you say "my friend did this," they think you're really talking about yourself. Sort of like the theory that all the people in your dreams are you. 'Cuz if you had friends, wouldn't you be talking to them instead of her?

My "problems" must have really confused her. Sometimes I'd tell her it was just too bad to talk about. I'd turn my head toward the wall, and through teary eyes I'd watch the clock. I'd either confess or "feel better" by lunch.

When I finally realized that the "class readmittance slip" the counselor issued was always in pencil, our sessions got significantly shorter. I started showing up at school an hour (or period) late and stopping in for a five-minute chat and a readmittance slip. If the teacher (whose class I was readmitted to) just looked at the slip and didn't take it from me, I could change the date and use it later, completely skipping the middleman guidance counselor.

All this is not to say that I didn't have problems the school counselor and I could have discussed, but would you share anything with someone that gullible?

*   *   *

My first committed relationship with a therapist was when I took my four-year-old son to a family counselor after I suspected he'd been molested by the babysitter's brother. In her opinion as a professional doctor, he had not. (Which means he hadn't confessed to the hand puppets.) In my opinion as an amateur mother, she was wrong. She tried to reassure me that any maladjustments he might be displaying were solely the result of being raised by an anxious, poverty-stricken, teenage lesbian.

"He's fine," she said. "You're a mess. I'll make an appointment for you to see me on Tuesdays."

Since I couldn't stop sobbing, I had no choice but to agree. (A lot of my relationships start that way.)

She was a grandmotherly woman whose name I won't mention here (because I've forgotten it). Just like my own grandmother, a look from her was all it took…to fill me with shame. And because I had no other experience to compare it to (if you don't count math avoidance), I thought that's how therapy was supposed to be. Also true of a lot of my other relationships. But our sessions together helped me to discover I was having panic attacks. I had one every time I even thought of seeing her.

We eventually stopped seeing each other, citing irreconcilable differences. I felt that as a straight and very old woman, she couldn't understand my young queer self. We didn't always see eye to eye about which things were my problems and which were my assets. She felt she couldn't help me if I refused to leave my house and kept canceling appointments.

*   *   *

Another school counselor story: In college the women's studies program had a volunteer therapist. Background: A beautiful but alcoholic woman I was in a fledgling relationship with died after lubricating her driving skills with a six-pack. Foolishly, I ran home to my mother. With philosophical aplomb my mother remarked, "The death of someone your age makes you think of your own mortality." While I explained what Cricket's death did make me think of, my mother did everything but cover her ears and hum, rub her belly, and chew gum. I ran back to school. Once again I found myself in the school counselor's office—the volunteer therapist in the women's studies department. I poured out my mangled heart to her: my rage at my mother, my grief over losing my lover (and anger at her recklessness), and the stress of being a lesbian boat adrift in a sea of straightness. She nodded, therapistly. "You're suffering from PMS."

*   *   *

I often wonder, after so many bad tries, why I kept at it, how I held onto the belief that there was a therapist out there for me. (I think that about my other relationships too.)

I saw men (therapists) for a while, believing by personal bias and personal experience, that straight women are at the evolutionary bottom of critical thinking. Straight men are at least sane enough to not be involved with each other. A male therapist (I rationalized) would understand my lust for women. Secretly, I was afraid of this inner child that women therapists kept trying to introduce me to. I was also afraid of their pink offices, their inspirational needlepoint samplers, and their nice, quiet voices. I knew they wanted me to be nice—nice and quiet—too. I knew a man would understand not wanting to be nice. But as it turned out, straight men and I weren't able to interest each other enough to engage in effective therapy.

After almost a year of weekly sessions, one man flipped through my chart while we spoke. He interrupted my stories. "Debbie? I forget—is that your sister or your girlfriend?"

I would respond to most of his therapeutic advice by rolling my eyes and saying, "What would you know?" Not even my belligerence made me memorable. I just stopped showing up. I doubt he noticed.

*   *   *

Now I knew it was a lesbian therapist I needed. That knowledge eventually led me to the therapist I have now. She helped me to see how fucked up I am. She helped me to not care. I've been seeing her for almost a decade.

My romantic relationships have never lasted more than three

years. Probably because I can't get my lovers to follow the same rules as my therapist: (1) Let me do all the talking. (2) Pretend you're listening, even if you've heard this story a million times before. (3) Let me make all the rules.

*   *   *

Before I found Dr. Right I interviewed a couple of therapists. Mostly we rejected each other due to financial incompatibility. They wanted money. I didn't have any. Because I live in a small town and the queer community is even smaller, I bump into some of these ex-interviewees. Some of them are friends of friends and/or lovers of lovers. Because I've been monogamous with the same therapist for so long now, they don't remember me or my problems (aside from the problems that my friends or lovers are affected by and/or complain about). I remember them. One in particular made herself unforgettable. I'll call her Dr. Sue.

Dr. Sue sees clients in her home. At our initial free consultation, I mapped my psyche, complete with speed bumps of childhood traumas and bad relationships. After, when she explained that her sliding-scale fee structure didn't slide out of three digits (before the period), I pulled my butt off her comfortable couch and mapped my way to the door.

Little did I (or her other clients) know how significant that comfortable couch would come to be. Several months and bad relationships later, I was settled in with Dr. Right and in a serious relationship with my then-lover, let's call her Relizabeth. Relizabeth and I were committed (which is codependent slang for *deluded*). Things looked good for me. Therapy was good. My relationship was nonviolent. I had a coparent and was inching toward the upper end (or at least the middle) of the poverty index. I had friends who were useful for more than making up stories to get me out of class.

One of my friends (OK, an ex) was friends with Dr. Sue. They had weekend potlucks at Dr. Sue's house. Hungry for more "married-couple" things to do, I mentioned Relizabeth and I would love to join these potlucks. But we never did get an invitation. Later I realized my friend (ex) never wanted to do things with Relizabeth and me as a "married couple." She really only wanted to do friend things with me alone. Go figure.

Twice when I was out of town Relizabeth went to the potluck without me. Relizabeth said she was lonely and had insisted on going. But when I was in town the potlucks either didn't happen or no one would return our calls in time. Very mysterious. I suspected my friend (ex) of having designs on Relizabeth. I could not have been more wrong.

There is an airport in the small town I live in. For the same price as an airline ticket to my small-town airport, you could fly to the nearby major city, stay in a nice hotel, have an expensive dinner, buy a car (to drive the hour and a half to my small town), and still have spare change. So that's what all my out-of-town friends do.

One night I was driving to pick up an old friend from that other airport. He wanted to cruise all the gay bars (and probably every bathroom listed in *The Damron's Guide*) in the glittering city before we came back to my rural sex-free town. In gratitude, he was buying dinner and paying for a hotel (though not, unfortunately, buying me a new car) with the money he saved. I figured we'd get a few hours of playing catch-up in before I disappeared into a book and he just disappeared. We'd drive back in the morning.

Relizabeth sent her regrets. A bunch of women were getting together at Dr. Sue's house to watch lesbian videos. Other than that one hour two years before (which I never mentioned to Relizabeth), I had not even "met" Dr. Sue. Relizabeth said they would be staying up very late drinking and had been encouraged by the host to bring sleeping bags so that unfit (drunk or overtired) drivers could sleep over. She extolled the virtues of childhood slumber parties.

After my friend left, Relizabeth confessed she'd slept with Dr. Sue. She denied ever having claimed there was a movie slumber party.

"Do you want me to leave?" Relizabeth asked.

"And go where?" I asked, stomach lurching.

"You know where," my lover smirked.

I alternated between telling her I wanted her to shut up and leave me alone and demanding she tell me all the gory details I didn't want to hear. It turned out she'd told Dr. Sue we had an open relationship. Dr. Sue, who was calling every hour on the hour, soon discovered otherwise.

Relizabeth told me she felt that her "session" on the couch with Dr. Sue made her feel closer to me. "I did it for you," she said—which was the same jabberwocky she spouted every time she did something that truly disturbed me. The more she talked, the more baffled and queasy I became.

I told her I needed a week or two to think about what I wanted to do and whether our relationship was worth saving. During that time I expected her to have no contact with Dr. Sue. No phone calls, no clandestine meetings, etc. This started an onslaught of tears—not that I might leave her, but that I would interfere with her new "friendship."

Yes, I agreed that she could call Dr. Sue and explain my conditions. I waited for an hour while explanations, tears, and sweet talk ensued. Dr. Sue did not like my plan. She thought we should all get together for a clearing talk. After I made it clear I didn't care what she thought, Dr. Sue agreed not to call or try to contact us for two weeks. Her resolve lasted three days.

For reasons I cannot explain to my own therapist (let alone to you, dear reader) I agreed to meet for coffee so that we could each tell "our side" of the story. Chalk it up to the lesbian compulsion to process. After four French-press pots of black coffee I agreed to a conditional friendship.

My conditions: (1) They never have sex again—which, as far as I know, they never did; and (2) They never be alone together. As the only way I could guarantee that they weren't alone was if I was there…we'd have to be a threesome, a strictly platonic threesome.

So my conditions were also my punishment (not unlike most of my relationships). I didn't sleep for two days. I knew I'd made a terrible decision. Only later I realized that the terrible decision had been drinking four pots of coffee by myself.

Surprisingly, Dr. Sue and I are still friends, while Relizabeth and I are barely on speaking terms.

*   *   *

When I said I've been monogamous with the same therapist for almost ten years, I meant that I see only her. I know she sees other clients. I try not to picture it. It's too disgusting. But just as you should never brag about how great your lover is (it only tempts your friends), it's not safe to boast about great therapy.

A friend, Rjanet, called me from L.A. in tears. (It's a terrible town, I know, but nothing to cry about.) Her mother was in the hospital, and she'd flown there to help out. She needed to process all the old and new issues that had come up. She just wanted to decompress, sort it all out. Could she have the name of my therapist? One session should be enough. I hesitated.

No, I didn't hesitate. But I should have. One decompression session turned into six (that was all her insurance would pay for). By the end of six sessions, Rjanet was "in love" with my therapist and spent all of her tears on that instead of her crappy parents. That was two years ago.

It's weird when your friends see the same shrink as you. They tell you things about your doctor you don't want to know. If I went seven years without knowing the names of my therapist's cats, did I really need to find out now? Rjanet knew the cats and what was most recently planted in my therapist's garden. I knew her lover was a cop. Since my sessions were right after lunch, I had actually seen her. Many times. Two points. Aha! Damn. Rjanet knew the names of my therapist's nieces. But did she know that she hated tomatoes because her father once made her eat something she drowned in ketchup? Aha! Rjanet knew the names of the teddy bears in her office. Stop! The teddy bears have names? I did not want to know this. It's bad enough that teddy bears line up along one wall of her office. Dr. Right suggested once that I might want to hold one—and was rewarded with a remark of such un-teddy sentiment as to cause her fuzzy, stuffed heart to skip a beat. She actually blanched.

I have a favorite sofa pillow to hug. I am not a teddy bear person. At home I sleep with a stuffed gorilla. But that is not the same thing at all. Not at all.

Dr. Right is nice—maybe even quiet—in a sorta butch way. (And yes, she did introduce me to my inner child. It was every bit as horrid as I expected.) Her office isn't pink. But there is a huge unicorn mirror in the lobby. The walls of her office are covered with inspirational posters. "Love Yourself," one says in huge letters with a lot of smaller, annoying how-tos. When I can't think of anything to talk about (or rather when I can and don't wanna), I am fond of reading and ridiculing these aphorisms aloud.

I also read aloud the titles of books on her shelf: *Courage to Heal; Dance of Anger; I'm OK, Who Cares About You?* and my personal favorite—this one always stops me—*The Joy of Stress.* The rant that seeing it starts is good for about five minutes of avoidance. The trick is—can either of us remember what I was talking about before

I started reading titles? Dr. Right's pretty good at this game. But sometimes I can stump her.

I ask Rjanet if she had ever noticed *The Joy of Stress*. After that, how could she see anything else?

The next week I'm reading the book titles on the shelf, and I notice one is turned around. It's *The Joy of Stress*. Dr. Right grins. She admits that Rjanet turned it backward to "see if I would notice." I decide I like it better that way.

A few months ago Rjanet reawakened the sibling rivalry I thought we'd laid to rest. She referred her stressed-out friend Rrebecca to *my* therapist. It's like a plague. Where will the madness end? It turned out that karma was swift. Rjanet's stressed-out friend was stressed out about being in love with Rjanet.

Rjanet and Rrebecca both thought it was hilarious that Dr. Right kept a straight face while they whined and whined, each unwilling to make the first move, paralyzed by fear of rejection. It took a month for them to get together. It took two months for them to break up. The rivalry and therapy bills seem likely to last a long time.

Rrebecca turned *The Joy of Stress* back around.

"Let's see what Rjanet thinks about that!" she smirked to me.

I haven't heard if Rjanet noticed. I don't really care. I've thrown a shovel of dirt on my rivalry feelings. I see a lot of wriggling happening in that dirt, but they're not my worms anymore. Unless we all show up at the same hour, there's enough doctor to go around. When the meter's running and the couch is mine, I've got plenty to talk about without regressing to the high-school drama of discussing friends' problems.

*   *   *

After almost four years and so many disturbing things that "she did for me" that I'm still talking about them in therapy, Relizabeth and I broke up. Timing is everything. We had been waiting almost three of those almost four years for her insurance settlement due to a job-related accident. We had spent most of our turbulent relationship spending that imaginary money.

We had planned a coast-to-coast train trip that included lengthy stops at such wonders of the world as the Grand Canyon and New Orleans strip joints. And a side trip to meet her family, who had only objected to and finally accepted our relationship by phone.

We also planned to take a cruise with our son and some of our friends. We gave our best friend Dr. Sue a cruise ticket for her birthday. She was delighted. (Secretly though, she seethed and squirmed, feeling it was too extravagant. Finally, when it was too late to redeem the ticket, she refused to go.) Our richer friend Rsarah was also coming, but she could afford to pay for her own ticket.

Although Dr. Sue had a thriving practice, she was deeply in debt. She frequently borrowed money from loan shark Peter to pay loan shark Paul. The only way she'd ever get caught up is to charge her clients the same rate of interest the loan sharks charged her. And break their legs if they don't pay.

Train, then boat. Relizabeth and I had barely pulled out of the train station when she announced she was leaving me. It put a cramp in our romantic vacation. When her mother threw her arms around me and welcomed me to the family, I had to beg for aspirin. I called my therapist from every pay phone.

Before the Love Boat set sail, everything that could change had. Relizabeth had a new lover, a local blues diva whom Relizabeth had denied making eyes at during a Pride Day concert. I was in love with Rsarah—although the interest Rsarah had shown in me while I was in a relationship with someone else (Relizabeth) dwindled significantly when I was available. Rsarah backed out of the cruise. It would be too weird to share a cabin with Relizabeth, she said. With Dr.

Sue's cancellation, that left just our original ex-family unit.

Relizabeth's lover had a sudden fear of potential reconcilation and forbade her from going. That left my son, me, and three cruise tickets I couldn't return.

I invited my therapist. She declined but suggested I take something from her office as a substitute.

"Like what? A pencil sharpener?"

Her office is littered with teddy bears and hand puppets. But I had previously made it clear what I thought of teddy-bear therapy. She brought over a beautiful raku figure of a woman. It rattled. Fat rattle-woman beamed at me. It was as fragile as I felt.

"Take this."

I swaddled fat rattle-woman in socks and HOTHEAD PAISAN T-shirts. For the plane trip, she was definitely carry-on luggage. But when people started jamming things into the overhead bin, I panicked. Fat rattle-woman rode in my lap.

Giving me fat rattle-woman was the most stressful thing my therapist has ever done to me. Perhaps she thought it would take my mind off my other problems—if I spent every waking moment thinking, *What if it gets broken?*

In the cabin I put it on the dresser. But ships rock, and I found fat rattle-woman on the floor. Still smiling, unbroken.

I could put her in the porthole, so she could see the ocean and fall, if need be, onto the bed. *What if she got stolen?* (Not likely, I know, but I told you I was obsessed.) I could put her under my pillow, but what if I forgot she was there? Crunch. I shook fat rattle-woman but found no answer in the sound of the rocks in her head.

What did my therapist want me to do with this fat rattle-woman anyway? Take her to dinner at the captain's table? Scuba diving?

I reswaddled her in socks and HOTHEAD PAISAN T-shirts. She spent the whole week in my suitcase. I spent most of it crying in a deck chair and avoiding Richard Simmons. Somehow my travel agent had failed to mention that Richard Simmons and friends had booked half of the cabins for a fun-filled, fat-reducing cruise.

In spite of my HOMOCIDAL LESBIAN TERRORIST T-shirt, large women continually came up to tell me I was late to an aerobics class on the Lido deck. I invited them to meet me at the midnight chocolate buffet (off-limits to Simmonites), and I recited every "Love Yourself" aphorism I could recall from my therapist's sappy poster.

She decided to leave her baggage behind.

Ursula Roma

I Dated a Therapist
Meredith Pond

Once upon a time, I dated a therapist. A therapist who looks a little like Cris Williamson—you know, filling up and spilling over in all the right places. She lives in Baltimore, so I commute from D.C. and spend a lot more time at the National Aquarium in Baltimore's Inner Harbor than I really want to. The things we do for love.

The shark tank is her location of choice when she isn't at the office tending to her clients' broken hearts and soap-opera mood swings. She loves to go there at feeding time—not the office, the shark tank. Lemon sharks are her favorite, she says, because the name sounds like kids' candy. At the aquarium, I learn there are 350 species of sharks. All of them have teeth like razor blades and no candy.

Actually this therapist and I met at the shark tank for our first official date. I remember that afternoon. Wandering through the aquarium's labyrinth of walkways and scaffolding, we stare at the walled-in aquamarine water packed with fish of all colors, shapes, and sizes swimming in circles and chasing each other around, occasionally swallowing a neighbor whole.

I'm not much of a fish person. I'm an earth sign. I know salmon…that's about it. And I like it with béarnaise sauce. But she can name them all, like nieces and nephews: parrot fish, lion-fish, angelfish, jellyfish, squid, eels. Do you know there are 10,000 animals at this aquarium? I'm hoping we don't have to look at every single one. She even spots an octopus hiding behind a rock. In her ocean-blue tank top, she is a walking encyclopedia in lace-up leather sandals and no bra. Definitely a Pisces.

We have known each other since spring, when both of us volunteered at the local queer film festival. After that we met for espresso and matinees with mutual friends from the organizing committee and then alone together at the nighttime movies. We eat out first—seafood of course, usually oysters or shrimp and catfish. She goes for the bottom feeders big time.

So everything is normal in the getting-to-know-you department. Slow but normal. As I think back, I guess I expect her to pump me about my childhood, searching for telltale traumas. That never happens, which is good because I prefer to be probed in other ways. I fantasize that we are pacing ourselves for the long haul. That means we never meet at her apartment or mine. It's movies, movies, movies—a different theater every time. She's into creature flicks: *Jaws, Anaconda, Piranha, Lake Placid,* and, of course, the classics when they are in town: *20,000 Leagues Under the Sea* with James Mason as Captain Nemo and *Moby Dick* with Gregory Peck as Captain Ahab. Personally I never recovered from watching Monstro the Whale swallow old Gepetto and his raft in *Pinocchio.*

I consider objecting to sitting through *Moby Dick* twice on a Saturday afternoon downtown, but she likes to slouch in the back of the theater and make out. A hole ripped in the bottom of the popcorn bucket and placed strategically over her crotch, especially if she is wearing a skirt, is fun for me, so I don't complain. But I'd rather watch movies and then go *home* and make out.

One afternoon, after watching the thrashing around and biting and tearing asunder of huge chunks of raw meat at the shark-feeding snarf-o-rama, she kisses me hard. She says *I want you. Take me home.* I say sure. Now I'll finally find out where she lives. In a few minutes we are unlocking the door to her upscale apartment near

Charles Street. I carry her over the threshold. She sucks on my neck like a lamprey.

Her Caribbean motif is applied with a Baltimore flair—wicker chairs, carved conch shells, sand-colored cushions, and carpeting the color of Sapphire Bay in St. Thomas blend in with a huge Orioles poster and a coffee-table book on the rebuilding of the Inner Harbor. Surprisingly I don't see a fish tank anywhere. Ficus trees and date palms are set at the corners of the living room as if they are holding down the floor, keeping it from floating up like a jade cloud. Over the windows, perky spider plants burst out like green-and-white peppermint sticks. The place smells a little fishy even though she doesn't have a cat. Her dog, a Pekingese named Neptune, would never tolerate a cat. She told me that bit of information on day one. Of course I didn't meet Neptune until a few minutes ago. The dog doesn't seem to like me much, pulling at my sneaker strings until the plastic thread guards come off.

Neptune sports a little black box around his neck. Every time he barks inappropriately, he gets a tiny shock from the electrodes attached inside. This is a hard way to learn to be quiet—or maybe it's puppy-dog S/M. I hope there's nothing similar in store for me, or any of her clients. After a peek in the mistress's kitchen, I figure out the smell. She likes canned sardines and jars of creamed herring. A benign obsession, except that the cans are open, the sardines are old, and the lids are off the herring jars.

Unapologetic, she serves white wine from a box in the fridge and leads me into the bedroom. Our clothes disappear, and we tickle each other, giggling, out to the balcony. Not as dark as the movie theater but dark enough without the moonlight. She switches on the heater to the hot tub. Bubbles rise to the surface of the water. Steamy. Our wine glasses are touching on the deck. A mermaid in a past life, no doubt, she is at home in the water, ducking, undulating, playing with the water jets. Me, I could use some water wings and a snorkel. I'm big on the breaststroke and keeping my head above water. She should pay attention to my metaphors. I'm not much of a swimmer. Besides, when water gets up my nose, I sputter and gag and get burning sensations between my eyes. How attractive is anyone with sopping wet hair? I long for a blow dryer and sex on dry land.

An orgasm explodes like an underwater volcano. Was that her or me? I push to the surface for air like Shelley Winters in *The Poseidon Adventure*. I'm breathing hard, lying on the deck huffing and puffing like a beached whale. I need a towel. She is parading around pleased with herself, dripping and happy like a circus seal after a bucket of fish. *Wait, I'll get a ball for your nose.*

The water bubbles in my ears won't pop, no matter how much hopping up and down I do. She offers an impromptu ear-candle treatment with a rolled-up newspaper. *Gee, thanks, but I really have to leave.* So the evening ends abruptly.

She gives me a peck on the cheek. *Good night. I'll call you soon.*

I haven't seen her since. She's probably going for a bigger fish or a smaller pond.

I never really liked Baltimore that much anyway. Besides, Washington has its own National Aquarium in the basement of the Commerce building near Constitution Avenue where shark-feeding is Thursdays at 3.

I'll be waiting for you.

Techniques for Testing Your Therapist
Cassendre Xavier

I require focus from my therapist. Focus and an iron hand. I'm the queen of nonsequiturs and changing subjects when the subject gets a little uncomfy. You know, when I'm feeling my feelings. And my feelings about my feelings. And my feelings about my feelings about my feelings, and my…well, you get the idea.

So for these tough "feelings" times, I refer to my highly defined, Pentagon-level developed aversion and distraction techniques, which my therapist ought to be tops at noticing and disarming immediately. This is no small task. Therefore, work must be done to select the proper womyn for the job.

As a favor to the lesbian community—as an act of true, genuine, totally vulval womyn-love—I am passing on these time-tested techniques, these completely Sapphic and Steinesque clitoral nuggets of wisdom, to you.

May they succeed in finding you the best, sharpest, most on-guard therapist. (Helpful hint: This type of therapist works best with those of us with a penchant for "dissociation." And if you know what that word means, it's probably taken you a week to read this paragraph…but I digress. Where was I?)

1. *The Compliment Test*
Now this is the best one. (There's a reason it's number 1.) Pay her a compliment. If she dwells on the compliment too long, ditch her.

Sounds cruel, but ya gotta do it, sister. Feel the Power of the Mother give you the strength you'll need to find a shrink who can stay focused on the subject at hand. And it (the subject at hand) ain't her scarf.

I had a session once, *one* session, with a woman whose pendant I'd complimented. Ten minutes she stayed on this subject. Ten. Now granted, I made no moves to stop her. But that wasn't my job. She was kind and sweet. She was responsible and articulate. She was thoughtful and considerate. And she was cute. But she failed the test, so I had to say, "Buh-bye, now. Buh-bye!"

2. *The Sudden-Observation-of-Decor Test*

In the middle of the session, mention something in the room. Say something like, "Hey! Has that plant always been there?" Just like that. Just blurt it out. If she acts like nothing happened, it's over. You need someone who's going to notice you've suddenly changed the subject. For example, right in the middle of one of my sessions with The Best Lesbian Therapist in All of Philadelphia, I said, "You know what, I've never noticed that poster before. Has it always been there?"

And you know what The Best Lesbian Therapist in All of Philadelphia said? "Yes, it has actually. Now, Cassendre (I loved it when she said my name!), I've noticed that you've changed the subject. Do you want to talk about that?"

At this point, a big ol' grin would spread across my face as The Best Lesbian Therapist in All of Philadelphia and I then proceeded. I stayed with her for years. In fact, *she* deserted *me*, by moving, with her partner, to New Mexico. I will never understand how she could ruin such a perfect relationship as ours. That she would leave me for a pesky little retirement and her partner of 19 years is something that will take me years and years to recover from. It still hurts to this day (sniff). Hold me.

3. *The Great Boundary Test*

I like to know that my shrink can take care of herself. If I'm supposed to do it, shouldn't she too? If not, I certainly can't look up to her, and I wouldn't *dream* of taking advice from her.

There are a few very effective ways of testing your prospective therapist's boundaries. Some of these are a bit more advanced than others, but every dyke can do them, and every shrink will either pass—or fail miserably. One of the two. Here's what you do. After two or three sessions with your new therapist (she's passed the first three tests during the intake session), ask to spend the night at her place.

I like to say, "Hey, how 'bout a sleepover at your place, huh? Some of *your* friends, some of *my* friends, just us girls—I'll bring the hot chocolate—it'll be fun. C'mon!"

Of all the tests, this is my favorite. Absolutely the most fun. Simply because of the various shades of red and pink their faces get and all the new deep-breathing exercises I learn from watching them.

4. *The Anger Test*

And last, an extension of The Great Boundary Test, The Anger Test basically lets you know where you stand with your therapist insofar as the power dynamic is concerned. If you do little things that ought to piss her off, like show up late for every single session, she should tell you about yourself. If she doesn't, then you can't really have any respect for her, now can you? Of course, you can't.

I hope these tips help you find the lesbian therapist of your dreams. And remember, trust the process! Or something like that.

©2000 T.O.SYLVESTER

After therapy, I dumped the dish and started dating other spoons.

Paying for Lesbian Foreplay
Myra LaVenue

Even though I had a lesbian barber, a lesbian veterinarian, a lesbian picture framer, a lesbian primary care provider, a lesbian landscaper, a lesbian soccer team, a lesbian chiropractor, a lesbian financial planner, and lesbian housemates, something was still missing. When my friend started lauding her new therapist, who happened to be a lesbian, it hit me. The missing link was therapy.

I jumped on her immediately. "What's her name?"

"Evelyn Fielgud," my friend replied.

It took some juggling of my schedule and finances, but I finally got an appointment to see her. I nervously entered her office and sat at the far end of the couch. Upright. Her office contained a desk in the corner overlooking a view of downtown Portland, a bookcase filled with…books (duh!), her chair, two end tables, and *the* couch.

She started off the session with a question I hate (even more than the famous job-interviewing zinger, "What do you see yourself doing in five years?"): "Why are you here, Ms. L'amour?"

That question may throw most emotionally disturbed lesbians, but I was ready for it. "Um, can you call me T.J.? Ms. L'amour makes me sound like a drag queen. Why am I here? I'm here to pay for lesbian foreplay."

The therapist looked startled, but before she could speak I clarified, "You know, lesbian foreplay? Two women talking all night? OK, so you didn't get it. No biggie. I'm really here to find the answer to the eternal lesbian question: 'Am I butch or femme?'"

"And what makes you think you have to be one or the other?" she asked, as she shifted in her chair. Her appearance was annoyingly androgynous, which threw me into confusion. Was she a top or a bottom, I wondered.

"Well, I guess the main reason I want an answer is so I can reply to the lesbian personal ads I keep reading. They *all* ask for one type or the other. And after I figure out the butch/femme thing I still have to find out if I'm more comfortable on top, on the bottom, or side by side. Jesus, the other day my friend was telling me how she met a butch bottom...a butch bottom! I mean, what the hell is that? Does that mean she would need to be with a femme top, or would an androgynous side be OK for her?" Damn these couch pillows...should I face her or sit forward? Did she notice how my pants were bunching under my butt?

"Would you like my input?" she questioned, and then with my eager nod, continued. "I think we are all able to be both butch and femme. These roles we take on are merely constructs of our own minds and are built over and over again with each new encounter. With one lover you may feel more butch, whereas with the next you're the femme. By trying to actually label yourself as one or the other, you ultimately limit yourself to expressing only half of you. With the right lover, and communication, you can be both butch and femme, depending on your mood, as can she." The therapist ended her brilliant dissection of my question and sat back smugly.

"Well, huh," I replied. "For being 'constructs of our own minds,' we lesbians sure have developed entire dress codes and behavior standards, not to mention associating certain roles with certain sexual positions." I paused, looked at the clock.

Sheesh, it's only been five minutes? God, what was I going to talk about next?

Oh, no, she was looking at me again. Like I was about to say something so amazingly out there that she could write a paper on her treatment of me and win some professional award.

"OK, so, I've been stressing a lot lately about...about...mastur-bation." I could feel the heat on my cheeks as I broached this sub-ject. Sex has always been a somewhat private thing for me to dis-cuss, but I knew I had to plunge in. After all, I *was* paying this woman to help me. "You know, I've been using my right hand for years. Years! And I always use the same position, and put on the same music...well, I'm sick of it. I don't turn myself on anymore. The passion's gone. I feel guilty because, you see, last night, well...I cheated on myself and used my other hand. And it was fantastic! Now I can't seem to get the right hand to even pick up a pen, much less use a fork. Do you have any ideas on how I can get over this momentary hiccup in my relationship with myself?"

"This is a challenging question for yourself, and I congratulate you on your courage in dealing with it, especially in our first ses-sion," my therapist smiled, and nodded her head in praise. "You'd like to hear my ideas on that?"

"Please," I replied.

"You say you're feeling guilty about your switch in masturbating partners. However, I feel you should focus more on the reasons for the switch. Your right hand and you were having problems—*are* having problems—and the switch to your left was just a symptom of those problems. Rather than condemning yourself for this sup-posed infidelity, why not encourage a more open relationship between you and both hands? After all, you are all part of the same body, and the only thing standing between you all and mutual sat-isfaction is communication. Let your right hand know how much you still care...that it has *not* been replaced by the left. With the right level of discussion you should be able to move into a newer and more satisfying sexual sharing that includes all three of you! Why not?" Leaning back in her chair, my therapist looked at me encouragingly, her eyebrows raised, as she invited me to think about the possibilities.

"I never thought about using both hands! Wow, what a cool idea…I wonder if the right hand would go for it. Hmm, this gives me a lot to think about." I averted my eyes from her stare and read the titles of a few books on her bookshelf: *My Body, My Mind, My Heart: The Healthy Three-Way; Women Who Love Women and the Women Who Love Them; I Am My Own Best Lover; Alone Again: Breaking the Myth of the Old Maid Stereotype; Women Are From Venus and Women Are From Venus;* and *Lesbians and Their Lovers: Easing the Mother Hunger.*

Silence descended once again. The clock ticked and I focused on it momentarily, noting I had 25 more minutes in my session. Was it supposed to be this quiet?

I sighed and spoke. "I must confess that I just love sex. I came out about five years ago, and I can't seem to get enough of it. The problem is—how do you get to the point where sex is a possibility? I mean, hell, sometimes I can't even tell if I'm on a date or not."

"Describe a time when this happened," she requested.

"All right, take last week, after a soccer game, right? There's a new lesbian on our team, and she and I are always flirting as we warm up before the game. At least I *think* we're flirting. Anyway, last week at the end of the game, we were talking about the game, and people were packing up and leaving. Soon it was just the two of us. So she asks if I wanna grab a cup of coffee and finish our discussion. I say, "Sure." At the coffee shop, we're so engrossed in each other and our conversation, which by now is way off the topic of soccer, that we almost forget about eating. So I say, "Shall we grab some dinner?" and she totally agrees. Once we hit the vegan diner around the corner, we run into a couple of her friends. Before I know it, they're joining us, and the twosome becomes a foursome for dinner. At the end of the meal she says, "See ya later. Thanks for the talk." So what the hell was that? A date? A post-game stretch? Two new friends grabbing grub? Beats the heck outta me!" I comb my fingers through my hair in frustration.

"My question for you is—why do you feel the need for a definition? Is there a part of you that must have an answer to whether she likes you, whether she is attracted?" Her questions came at me, so pointed and thought-provoking, that I looked away again to think.

I couldn't help thinking that each minute I didn't talk or hear something from her was money. Let's see, $80 an hour divided by 50 minutes equals $1.60 per minute. At this point I was down to about $32 remaining in the session. Talk about time being money!

"So I guess I'm black and white, and…yes, I do want to know if she's attracted…if she wants me too. Because then I won't look like a clingy U-Haul lesbo if I call her for another date." My brows furrowed. My hands twitched in my lap as I glanced quickly back at my therapist.

"Well, that's a whole session in itself: your desire to avoid rejection and how you cover it up with this charming exterior. Have you ever thought that maybe you've just made a new friend?"

"Yes, but I applied my fork theory to this situation."

"Your fork theory?" she asked confusedly.

"Yes. You see, usually when a new lesbian comes into my life I go down a path and choose a series of forks in the road at various points of the relationship. The first fork is attraction. If I'm attracted to her, I take that road. Then I get to the chemistry fork. I figure if it's there, at some point in the first two weeks we'll attack each other. If not, then it's take the friendship fork and stay on that path. If we have chemistry, then it's on to the dating fork, which can sometimes come *before* the chemistry fork. After the dating fork is the living-together fork, then the partnership fork, and the parent fork. And each of these can at *any* time divert *back* to the friendship fork. I know it's confusing, but I just try to apply a little logic to dating in this society of women in which I find myself."

"Let's leave the fork theory alone for now. I'd like to know if you think you have a way with women, to put it in old-fashioned terms."

"My last name is L'amour for a reason," I joked. "OK, seriously, I know that I never have a problem meeting women or finding dates. If anything, I'm usually *too* busy when I'm single. It's like I'm a bright light, and I attract all these...moths...and all I'm looking for is that one butterfly in the bunch." I spun my analogy and then wondered if butterflies even come out at night.

"What is this, the bad poetry hour?" my therapist replied with a smile on her face but more than a touch of sarcasm in her voice.

"Hey, am I paying for this abuse?" I laughed. "It's not a poem— it's an analogy."

"As analogies go, I guess it's a pretty good one! But as a poem, it's bad," she teased back.

"Poem or analogy, the truth remains that I do have a way with women and a hard time remaining single. I've had so many girl-friends with so many interests that I now know a lot about a wide range of topics: watching competitive beach volleyball, meditating at 6 A.M., designing quilts, knowing which Indigo Girl is a lesbian, living life the Martha Stewart way, responding with a straight face when someone's telling me they're a witch, wearing the right thing to a summer solstice ceremony, making your own drum from the hide of an animal that died of old age, eating wheat-free/dairy-free/caffeine-free/meat-free meals, healing a new piercing, navigat-ing an open relationship, maintaining a positive outlook when your girlfriend wants to include her ex in everything you do together, getting a good seat at Lilith Fair, snowboarding with rad peeps, chanting 'Om namah shivaya,' and performing tantric sex."

"Tantric sex! I've heard a lot about that recently."

"Boy is *that* one a doozy! Let me just tell you, tantric sex is just another way of saying, let's take the next six hours to have *one* orgasm."

"Really?"

"Yeah! It's touching, touching, touching and then *finally*, when your head is nodding with sleep and your fingers are getting tired and your mouth is dry, *only* then does she touch you in the holy spot. And then you come like a freight train! Holy Mother of Jesus! But I don't recommend it for today's busy lesbian! It lasts as long as the Dinah Shore Tournament…only with a lot less stimulation!"

"What you're saying is that you never take time to be alone…you're always with a woman?"

"Um, no, well, I mean…what are you trying to say?"

"I'm asking if you're a leapfrog lesbian. You know, moving from one relationship right into the next without trying life on your *own* lily pad for a while."

"I don't see anything wrong with moving from woman to woman. Call it serial monogamy or call it following your heart…it's what I do. My friends say I make serial monogamy look like an extreme sport. But, hey! I believe life is so much better when you're in a relationship. Hell, I'm always matchmaking for my friends because I love seeing them in love too. My motto is 'I'll either fix you up, or I'll do you myself.'"

"Doesn't that lead to a lot of people dating each other in your social group? Do you date your friends' ex-lovers?"

"No, I have a few rules about that stuff. Basically I won't date anyone that anyone I know has ever dated. It's tricky, but so far I keep finding fresh faces. And sure, the rest of the group does get incestuous at times, but the drama beats the heck outta TV."

My therapist looked at her clock and replied, "I'm afraid our time is up. Would you like to continue working with me?"

"I think so. I mean, why not? My mind is an open mouth, I

always say. That should give us food for a hell of a lot of sessions."
But at the same time, I thought to myself that a therapist is like
having a paid audience. They have to listen to you, and there's a certain ego stroking that comes with being listened to.

"All right. Is next week at this same time good for you?" At my
quick nod, she said, "Then I'll see you next week."

"That's cool. Thanks." I grabbed my jacket and headed for the
door. My life felt complete now. A lesbian therapist was just what I
needed. My silent partner on every date and an advisor to me on every
topic. She would be my id—no wait, my ego, or my superego? I never
can remember which is which. I made a note to ask her next week.

As I began to cross the street in front of her building, I paused
and looked back reflectively. A sign in her window read, LESBIAN
THERAPIST: I'LL FIT YOU IN AND GET YOU OUT.

Kris Kovick

Therapy Audition
Riggin Waugh

I quit therapy a few years ago because, financially, I had to choose between my therapist of eight years and my cleaning boys of six months. I loved my therapist, but frankly, my cleaning boys were cheaper, and truth be known, they made me feel better about myself.

But now my lover and I are having problems, so we're auditioning therapists. Trying to be optimistic, I say we're going to therapy "to get fixed." My lover thinks this makes us sound like cocker spaniels on our way to the vet.

So what are we looking for in a therapist? Well, she must be kind, she must be witty, very sweet and fairly pretty, take us on outings, give us treats, play games—Oh, wait a minute, that's Mary Poppins. We'll settle for a dyke who doesn't get on our last nerve or charge us an arm and a leg.

When my lover schedules the first audition she tells our prospective shrink that we're looking for a lesbian or lesbian-friendly therapist. My lover's the diplomatic one. I want a dyke.

It's a spacious office uptown—across from the zoo. The audition is free.

"How are you?" she greets us.

Oh, we're fucking great. That's why we're here—because life is fucking wonderful. "Fine, thank you," I respond, "and you?"

She asks us each to talk a little about ourselves, our family history, our relationship history, and *the problem*. The problem is that my lover's 15-year-old daughter has moved in with her, and our time alone together has been cut drastically. For reasons too numerous to mention, we can't move in together.

The therapist says, "You have a unique problem. Most couples come to see me because they're having problems communicating. You two seem to communicate very well. You just have this 'given' with no apparent solution."

"Well, we were kind of hoping her daughter could come live with you," I say. My lover and the therapist laugh. They think I'm kidding.

As the session nears its end the therapist asks if we have any questions for her.

I look at my lover. My lover looks at me. We both know the question. We got this therapist's name out of the gay newspaper, but we don't know if she's queer. I know my lover will not ask. "Are you a lesbian?" I blurt out.

"I was afraid you were going to ask that." The therapist proceeds to beat around the bush. "What I usually tell people is—Does it matter? Some of my clients are gay and lesbian, and some aren't. So, does it really matter?"

Well, hell yes, it matters. It's a fair question. Not too personal under the circumstances. After all, she advertised in the queer paper, and she expects us to tell her the most intimate details of our lives. It's not like I asked her if she's a top or a bottom, for chrissake.

I look at my lover and joke, "Write that down, honey. Not comfortable with own sexuality." My lover, I can tell, wants to disappear on the spot.

The therapist offers to see us for, say, six sessions but has already said that she doesn't know what she can do for us. In other words, we're no more encouraged than we were 50 minutes ago. Would we go to a dentist on those terms? I think not. We thank her for her time and leave. Needless to say, she does not pass the audition.

Next?

How I Spent My Bummer Vacation
Anne Seale

Two weeks ago my lover Sherry and I borrowed my parents' 30-foot Winnebago and set off to see America. I had a month of vacation saved up, and Sherry was between jobs.

We left our apartment in Cincinnati on the last Saturday in April. At noon on the first Monday in May we rolled into San Francisco, which was the part of America we really wanted to see.

Using *Women's Traveler '99*, we promptly located a lesbian bar. It was harder to find a parking space, but we did, blocking only a foot or two of someone's driveway. After jogging the 20 blocks back, holding hands because we could, we found ourselves enjoying a couple of cold ones while chatting with the bartender, Helene, as if we'd known her forever.

Helene was everything we'd expected to find in a San Francisco dyke. She was sexy, sassy, and androgynous to the max. She told us she'd moved to the Bay Area from a small town in Georgia six years before. She still had the accent.

The bar was empty except for us, so Helene had plenty of time to fill our eager ears with tales of life in "The City," replete with political demonstrations, pride parades, and parties to die for. It made Cincinnati, which doesn't do too badly in the pride category, sound like Nowheresville.

After a couple of beers I needed to hit the bathroom. When I came out—and I wasn't in there long—Helene had rounded the bar and was sitting on the stool I had just vacated. Her hand was resting on Sherry's shoulder, and her cropped head was much too close to Sherry's curls. They were speaking in low tones.

I shouldn't have been surprised. This scenario took place fairly regularly back home. Sherry soon got bored, however, and returned after a couple of nights. But that was back home. This was *San Francisco!* I needed to act fast.

"So, Sherry," I said loudly as I approached, "I'm hungry. What say we go find a restaurant and eat?" I figured Sherry would jump at the suggestion of a restaurant meal. She'd been out of sorts for days because I'd insisted on cooking our meals in the motor home. I mean, who can afford to eat out after you buy all that gas?

Sherry swiveled to face me. Her cheeks were flushed, much like they had been on those occasions back home. She frowned and said, "Eat?" as if it were a lewd suggestion.

Helene turned slowly, lifting her heavy-lidded eyes to the "Miller Time" wall clock above the dance floor. "Geez, Dar," she drawled, "it's only 3:30. What's your hurry?"

She'd been calling me Dar all afternoon, even though I'd introduced myself as Darcy. I'd thought it was kind of cute until now. "Geez, *hell*," I snarled, "it's 6:30 in New York, and I want my supper. C'mon, Sherry."

Sherry took a full four seconds to think it over before saying, "I'm not coming with you, Darcy."

I pretended I didn't hear. "How about Chinese? I'll bet they have some damned good moo shu chicken in this town." It was Sherry's favorite. When she didn't answer, I added, "We can come back here afterward." I was lying, of course. No way was she straying back into Helene's magnetic field if I had anything to do with it.

I was trying to recall Sherry's favorite kind of pasta when she spoke. "I'm not coming with you at all, Darcy. I'm going to stay in San Francisco. They're looking for another bartender here, and Helene is sure I can get the job. She's offered to put me up for a while."

They'd settled all this while I was peeing? "But what about…us?"
I asked.

Sherry took a deep breath and let it out. "I hope we can still be
friends."

"Well, why not?" Helene chimed in, "We can all be friends. Give
us a ring once in a while, Dar." She pulled a card from her shirt pocket and held it out. I was impressed—I'd never known a bartender to
have a business card before. Made sense, though. When patrons were
struck with sudden lust for each other and asked for some paper to
write phone numbers on, she could hand them her card. If the
romance didn't gel, maybe one of them would phone *her*.

I took the card, inspecting it carefully while I tried to think of
something that would bring Sherry to her senses. "Helene Lauffer,
Mixologist," it read, followed by an address, phone number, and
"Available for Private Parties." I'll bet!

I tried locking eyes with Sherry. "Honey," I moaned. "I love you.
I need you. Won't you please come with me?"

The eye-lock ploy didn't work—Sherry looked up, she looked
down, she looked sideways. After a minute Helene put her arm
around her, and Sherry sank into it. I had my answer.

Helene grinned nastily. "Say, Dar, why don't you drop Sher's
things off here," she said, "on your way out of town."

I knew I'd think of a scathing reply in about an hour, but waiting around for it seemed like a bad idea. I stuck the card in my
jeans pocket and left the bar. The weather had turned cool and it
was raining, making the 20 blocks to the Winnebago seem like
120. After removing a sodden ticket from the windshield, I drove
the motor home out of the parking space and back to Cincinnati,
eating nothing and sleeping hardly at all. I made it in two days and
17 hours.

As soon as I got home, I pulled Helene's card from my pocket—

I was still wearing the same jeans—and dialed her number. After four rings, an answering machine clicked on and Sherry's voice said, "Helene and Sherry can't come to the phone right now. We're probably in the sack. If this is Darcy, *where are my clothes?*"

I cut the connection and flipped through the Rolodex to find the number of Erika Nisson, Sherry's therapist. I called, telling the receptionist I was desperate and needed an appointment, like *now*. When she offered an hour the following Tuesday morning, I almost told her I'd be working, then remembered that I had two more interminable weeks of vacation.

"I'll be there," I said.

Later, as I was folding Sherry's clothes into boxes for mailing, the telephone rang. It was Dr. Nisson. "Are you the Darcy Ford who is in a relationship with Sherry Bouchard, one of my clients?" she asked.

"Not at the moment," I said.

"Ah," said Dr. Nisson, as if she weren't surprised to hear it. "I'm sorry, Darcy, but I can't see you."

"Why? What did she tell you about me? Was it that thing with her parrot and the oscillating fan? It was her fault as much as mine!"

"Actually it's a matter of professional ethics," she said. "I can counsel you and Sherry jointly, however. Do you think she'd agree to that?"

"No." Everything else being equal, Sherry's commute would be a killer.

"Then why don't I give you the name of another therapist."

"Another therapist? I need to talk with someone who *knows* Sherry, Dr. Nisson—someone who can tell me how to get her back. Oh, please, doctor, I miss her so much. I can't go on!"

She paused, maybe scanning her list of professional ethics for a loophole. Anyway, she found one. "Would you consider joining a therapeutic group?" she asked. "I facilitate one in conjunction with a colleague, Dr. Jack Gonzalez. If you register as his client, you could join. It meets tonight, in fact, and there happens to be an opening."

All I heard was *Jack*. "A guy?"

"He's a gay man, very competent." She sounded a little snippy—here she was knocking herself out to accommodate me, and I was quibbling over body parts. "The group includes persons of both genders. We feel, Jack and I, that it's best to be as heterogeneous as possible."

"You have heteros too?" I was beginning to rethink the whole thing.

"No, we don't. The participants are mixed as to sex, age, and type of neuroses, but we're all gay. Look, Darcy, why don't you come by this evening and see if our group fits your needs?" When I didn't answer because I was still rethinking, she added, "Perhaps you aren't quite as desperate as you led me to believe."

"Oh, I'm desperate all right. I can't eat. I can't sleep. Who knows what else I can't do that I haven't even tried yet because all I've done for the last three days is drive!" The word *drive* came out as a scream.

She quickly gave me an address and ran through some rules that included always being on time and never talking outside the group about anything I might hear during the session. Then, sounding slightly apologetic, she explained the payment schedule. I agreed to everything.

After hanging up I found I'd regained some hope. I finished packing Sherry's things but didn't mail them—I stacked the boxes on the closet floor to be unpacked when she got back. Before I left for the group that evening I was actually able to keep down a handful of Corn Chex, the only food I could find in the house except for a can of peas.

There were seven or eight people milling around when I got there not only on time but ten minutes early. I recognized Dr. Nisson—I'd met her last year when Sherry and I had run into her at the food co-op. She recognized me too and came over, dragging with her the big, bearded man she was talking to. He turned out to be my new therapist.

"Welcome, Darcy," Dr. Gonzales boomed after our introduction, "to our humble group." He didn't act at all embarrassed to accept my check.

He introduced me to the others in the room, plus a couple of late arrivals—I hoped they weren't equally careless of the confidentiality rule. Then we were herded to some folding chairs that had been arranged in a circle. Everyone gave me big smiles to make me feel at home. I smiled back, stretching it wide to embrace them all. Such nice people!

Dr. Gonzales asked who would like to begin sharing this evening. There was a long pause while everyone studied their laps. Then a young woman a few chairs to my left stood up and said, "I ate some lettuce this week, romaine." Everyone murmured congratulations. She sat.

Immediately a tall fellow who'd been introduced to me as Paul stood and announced that he hadn't had "the pain" for five days. Immediately after saying that, he screamed and fell on the floor, clutching his right side. I didn't feel it was my place as the new kid to help him, so I looked to Dr. Gonzales, who simply watched the fellow moan and writhe. Dr. Nisson was making notes on a legal pad.

Finally an elderly woman next to me whispered loudly, "Pay no attention, dear, it's all in his head."

As Paul continued to writhe, a woman whose name I'd forgotten spent ten minutes recounting vivid and detailed memories of a childhood that was so horrible, I wanted to block my ears. The others in the group must have heard it all before—two of them started an independent conversation, and another yawned.

She finally finished and collapsed, sobbing, in the arms of her neighbor. I was considering doing the same when a balding man across the circle leaned forward and stared at me for a long time before whispering, "She phoned again last night."

I was about to whisper, "Who?" when Dr. Nisson said, "Your mother?"

He nodded and, to my relief, turned his gaze on her.

"You remember, don't you, Ambrose," she said, "that your mother died six years ago."

He nodded. "She called last night and said that I killed her."

"You know that you didn't kill her, don't you, Ambrose?"

"I didn't?"

"No. Try to remember what happened."

"Let's see." His brow furrowed. "I invited her to my apartment for lunch. It was a Saturday."

"That's right."

"We sat down at the table. I passed her a plate of sandwiches. She took one and bit into it."

"And then what?"

"Oh, yes! That's when I told her I was gay. She choked to death."

"That's right, Ambrose. It wasn't your fault."

"I'll tell her that when she calls tonight," he said and leaned back in his chair.

What am I doing here? I thought. *These people have real problems. What am I going to say when it's my turn? That instead of coming back to Cincinnati with me, my lover chose to stay in San Francisco with a sexy bartender from Georgia?* I could imagine them saying in unison, "So who wouldn't?"

I stood up. "Excuse me," I mumbled. They all turned to look at me with empathy on their faces, ready to listen and support.

I licked my lips. "Where's the ladies' room?"

"Down the hall, to your left," said Dr. Nisson.

I nodded and walked out. On the way home I decided that I didn't need therapy, I could deal with this situation all by myself. I was sorry to lose Sherry, but I could get along without her, no problem.

It'll actually be wonderful, Darcy, I told myself as I pulled into a McDonald's drive-thru. *You'll be able to do anything you want! You can buy real butter! You won't have to play Crazy Eights with Sherry's mom! Oh, and best of all, never again will you have to watch World Championship Wrestling!* To celebrate, I supersized my fries.

As soon as I got in the door I dialed the San Francisco number again, with my finger on the disconnect button in case Helene answered. She didn't, but Sherry did.

"Darcy," she said, "I'm so glad you called."

"Yeah, I'm sorry about your clothes. I'm home now, and I'll be mailing them in the morning."

"No, don't!" she said. "This isn't exactly working out. Will you send me money for a plane ticket?"

I didn't hesitate a millisecond. "I'll wire it tonight."

"Thank you. I've done it to you again, haven't I, Darcy?" she said, "I feel really guilty."

"I know. Do you think you can be happy back here after living in San Francisco?"

"Yes! This place sucks. Helene doesn't even have a TV. I didn't like tending bar either. Know what they made me do? *Wash glasses!*" She paused for effect, then added, "I really do love you, Darcy."

"I know."

"It's just when another woman talks sweet to me, I forget all about you. I forget how wonderful you are and how well you take care of me. I forget everything. It's like I have to get all the love I can from as many women as I can, as often as I can. Do you know what I'm saying?"

"No, but it's all right."

"I'm really messed up. I don't know what I'm doing. I need to talk to Dr. Nisson."

"I called her."

"You did?"

"I was feeling pretty messed up too. She suggested joint therapy—you and me. What do you think?"

"If you want to."

"I do."

"Darcy, will you do me a favor?"

"Sure."

"Will you watch wrestling tonight and let me know who wins?"

We exchanged endearments and hung up, and that's pretty much the end of the story. As I cross the room to switch on the TV, I'm seriously considering taking another stab at the therapy group, for a couple of reasons:

1. I paid for a month, and

2. I was wrong. I'll fit right in.

Watch Your Head
Sue Weaver

I never thought I'd long for a confessional until I was stuck under the brightly lit scrutiny of a psychiatrist. With the first sympathetic smile, I began to yearn for a dark closet, a sliding door, a few beads, some prayers, and best of all, redemption by the end of the afternoon. Sure, follow-up visits were expected, but my priest never pestered me about confessing the same sin weeks in a row, and he never looked at me like Stan, my shrink, did, his eyes like augers boring through the surface in search of any little insecurity, any sore spot. And he certainly didn't say words like *fuck* and *dick* all the time the way Stan did. Not to me, anyway. What he did on his own time was between him and his god, and I don't want to hear about it or read it in the paper.

Before you get too attached to the idea that I'm a complete moron or some kind of religious nut, let me say that I understand full well that psychotherapy is not supposed to be anything like confession. But in my mind—in my 18-year-old mind—they were definitely linked, one extending from the other. The Catholic Church had failed to strip me of my perversion—which at this point manifested itself as a tendency to be found less than fully clad with a perky blonde cheerleader (what was I thinking?)—and was, therefore, replaced by Dr. Stanley Payton, psychiatrist.

Dr. Payton, or Stan as I had always called him, was a friend of my dad's. My folks sent me to him to "make me better," and I don't mean make me *feel* better. I guess they figured that if threats of eternal damnation hadn't gotten to me, they may as well give Stan a shot at psychological manipulation and at the very least, I suspected, gain an inside line on what I was up to.

Stan's office was in a beautiful old Victorian house, a meandering three-story monument to the intricacies of the past. It had elaborately carved shutters and lots of tight little railings. These delicate details were skillfully enhanced by thousands of tiny brush strokes. The front steps had a deeply worn groove right up the center, and the sturdy handrail was smooth from the caresses of years. It was practically a miracle that I managed to get a splinter.

The first time I walked in the front door I got lost. Right away I thought that was a bad sign. I wandered around the maze of the first floor for a few minutes until a podiatrist's receptionist guided me to a wooden staircase and then mutely pointed upward. The staircase curved gently at first, and then the last flight narrowed and tucked in tighter. At the very top of the landing on the third floor there was a sign on the low ceiling that read "Watch your head." Upon emerging into a rather full waiting room I realized I was the only one laughing.

Self-consciously I cleared my throat and looked around the windowless room at the other patients who quickly dropped their heads toward the magazines on their laps. Where I came from, it was a commonly held belief that only "crazies" went to psychiatrists, but these people looked normal enough. I wondered if they were thinking the same thing about me. I sat down next to one of the four closed doors, picked up the nearest newspaper, and nervously pretended to read it. I could vaguely hear talking going on inside the room but was relieved that I couldn't make out any of the words because not only did I not want to know the dark secrets of others, I didn't want anyone to hear me either. Not that I planned on saying anything.

The building's outward beauty made entering Stan's office all the more shocking. The furniture looked like he had bought it used from a Days Inn, the carpet was orange shag and had probably come from Crazy Eddy's Carpet Remnant Warehouse sometime in the mid 1970s, and there were two almost identical "office" plants, both ailing, in cheap plastic pots. After what seemed an eternity I looked at my watch. Oh, God, only ten minutes had gone by. Ten down, 40 to go. So far he had done all the talking and I had managed to get by with smiles and nods, but I could tell that wasn't going to last.

Stan tried to set me at ease, but everything about being there made me nervous. He chatted on and on about my family.

"Your little brother just got a new dog, didn't he?"

"Yes, sir," I answered.

"It's a beagle, isn't it?"

"Yes sir, it's a beagle."

"Good dogs, beagles."

"Yes, sir, I'd have to agree."

"I like beagles."

"Me too, sir."

"I like them, but they howl, don't they?"

"Yes, sir, they do."

"Does Rob's new dog howl?"

"Yes, sir, he does."

"Beagles are loud too."

"Yes, sir, they are."

"They go like this, don't they?" and Stan leaned back in his chair and let out a tremendous howl, "Ooow, ow, ow, ow, oooooww."

And then he did it again, this time cupping his hands around his mouth. I looked at him in absolute horror. I couldn't make him stop. He thought it was funny, but I was the patient who had to walk out there through a waiting room, which would, no doubt, be full of people.

When the time came to open the door, it was exactly as I feared. There were probably only three or four people there, but when they quickly looked up at me it felt like 30 or 40.

I should have just said it out loud, "No, I don't think I'm a dog, it's the psychiatrist who likes to howl!" but they'd never believe me. Instead I bolted across the room, pulling out my car keys as I strode. They jingled very much like dog tags. Too quickly I rounded the corner and whacked my head on the low ceiling just beside that very informative sign.

Jane Caminos

Dollars and Sense
(or Why You Should Never Confuse Your
Girlfriend With Your Therapist)
Zonna

"**I** don't know where to start."

"Well then, start at the beginning."

"I don't know where that is."

"All right. Start anywhere. It doesn't matter. We'll sort it all out later."

"I feel funny."

"We've been together for five years. What's there to feel funny about?"

"This is different."

"Come on. Out with it."

"OK…Well, there's this woman."

"Woman? What woman?"

"It's not what you think."

"It better not be."

"I can't do this."

"Yes you can. Come on, we agreed. Therapy costs way too much money. We've both been going long enough, we know all the tricks. We can do it ourselves. Who needs a therapist? Come on. You were saying…"

"Well, OK. There's this woman I met at work."

"Is she cute?"

"What? I don't know. I didn't notice."

"Yeah, right."

"Look, I can't do this if you're not gonna be objective."

"OK, OK. Go ahead."

"Maybe this is a bad idea."

"No it's not. I'll be objective, I promise."

"So, I met this woman at work. She reminds me of my mother."

"Is that a good thing or a bad thing?"

"What? I don't know."

"How does she make you *feel*?"

"I'm not going there."

"Oh."

"Just let me tell you what I want to, OK?"

"OK."

"I forgot where I was."

"You met this woman at work who reminds you of your mother, whatever that means."

"You're making fun of me."

"No I'm not."

"Yes you are. You're judging me."

"Don't be silly."

"You're minimizing my feelings about this woman—"

"You have feelings about her?!"

"You know what I mean."

"No I don't. What feelings?"

"That's not what I meant."

"Are you cheating on me?"

"No!"

"Then what's going on with this woman?"

"Nothing!"

"How can I believe you?"

"Don't you trust me?"

"Trust? How can I trust you when you've been fooling around with this woman. I'm not blind, you know!"

"What?"

"I knew there was something going on."

"Nothing's going on. What are you talking about?"

"Then who is this woman? And why is she so important to you?"

"You've got it all wrong. I knew this was a bad idea. Stop crying."

"I'll cry if I want to. Don't touch me."

"Please—I swear I'm not cheating on you."

"I don't believe you."

"You have to believe me. Have I ever lied to you?"

"How do I know? I should've listened to my friends."

"What?"

"They told me you were no good."

"Who told you?"

"Everyone."

"Everyone?!"

"Why didn't I listen? Five years…How many other women have you had *feelings* for, I wonder. I'm such an idiot."

"This is ridiculous."

"Now I'm ridiculous? Why did you ever move in with me if you think I'm so ridiculous?"

"No, not you. This. This whole argument."

"You're just saying that because you were caught red-handed."

"I was not!"

"Oh, so you've managed to keep it a secret then."

"There is no other woman!"

"I can't believe you thought you could fool me. I know you too well. I could see it in your eyes."

"I can't believe everyone told you not to date me."

"You probably never loved me. I was just convenient or something."

"Why'd you go out with me if everybody said I was such a bum?"

"Because I was a jerk."

"What are you doing?"

"Packing."

"Packing?!"

"I'm not staying here."

"What? You can't be serious."

"Oh, I can't? Just watch me."

"Stop it. Come on, talk to me."

"There's nothing to say."

"I'm not cheating on you. There is no other woman. What can I do to prove it to you?"

"Nothing. You've done enough."

"Put that down! Hey, that's mine."

"No it's not."

"Yes it is. My mother gave that to me for my birthday."

"No she didn't. Sara gave it to me for Christmas."

"No. Look, it wouldn't even fit you."

"Is that a fat joke?"

"What? *No!*"

"Great. Fuck some girl behind my back *and* make fun of my size. Is she skinny? Is that what this is about?"

"No!"

"You said size wasn't an issue. You said you thought I was pretty."

"I did! I—I do!"

"Then why are you seeing someone else?"

"I'm not."

"Take your stupid shirt! I don't want it. I don't want anything of yours. Here, take your stupid ring too."

"Hey! Don't throw that! Hey! Now look what you did—it went right down the heat vent!"

"Who cares?"

"What do you mean, who cares? I bought that for you!"

"Why?"

"Because I love you, you shithead! I can't believe you threw it down the vent."

"I didn't aim for it, you know. It just happened."

"Damn…I can't believe you did that. I would never throw away something you gave me."

"You wouldn't?"

"Never. I love you."

"You do?"

"Of course I do."

"Then you're really not seeing anyone?"

"No. Hand me that screwdriver."

"What about that woman?"

"What woman? Here, hold this. Maybe I can reach in far enough to grab it."

"The skinny one from work."

"Mary? She's not skinny."

"She's not?"

"Not really, no. Damn…I can't even see it."

"Am I pretty?"

"What? Of course you are."

"Really?"

"Really."

"And there's no one else?"

"There could never be anyone else. I give up."

"On me?"

"No, on the ring. I can't find it. Help me up."

"Stay there. You look sexy like that."

"Oh yeah?"

"Yeah. I'll bet that Mary never did you on the floor like this, hmmm? Her knobby knees would probably make too much noise."

"She doesn't have knobby knees."

"How do *you* know what kind of knees she has? When did you see her knees?"

Cost of therapy session you tried to avoid: $95.

Costs involved in fixing what you broke: heating technician to retrieve the ring, $165; dinner to prove you still love her, $85; surprise vacation to prove it better, $456; six follow-up therapy sessions each to work this whole thing out of your systems, $1,140.

Total costs incurred from your stupid idea: $1,846.

My Favorite Mistake
Allison J. Nichol

Grey says that if Marv Alpert and Monica Lewinsky had just met each other first, they could have saved us all a lot of heartache. He thinks it is more than coincidence that they were both arrested in the same hotel. He has cable. He is telling me this as I circle the parking lot of Paris Dance for the ninth time.

"Geez, there is never parking here," I said, as I swung the BMW out onto Montrose Avenue and began the long tortured process of parallel parking.

"Hey look," Grey said, pointing to the bumper sticker on the green Aspire in front of us, "Jesus Saves, don't ya know?"

"Yes, too bad when he was saving them he didn't also teach them how to park," I said, barely missing the side as I pulled the car back one last time and put it in park.

"We could go to Sidetracks instead," Grey said, fidgeting with the button to the convertible top.

"Coward."

"Am not." Grey looked over my shoulder across the street to the bar's entrance. "OK, well maybe a little. Just stay close to me in case this is a man-hating crowd tonight."

"I will. I will. For God's sake, you do this every time we come here. What do you think is going to happen, anyway? It's not like you haven't been here before."

"I know but that was like on a Sunday afternoon to watch the

Bears game, not a Saturday night," he said, clinging to my arm as we dodged the traffic.

"I need you here with me tonight in case Julie shows up or in case her crowd is here. Besides, I haven't really seen you since you got back from the East Coast."

"Well, maybe your crowd will be here," he said, puffing up his minimal chest and straightening his WILL WORK FOR LIPOSUCTION T-shirt as we joined the small line at the front door.

"You are my crowd. And why didn't you call me from New York, anyway? In my hour of need and everything," I said, dodging the elbows of the woman in front of me as she and her girlfriend began their Saturday night fight early.

"I know, I'm sorry…again. But with the book tour, and the readings and signings…it was just overwhelming and unending. I really am sorry."

"OK, OK. But if you say 'I feel your pain,' I'm gonna smack you." We made our way through the door to the bouncer.

"Ten dollars," the decidedly butch-daddy–looking woman said from behind the small table.

"*Ten dollars?*" Grey said. "Ten dollars to get into a bar?"

"You got a problem, buddy? Is there a problem here, pal? You think maybe you should go to another bar?" The woman began to stand halfway up.

"No problem," I said thrusting a 20-dollar bill in her direction. "But why is it ten dollars anyway? Isn't it usually five?"

"Show tonight."

"What kind of show?"

"Ten dollars," she said, slipping the bill into the metal cashier's tray.

We zigzagged our way through the crowd to the back bar. We found two small but empty seats at a table right in front of the dance floor. The 20-year-old attitude-in-a-tank-top sneered at us as we ordered two Evians.

"OK, now spill it, sister. What happened between you and Julie, and don't you think couples counseling is a little extreme for a woman you have only been dating for four months?" Grey asked.

"Well, no. Why extreme? I really like her, Grey. And it's been almost five months."

"Why did she leave again?"

"I told you. She couldn't find the thermometer."

"I see. Yes, I remember that now from your voice-mail. Was she sick or something?"

"That's hardly the point, now is it?" I searched the crowd with my eyes for any sign of her while twisting the caps off of the Evian bottles.

"Oh. It's not? Oh, OK."

"No. The point is that every breakup has to be about something."

"So therapy? Counseling? You? Really? I don't see it."

"Why not counseling? What do you mean you don't see it?" I said, sipping my water. "And when did we all agree to pay $3 for a bottle of water?"

"Who is your therapist? Do you like her at least?"

"She's fine. I don't pay that much attention really. I just go for Julie," I said.

"What's her name? Your therapist."

"I'll tell you. But no laughing. You have to promise." I looked away.

"Why would I laugh? Oh, my God, is it somebody I know?" Grey asked, leaning across the table whispering.

"Not until you promise."

"OK, OK, how bizarre. I promise not to laugh." Grey crossed his index finger over his heart like a schoolboy.

"OK, her name is Sugar Jarz." I turned away toward the dance floor.

"What? What did you say? Sugar Jar? Oh, my fucking God. Your therapist's name is Sugar Jar? You're lying." Grey grabbed his stomach hard, trying not to burst out laughing.

"Not Jar, Jarz…J-A-R-Z. Jarz," I said, starting to laugh.

"Oh, yeah, that matters. Sugar Jar, oh, man," Grey squealed, spewing water across the table.

"All right, it's not that funny." I wiped the water from my cheek and the corner of my eye.

"How in God's name did you find her?" Grey asked, wiping his face and then the table with a napkin.

"I just got her name."

"Uh huh. Sure."

"OK, Emma recommended her," I said, turning in the seat to face the dance floor again.

"Oh. My. God. You are going to a therapist recommended by your ex. Honey, I spent way too much time in New York."

"She is not my ex. She is several exes ago. The statute of limitations is up on that now. Now we're just two white girls who used to know each other," I said, bouncing the empty Evian bottle on the table in rhythm to Shawn Colvin's "Get Out of This House."

"At least she's not a lesbian."

"This is me saying nothing."

"No, please please please tell me she's not a lesbian."

"I don't know. I never asked her."

"You are so lying. I cannot believe you are seeing a lesbian therapist."

"And why not? Anyway Julie likes her—that's all that matters," I said.

"Do you call her that? Sugar?"

"No, it's sort of awkward, actually. She asks me a question and then I answer it, and when it comes to the part where her name would naturally go, I just sort of stop. It makes us all a little uncomfortable," I said, hitting the Indiglo function on my watch to check the time. "When is this show we paid all this money for starting anyway?"

"How is the therapy going? Do you think you can save the relationship?"

"Not a chance."

"Really? Why not?"

"What do you mean why not? You know Julie, she's totally wacko."

"Then why are you still going?"

"Because I'm wacko too," I said.

"Yes, but in a much more meaningful and interesting way." Grey turned toward the dance floor as the lights began to dim.

"Of course," I said.

"What do you talk about when you're there? Is it really weird? Do you tell her your deepest secrets?"

"Why on earth would I tell her my deepest secrets? I don't know her from Adam. Besides, if I did that, I wouldn't need you, dear."

"But I thought you were supposed to be honest in therapy," Grey whispered, as the announcer came on stage.

"You are? Oh, I don't think that's right."

"What does Julie say? Is she feeling better? You never really explained the thermometer incident to me. What happened, anyway?"

"She says it was about the thermometer, but really it was video Elvis that started it all." I put on my glasses.

"Video Elvis? What the hell is video Elvis? My God, what have you been doing since I left? Who are you?" Grey said, leaning all the way across the table, whispering loudly.

"Shh, it's starting."

"No way, sister. You can't say video Elvis started it all and then shh me."

"Shh, I'll tell you at the break."

The MC, a tall redhead dressed in a vintage tuxedo, read some announcements and then introduced the first act. From behind a makeshift green faux-velvet curtain stepped several women dressed as the Village People. As the familiar sound of "YMCA" began to blast through the speaker system, the women began dancing around each other and lip synching. Unfortunately, two of them were a moment behind the others, giving the whole performance that dubbed-kung-fu-movie effect.

"Oh, this act is so tired, it needs a pillow," Grey whispered, as we started to giggle.

"Shh," I said, "want to get us killed?"

The women continued, and the crowd started to follow with the familiar YMCA letter moves, done even at suburban heterosexual wedding receptions now. They left the stage to thunderous applause.

Then out walked two women dressed as nuns handcuffed together. "This should be good," I said. The song "Sisters" began to play. As the one on the left mouthed "Sisters, sisters, there never were such devoted sisters," the one on the right fell to her knees and disappeared under the front of the other's habit. The one left standing started to thrust her hips forward and back in a motion familiar to all.

"Oh, my God, lesbians do that?" Grey asked.

"Yes, just usually not on stage."

Just as the one standing gave her last big thrust, the one under the habit emerged just long enough to join in the final, slightly amended line, "Lord help the mister that comes between me and my gal."

"I don't know how much more of this I can take," Grey said. "I mean, men doing women is one thing, but women doing drag? I'm not getting this."

"OK, one more, then we are out of here."

Out stepped two women. One was dressed in a business suit and wore a blond, highly sculpted wig. The other, a much younger woman, was dressed in jeans and a T-shirt that said GOT VODKA? over a picture of Sandra Bernhard. The women held hands and started to skip across the stage, mouthing the words to "Just Two Girls From Little Rock."

Grey started to howl. "They're doing Hillary and Chelsea."

"All right," I said, "that's it. I can't take it anymore. We are going to the front bar. Follow me."

We made our way delicately through the crowd and rounded the corner to the front bar.

"Jesus. What a nightmare," I said, sliding into a chair by the front window.

"Hey," Grey said, "Did I tell you Brenda came by the house the other day?"

"What? Why on earth? What did she want, for God's sake? To borrow a cup of eye shadow? I have way too many exes," I said, flagging down a waitress.

"I don't know exactly, she was there to see Ronnie, not me. Big surprise. Anyway, just thought you might want to know. OK—now, now, now I want to hear the video Elvis story."

"Oh, all right. I told you we were in Vegas, right?"

"Yeah, you did tell me that. That in itself is funny." Grey ordered us two more waters.

"Yeah, yeah. So we are in Vegas, and, well, Julie hates Vegas of course because it's, you know, fun. So we are, or rather I am, playing slots. And I was having fun, winning a little, losing a little. Julie is just complaining the whole time about how tired she is and how much she hates gambling, blah blah blah. So I finally decide to give in, but as we're walking up to the room I see these other slot machines. So after I beg her, we walk over to the video Elvis slots. I put some quarters in and I won. Then—here is the really fun part—I got to play the bonus round. OK, so this thing spins around, and if it lands on Elvis then you win like 500 bucks. So it lands on Elvis, and these lights start going off and up pops a video screen with Elvis singing 'Heartbreak Hotel.' The young Elvis, you know, not peanut-butter-sandwich Elvis. I was so excited. All the money starts spilling out, and Julie starts scooping it up in those little buckets they give you. And I'm laughing, and then she scoops up the last of the money and she starts to walk away with it, toward the cashier. And I'm like, 'What are you doing? Where are you going with that?' And she just says nothing and keeps walking. She walks right up to the cashier with my money and cashes it in. Then she turns to me holding the hundred-dollar bills in her hands and says, 'I am going upstairs, and this is going with me. I need to save you from yourself.' I was just ballistic. Save me from myself? *Save me from myself?* I don't think so. So basically she went upstairs, and I played roulette till 4 in the morning. The day after we got back I'm lying on the couch watching the Bears game, and she said she wasn't feeling well. She asked me if I knew where the thermometer was, and when I said no, she said that was it and she was leaving."

"Oh, my God, what did you do?" Grey asked.

"You mean after the game? Well, nothing actually. I mean I thought she was just mad and that she would cool off and come back like she always did. But she didn't. Who leaves somebody over a thermometer? So I started calling around and finally found her at her sniveling little friend Ryan's house."

"That is too bizarre. You have the weirdest life of anyone I know." Grey patted my arm. "I'm really sorry."

"Well, I just get tired of living with the fun police, ya know?"

"Yes, of course you do," Grey said, putting on his jacket. "I hate to say this, but isn't it cheaper to just break up?"

"I'm beginning to think so. OK, let's go, I can't take this place anymore."

As we edged our way toward the door, we got caught in the crowd and found ourselves wedged in between the dance floor and the door.

"Damn," I said, "We'll never get out of here now until this show is over."

"Great," Grey said. "Well, it can't last too much longer."

The lights dimmed almost completely, and then out walked a

very tall woman dressed as the Statue of Liberty. She was draped in a cloth gown that was stiff from having been spray-painted gold. Her face, her hands, her torch lit by an inside lightbulb, everything was painted gold. The sounds of Cyndi Lauper's "Girls Just Want To Have Fun" started over the speakers. The lights brightened a little, and she began to move in slow motion across the dance floor. Between the lights and all the gold, I began squinting my eyes. She continued her slow sort of disco waltz across the floor, moving slowly in our direction. She seemed to be heading straight for us. In another two bars I knew. She smiled at me. Right at me. I froze. When she got close enough she reached out her torch and laid it alternately on one of my shoulders then the other as if she were knighting me. Then she turned and began to walk back to the center of the stage.

"She must like you, honey. She thinks you're her knight in shining armor. Good thing we stayed," Grey said.

"Oh, my fucking God" was all I could manage.

"What? What's wrong with you? I thought it was cute."

"I think that's her."

"Who her?"

"That's her, Grey. I'm sure of it. That's Sugar Jarz."

"You're lying. It is? Your therapist is a lesbian drag queen?"

"We have to get out of here before I pee my pants," I said, dragging Grey by the arm and diving into the thick crowd.

We fell out the door, howling. We were both doubled over in laughter, and tears began to slip from my eyes.

"Well, that explains the name at least," Grey said, panting and holding his stomach. He grabbed me in a bear hug, and still laughing, I lay my head on his chest.

"And that is the woman you thought I should bare my soul to?" I said, still trying to catch my breath. "I learned two things tonight, honey. One, I will never have a relationship that lasts longer than the expiration date on my cereal. And two, this therapy thing is definitely my favorite mistake."

Kris Kovick

The Interpretation of Dreams
Lorrie Sprecher

I borrowed a book on self-hypnosis because I thought it would be really great if I could hypnotize myself and remember my childhood in time for my next therapy session. But I felt like an idiot reading aloud into a tape recorder and even more ridiculous playing it back. I turned out the lights, closed my eyes, and tried to pretend that listening to the monotonous sound of my own voice was causing my right arm to lift up all by itself.

It's no good, I said, *this is not working. I definitely can't hypnotize myself.* So instead I tried to send out hypnotic suggestions to my shrink through the astral plane of my psyche, telling her to change her mind, to decide that hypnosis would be good for me.

Not only is it a really good idea, I told her inside my own mind, pressing my fingers into my temples as though I were wearing some psychic space helmet, *but it's really safe. Your patient is ready to remember, and hypnotizing her will be both good and safe. And it will bring you great fame.* I added that last part hoping to appeal to her narcissism. I figured everyone must have some, even a really well-adjusted person like my therapist. Though I guess when a shrink's got it, it's healthy self-esteem or strong ego boundaries or something. But who doesn't want a little recognition for what she does? It can't be easy being my shrink—I'm a difficult patient—and she deserves some credit.

It will bring you great fame, I told her, using all my psychic concentration. *Tonight when you go to sleep, you will have a vision in which Sigmund Freud himself speaks to you. In your dream, he asks you to hypnotize me. He tells you it will help me remember. He mentions me by name.*

I have a little narcissism too, and the idea of the prince charming of psychoanalysis knowing my name appealed to me. I also figured it would go a long way toward making me more popular with my shrink.

"Did you sleep well?" I asked my therapist the next evening.

"Fine," she said. "Why all the concern?"

"Oh, nothing," I said, "I just thought you might be hearing voices."

"That's your department," she said.

Not anymore, I thought, *not anymore.* And I wondered if I could hypnotize her in session if I talked in a monotone, just like reading that book aloud into a tape recorder.

"What's wrong with your voice?" she asked. "You sound funny."

"I have a slight cold," I said, "in the head. It keeps me from remembering important things."

"This wouldn't have anything to do with wanting me to hypnotize you, would it? I told you, and I'll tell you again, hypnosis right now would be too dangerous."

Oh, my God, I thought, *she really is psychic.* And I vowed to devote the entire time until our next session to sending out more hypnotic thought waves. I was so desperate I was willing to try anything.

I was her last appointment, and when we walked to the parking lot together I looked at the sky and saw a streetlight or a planet, which I decided could pass for the first star. And I said out loud but very softly, "Star light, star bright, first star I see tonight, I wish I may, I wish I might, that my therapist will agree to hypnotize me soon and I will remember my childhood."

"Good night," she said, getting into her car.

"I hope you have very pleasant dreams," I said. And getting into my own car I thought, *Oh, my God, it's already working.* Because I realized that I remembered that star poem from my childhood.

She waited for me to turn on my headlights before pulling out of the parking lot. At least I decided that's what she did. I watched the taillights of her car until they disappeared. *Taillight red, taillight bright, first taillight I see tonight, I wish I may, I wish I might, that my shrink will make it home all right.*

Because I wanted to believe in a psychiatric sisterhood.

Art Cannot Hurt You
Claire Robson

Pusch cycles toward the house of a therapist in Lexington, Mass. Her probation officer demanded that she make the appointment. With his soft, shadowboxer's insistence, he said that therapy is routine for repeat offenders, as if that would make it holy.

Pusch has offended—repeatedly. It is part of the work she only dimly understands but which she knows she must do. It is important. The business card in her shorts pocket says that she is "Pusch. Spontaneist," and she has found that spontaneity does offend. She has six convictions for indecent exposure in public places, which include the White House lawn, Times Square, and two Republican conventions. Pusch draws her line against misogyny by taking off her shirt when men take off theirs. She knows that her breasts are not radioactive, that art cannot hurt you.

Her wheels spin her into the suburbs, where the houses spread themselves out with an easy sigh and men in shorts appear like a rash. Clipping here and sprinkling there, they kill weeds and shroud suburbia in smooth lawns. A woman with a plastic Bread and Circus bag holds the leash of an embarrassed-looking weimaraner as it defecates in the gutter. Fast-pedaling Pusch sings loud and tunelessly to the tinny blare of her Walkman. The woman and the dog turn their heads to gaze after the dying wail.

As she swings by the final stop sign into Gate Street, where the therapist lives, Pusch sees a newly opened Starbucks. In that sink-ing instant, she knows that Mrs. Limme will own mugs with wry aphorisms. She pedals into Mrs. Limme's driveway and allows the loose gravel to suck her wheels to a stop. Scrunching her way toward a shiny blue Volvo, she looks for a place to lean her mountain bike. A garden hose snakes around the base of an old apple tree, and Pusch plants her wheels firmly in its coils. As she walks toward the front door, with its brass plate and fake carriage lamps, she considers putting Mrs. Limme off the scent by inventing a fictitious childhood, maybe even an entire alternate self. A trimmer snarls viciously from around the corner, and Pusch rings the doorbell.

The waiting room has the kind of bland, blond furniture that professionals buy for waiting rooms, with just the right number of plants. Music dribbles out of a speaker, sounding like tired pixies playing xylophones. Pusch picks at a scab on her knee and stares numbly at the inspirational posters till the door cracks open and Mrs. Limme's head appears. Her limp, brown hair is trapped in a silver barrette, and her face is fixed in a welcoming smile.

"You must be Pusch," Mrs. Limme says, opening the door wide. "Come on in." She sits down in a leather recliner and invites Pusch to sit anywhere she likes. Pusch thinks that maybe this is a test. She notices that Mrs. Limme is clutching a coffee mug that says "I love bears" and when she finally chooses a seat, on the edge of the couch, Pusch has to avoid a whole pile of them. The bears are glassy-eyed and tragic, and so, Pusch suddenly realizes, so is Mrs. Limme. They are all propped there in a state of synthetic fuzziness, waiting for revelation.

Mrs. Limme says that she wants to discuss the therapeutic process. She wants Pusch to understand that there is no conflict of interest even though the state is paying for Pusch's therapy. Her accountability, she says with a stern creasing of her brow, is always to the client. Her voice is quiet and automatic as she leans toward

Pusch confidentially. Her glasses slip down her nose, and she prods them into place with her index finger. Pusch sees much in this gesture and in the defenseless curve of Mrs. Limme's clean, pink ears. She understands that Mrs. Limme has allowed people to pour their misery into her head as if it were a jug, so that she and Mr. Limme (who owns a gas-powered weed whacker) can improve their house and travel to the Bahamas.

"Now," says Mrs. Limme eventually, "I've talked for quite long enough. Tell me a little about yourself." She reaches down for a notepad, pulls up an encouraging smile. "Maybe start with your family background." As Pusch searches for the right words, Mrs. Limme shifts her gaze to the left. Pusch suspects that there is a clock nailed somewhere behind her. It is time to tell the truth.

She says, "Art cannot hurt you."

Mrs. Limme's eyes swim up at Pusch from behind her glasses like stunned blue goldfish. Her pen stills and hovers. She sets her notepad on the coffee table and lays the pen on top. It rolls off and bounces onto the floor, but Mrs. Limme's eyes do not flutter a fin.

"What did you say?"

Pusch rolls up her sleeve to show the tattoo. "Art—not just the product, you know, more like…well…the spontaneous gesture, the passion, everybody's afraid of it, but really—well, it can't *hurt* you." She swallows and sits back on the couch, dislodging a koala bear that rolls onto its back and lies there with its legs sticking up.

Mrs. Limme looks at the bear with a smile that is neither welcoming nor encouraging. She looks at Pusch as if she has made an unfortunate joke. Her gaze shifts back to the place behind Pusch, and Pusch just has to turn to see what she is looking at. Pusch sees that there is another door there. On the door is a neatly pine-framed sign that has the words WAY OUT embroidered on it in blue cross-stitch.

"It's funny you should say that," says Mrs. Limme, but she

doesn't look amused. Her goldfish gaze returns to Pusch. "You don't want me to listen to your family history."

Pusch isn't sure if this is a question. "Nothing personal," she says. "It's just that I think there are maybe better things we can do with our time."

Mrs. Limme pushes herself out of the black recliner as if she's made a decision.

"I hoped someone would show up," Mrs. Limme says. "We all need someone, in the end. I just got tired of waiting, you understand. I gave up."

Mrs. Limme walks toward the Way Out. Next to the door is a table, and on it is the statue of a woman's body with the head and wings of a bird of prey. Mrs. Limme picks it up. "She's Babylonian," she whispers, holding the woman gently against her breasts. "She understands the nature of justice and confession. Art can be cruel too. You must know that." She opens the door.

Pusch looks over her shoulder at the heap of people crumpled on the back steps. They lie in surprised positions in business suits and Gap jeans. One of them still clutches his Starbucks travel mug. Nobody moves. Pusch makes one of those pointless calculations we resort to in stressful moments. She figures that at the rate of six clients a day there must be about two or three days' worth of bodies in that bloody pile.

"I gave them all a full 50 minutes," Mrs. Limme is saying (as if Pusch is about to accuse her of being unprofessional), "then I showed them a Way Out...permanent, you see. Otherwise they keep coming back. They keep coming back and they talk on and on, covering the same ground...They didn't suffer, you see—well, not by comparison...this is kinder than therapy in the long run." She holds out the statue so that Pusch can take it. "I'll show you where the phone is."

Pusch doesn't take it. "Not me," she says. Turning her back on

Mrs. Limme, she begins to walk away. "There are some things you just have to do for yourself."

Honey
Laura A. Vess

You called this morning,
a cold making your voice rough
and my throat sore in sympathy.

My therapist always said,
"You need to be more caring,
think about her needs,
be supportive,
give instead of take."

I waited for you, making hot tea with honey
but no lemon (you're allergic)—
then soup like my mother never made,
heating on the stove.

I left your favorite blanket
on the couch, turned up the heat
even though I was already too warm.

You called again,
said we needed to talk
when you got home—
you needed space,

we should see other people,
we can just be friends.

I agreed kindly,
fired my therapist,
burned the soup,
and put lemon in your tea.

Robin K. Cohen

You Gotta Have Faith
Yvonne Zipter

I wouldn't say therapy is a religion, but most lesbians, myself included, go to a therapist's office much more faithfully than they ever go to a church or temple. And for therapy to work, you do kind of need to believe that your therapist is a higher being: she is wiser than you are and/or she has access to some secret source of information. If therapists were merely mortal, why would we go? You might as well just talk to your mother about your problems. Except, of course, that dear old mom is exactly what many of us want to talk to the therapist about in the first place. That leaves the likes of Ricki Lake and Sally Jesse Raphael to turn to for advice, and I don't think anyone mistakes them for higher beings— although now Oprah's got that Angel Network thing going on, so even if she isn't a higher being, she's obviously got connections. Hard as it can be to hook up with the right therapist, though, it's even harder to get on *Oprah,* so really, your only viable option is to believe that the therapist is going to be smarter about your own life than you are.

What a disconcerting experience, then, when you discover that your therapist is, in fact, merely human. It throws your whole belief system out of whack, causing you to question all of your previously held assumptions—for instance, maybe Kate Clinton isn't really the goddess of humor after all? During the second-shortest client-therapist relationship I ever had, which lasted two sessions (the shortest relationship lasted only one session but had an extensive breakup period), I got to see the mind of a therapist at work. It was like that game Mousetrap, where you could see the ball rolling along myriad paths and over a variety of obstacles, but it was pretty clear where the ball was going to wind up ultimately : right under a trap.

I had gone to see this woman through a program at my job that provided short-term counseling benefits for free. It's a bit like the Supercuts of therapy: the price is appealing, but you never know who's going to be treating your hair—or in this case, what's under it. It seemed to be the place to work fresh out of therapy school while you were learning your trade, before you moved on to a big-ticket salon.

I had used this service a few times over the course of many years, mostly when I was having some problem on the job with which I wanted help coping, and not—surprisingly enough to the so-called moral majority, I'm sure—because I needed treatment for being a lesbian. This last time I went seeking advice about how to deal with burnout while I looked for a new job. When you've worked in one place for nearly two decades, either it must be a relatively decent place to work or you really do have some serious issues to talk about in therapy. For me, it was the former, and in that situation, you want to make sure you're not giving up Kansas for hell: the first might be a little bit boring, but the second is downright, well, hellish. I can think of a dozen hackneyed sayings that apply: Look before you leap. Out of the frying pan, into the fire. Better safe than sorry. A bird in the hand is worth two in the bush.

That's not quite 12, but you get the idea. I didn't want to just take any old thing to get away from a situation that had become like a second family to me, which is to say, it has all the dysfunction of your actual family, but the pay is better. While I looked for that new job—sent out résumés, consulted with a career specialist, networked my butt off, and so on—I thought it might be helpful to learn some mechanisms for handling the dangerously exhilarating work I was currently doing, such as making sure all the serial commas were in place in an author's work on the statistical inevitability of something or other.

The first session with this therapist was going along reasonably well, though she occasionally seemed to be missing the point that my life *outside* of work was actually quite fabulous and that it was the job that I was less than thrilled with. My first clue that she just wasn't quite getting it was that she started making suggestions like, "When you NordicTrack in the morning, why not read a book?" I suppose that's technically possible, since they do make a book-holding apparatus for the NordicTrack, but at the mere thought of this feat—the exercise equivalent of walking and chewing gum at the same time—the alphabet began to bob and weave before my mind's eye, and a little wave of motion sickness overcame me right there in the therapist's office. Despite her bad aim—repeatedly missing the target area of my dull work life and trying instead to liven up my wonderful home life with my best gal—I thought we were beginning to develop a rapport by the end of the "hour." I say "hour" in quotation marks because, of course, I actually mean 50 minutes. I think Webster's should add the phrase "therapist's hour" to their dictionary since they've already got "baker's dozen" and, if we're going to stick to time-related phrases, "New York minute," though I'm not quite sure what the latter is—a measure of time with a Bowery accent?

At any rate, whatever rapport we might have established the previous time evaporated in short order the second time. Having pored over my files between sessions and gleaned every ounce of information ever recorded about me by the SuperTherapists, the therapist decided that the reason I was having trouble leaving my job was because of an incident of childhood abuse. I sat in silence for a moment, stunned by the acrobatic leaps in imagination and logic this conclusion had taken: that, first of all, I was having trouble leaving my job and that, second, this abuse had anything to do with anything about my current situation. I spoke very gently to her, as one might speak to someone who seems dangerously delusional or extremely dull-witted, and described the reasons that I hadn't so far jumped at the chance to work at, say, Dunkin' Donuts or Molly Maids or whatever other jobs might be mine pretty much for the asking, since she didn't seem to understand that simply *wanting* a new job didn't mean you could just take whichever job you wanted. I also tactfully let her know that I was aware that such abuse can have far-reaching effects, but that someone working as proactively as I was at finding new work could hardly be described as crippled by this 30-year-old experience.

But this higher power had created her diagnosis and was now resting: She and I were done, and if I wanted to talk more about being bored with my job, I'd have to go see someone else—a long-term person—to talk about a three-decades-old incident first. God isn't the only one who works in mysterious ways. How did she miss the fact that sometimes when you say you want a banana, you simply want a banana, Freud notwithstanding?

What does it mean, though, do you suppose, that my first impulse, upon getting a new job, was to call her up and maturely say, "Nyah, nyah, nyah-nyah-nyah: I got a new job"? I didn't do that, of course, but the fact that I *wanted* to is no doubt directly connected to not being breast-fed. Why not? If wanting to contend with problems on the job is related to childhood abuse, how far-fetched is it to assume that wanting to give her the raspberry was connected to synthetic nipple use as an infant?

I can tell you this much, though: I'm not *even* going to speculate about what it might mean, according to that therapist, that when my old boss called and asked me to come back, I went. Sometimes it's better to be an agnostic—in therapy, as in religion, as in life.

I'm thinking of becoming a born-again neurotic. It's either that or lose my faith in therapy—and I don't think any of us wants that.

The Lavender Healing Center
Erin Cullerton

I sat on the waiting room couch watching the second hand on my watch go round and round. I was trying to forget how nervous I was. The waiting room was painted a pale, dusty pink color. Not exactly the color I would have imagined a bunch of lesbians choosing at a paint store, but maybe it had been in the free bin. And that, of course, would have been more fitting.

Nearly a dozen magazines lined the thin coffee table. When I picked one up a subscription card fell out. Someone had written "Sarah Loves Josey Forever" on it. It made me cringe. The topic of love was a sore one for me these days. So much so that I'd decided to go see a therapist. I could hear my friend Maria's voice now. "I think it'd be good for you, Max. You can't stay hung up on Syd forever."

But Syd had been my first girlfriend. I missed the way she called me her little "puppy dog" and the way she cooed "baby" in my ear late at night when she lay beside me. It didn't really matter that she'd moved to L.A. It just made me miss her even more.

The Lavender Healing Center was in an old rundown Victorian. As I sat on the couch beside the looming mantelpiece, I could hear women's voices coming from the back of the house. I imagined a happy collective of lesbians working together to solve the lesbian nation's problems. I thought of all the paperwork.

I glanced around the office trying to remember why therapy

could, in fact, be good for me. I listed the reasons in my head: (1) I was hung up on Syd; (2) I couldn't imagine falling for another woman again; and (3) women had begun to scare me. OK, I thought, that's reason enough. I forced myself to settle into the couch and picked up the only non–lesbian-lifestyle magazine on the table, a 1974 *National Geographic.*

I was just getting into an article on baby seals in the Arctic when a short, round woman with rosy cheeks greeted me from behind the frosted glass window. Introducing herself as Agnes, she said, "You must be Max!"

"That's me," I said, sounding cockier than usual. Shyness had a way of doing that to me.

"Do you mind filling out a few quick forms while you wait?"

"No." I shrugged my shoulders, and thought, *Like filling out forms is something I just love to do.*

"Good." She handed me the clipboard. "Your therapist, Laura, will be right out." She had begun to shut the window when the waiting room door creaked loudly. I jumped. Agnes chuckled. "Make yourself comfortable, honey. These old homes are just full of ghosts!" She seemed to find it amusing.

Remembering my nervousness, I squeezed my body deeper into the couch. I had almost finished filling out the form when I heard a soft voice to my left say, "Hi." I looked up. Standing in the doorway was a tall, extremely stunning woman who looked my age. She wore overalls and a baseball cap, and her hair was the color of the sky mid-sunset. She walked toward me and extended her hand. "I'm Laura."

My heart skipped a beat. It hadn't dawned on me that I might get a cute therapist. I thought they were all frumpy, skirt-wearing 40-year-olds; that they were all like my mother—someone I could bare my soul to. I felt my stomach tighten and thought, *Oh, shit, what have I gotten myself into now?*

"We're going to meet in one of the back rooms. It's right behind the bathroom," she said, inspecting my baggy pants and short hair. "I hope you don't mind the sound of the pipes flushing?"

I smiled weakly, shaking my head as she led me down the hallway. From behind, her walk was like Syd's—long and confident. The kind of walk that told you she was a woman who could dominate a situation.

When she opened the door to the room, I panicked. The two pieces of furniture—a chair and a polka-dot-print, love seat–size couch—were pushed extremely close together. Laura walked in confidently and sat down. I could feel her eyes on me as I made my way to the couch.

I glanced around the room while she pulled out a clipboard and placed it on her lap. Black-and-white photographs lined the walls, and a narrow skylight gave off a few inches of light. In an effort not to make eye contact, I studied the photographs intensely. My heart had just begun to slow down when she pulled out a tape recorder and turned it on.

"So, Max, tell me why you've decided to begin therapy."

I could feel the heavy beat of my heart again. I took a deep breath. The words were almost out when a sound like screeching mice, followed by a loud *whoosh*, filled the room. I braced myself on the couch.

"Oh, that's just the pipes," Laura said apologetically.

I cleared my throat, still trying to avoid eye contact. She was looking right at me and I could hear my heart reverberating in my rib cage. "I can't get over my ex-girlfriend." I said, almost too loudly to make up for the ringing sound that still filled the room. But as the words rolled off my chest I knew right then and there it was a lie. I could get over Syd; I was choosing not to.

"How long were you two together?" Laura asked, looking at me and totally ignoring her notepad.

"Only six months, but…" My voice trailed off. Suddenly I felt a little ashamed that I was so hung up on someone I'd only been with for six months. Laura swung her foot gently, waiting for me to finish my sentence. Her stare was sensitive but direct, and it sent chills down my spine.

"But," I continued, "she was my first girlfriend." At this, Laura's face smoothed into a warm smile.

"First girlfriend, huh?" There was something kind in her voice, something more friend than therapist. My body relaxed.

"First girlfriends are always the hardest to get over, but Max, you have to trust that you will get over her. What was her name?"

"Syd," I said, looking into Laura's face. I couldn't remember when a woman had ever looked at me so thoroughly. Did she do this to all her patients or did she think I was cute? The more I thought about her, the less I thought about Syd.

"Were you in love with Syd?" Laura asked, leaning forward for emphasis.

"I'm not really sure," I said honestly. I was in love with the idea of Syd, with the smell of Syd in my bed at night, with the comfort that Syd provided me. But was I in love with Syd the person? That was a good question.

"I don't know." It was the truth.

"Would you like some water?" Laura asked, leaning out of her chair and revealing the soft curve of her breasts from beneath her overalls as she reached for a cup. I remembered the woman on the phone the day I made the appointment telling me there was a possibility I might get a student intern. Of course, that's why she was so young. She was still a student.

I found myself watching the way she grabbed the cups. There was something delicate yet confident about each of her movements.

"Have you seen many patients?" I asked, unsure whether it was an appropriate question. But I felt like the room got ten degrees hotter as soon as I asked the question. Something about the way she looked at me between pauses made me giddy and nervous. But more importantly, it continued to make me forget about Syd.

"Yes, I've seen a few at this center and at another center, so far."

"Do you like studying people?" I asked, my eyes steady on her face.

"I like helping people," she replied, finding a pen and placing it on her clipboard. Then she poured us each a glass of water. Her eyes were a light almond color. I was completely transfixed by them.

"Have you done therapy before?" she asked, passing me a glass.

"No, I haven't, actually." I paused to take a sip of water. "I'm just a really curious person, which you'll soon find out." Somehow it came out in my most flirtatious voice.

What had gotten into me? I was practically oozing all over the couch. I had to remind myself that Laura was a total stranger. But I couldn't deny that I felt the same way that I had felt the first time I met Syd.

As the clock crept closer to 3 o'clock, my heart began beating rapidly. I knew what I needed to do. I grabbed my bag and paid Laura. "I'm not going to be able to continue therapy with you," I said.

Laura looked at me funny for a moment. It made me feel nervous. Maybe I'd been misreading her expressions.

"I'm sorry, I don't understand," she said, taking the cash from my hand. As our fingers brushed I felt a warm heat spread through my body. My confidence came back.

"It's nothing about you," I said, unsure of how to put it. "I mean it is about you, actually." I paused. *Just say it, Max.* "Laura, I think you're really…well, beautiful. And I don't know you, but I feel really comfortable with you, and I—I think I'd like to date you." Before today I had never thought I'd say those words again.

Laura placed the clipboard on the floor and took another big gulp of water. There was something awkward in the way she looked at me. I mean, I guess it was probably weird that a client was try-ing to ask her out.

"I don't know what to say, Max." She put the clipboard on the ground and folded my money into an envelope.

"'Yes' would be good," I said, feeling my rib cage start to tighten a little. Was I making an ass of myself? Oh, God, please tell me I wasn't. Had I completely forgotten how to read a woman? (Did I ever know how?) I looked down at the shit-brown carpet and wait-ed for her reply.

"I could be fired for something like this," she said, smiling weakly.

"Yes, but remember, I'm not coming back." I really couldn't believe how bold I was being.

Our eyes met, and we both just looked at each other for a moment. She was being cagey, but her fingers tapped the arms of her chair as though she were thinking seriously about it.

"Meet me outside the building in five minutes," she said, getting out of her chair and picking up her things.

A bright ray of sunlight spread through the tiny skylight. I looked around at the room, trying to remember the specific dimen-sions of the place that had pushed me toward the future. Then I walked out to my car and rested on the hood, waiting for Laura to come around the corner.

There is no there there, but I think I can handle it now.

Another Therapy Audition
Riggin Waugh

My lover and I continue to audition therapists in hopes of salvaging our relationship. This one is located in downtown Silver Spring, Md.

I have a bad cold, compounded by a lot of crying over the past 24 hours. My sinuses are clogged, my ears somewhat plugged, my brain a bit scrambled. Oversimplified, the problem with our relationship is that, due to circumstances beyond our control, my lover and I don't spend enough time alone together.

After a few questions about our history with therapy and why we're there, the therapist asks, "How's your sex life?"

Wow, she's really jumping right into this, I think. *Sex is not the problem here, except maybe not having enough of it. But I guess she knows what she's doing—she's the therapist.*

"Great," my lover says too quickly.

"That is," I add, "when we have sex, it's great."

My lover nods her head in agreement. "We only have it maybe twice a month."

I blow my nose.

The therapist looks at me questioningly. "Tell her what you like in bed."

God, did I hear her right? My head still feels pretty foggy. "Explicitly?" I ask.

The therapist nods.

I look at my lover and then down at my lap. Without looking up, I reach over and hold my lover's hand. "Oh, gosh. There's so much I like. I like it when she lies on top of me and holds my shoulders down with her hands and then kisses my neck real slow."

My lover gently squeezes my hand, which I take as encouragement.

I don't look up. "And I like it when she nibbles on my ear, then slowly moves her tongue down to my breast. She spends a lot of time making love to my breasts. Especially my right one; I think she favors it. I like it when she talks dirty to me. And we laugh a lot in bed. Like whenever she's on top of me, she asks, 'Am I too heavy?' and I say, 'You ain't heavy, you're my lover,' and we always laugh, every time."

My lover squeezes my hand again, almost urgently. I squeeze her hand back. I'm afraid I'm embarrassing her, but therapy's our last hope, and I'm going to do whatever it takes. I keep staring at my lap and go on. "I really like the way she grabs my ass when she goes down on me. And she does this thing with two fingers…." I finally look at the therapist, holding up my second and middle fingers to illustrate.

My lover starts to cough violently. Her face is quite red, and I hand her the bottle of lemon seltzer we brought with us.

The therapist looks a little pink too. "Well, you've told me quite a bit, but I asked, '*Do* you tell her what you like in bed?' It was a yes or no question."

Shaman Says
Meredith Pond

My shaman says I need to get out more. She says I need to move on and start dating again before my soul shrivels up like that old apple on the dashboard of my pickup. Move on. Explore my dharma, my karma, and my nightlife without pajamas. I tell my shaman that pajamas are good for me. So are mugs of hot chocolate on cold nights. And a Patricia Cornball mystery or two. My shaman disagrees. She thinks I need human contact. I say, with six billion people on the planet right now, human contact is overrated. She says it's not wise for a woman to disagree with her shaman.

Like a good mechanic under the hood, my shaman checks my aura every week. She says my second chakra looks like an overturned bowl of spaghetti, tendrils hanging out in all directions. Sometimes Tibetan 10W-40 pine needle oil does the trick. Other times it's eucalyptus leaf oil that keeps me moving on in spite of myself. I'm thinking breakups are like mythic battles between good and evil or light and dark. The problem is each party believes she is the good and the light. No one is ever wrong. The hard truth is that if I never bought new underwear again in my entire life, no one would know. My shaman says I need sexual healing. Let's just decide that sex is overrated and forget the whole thing.

Hey, it's not like I'm refusing to ask somebody out—I simply forget how. And even if I drink my Gingko tea and remember how, there's still *who*. Being in a long-term relationship means I didn't date anybody for a long time, just my girlfriend—my ex-girlfriend, and she doesn't count anymore. Oh, sure, I read the personal ads every Friday in *The Washington Blade*. "Loves to laugh" is still looking for Ms. Right. Her ad's been running now for six weeks. What makes her think someone will call her *this* week? The ad always reads the same. I'm waiting for her to drop the good-girl head games in her next ad: "Hysterical bottom seeks rough top for marshmallows and oblivion. Roast me, toast me, butter my biscuits."

My shaman is more in tune with me than a conventional therapist could ever be. She lives in a cave on weekends to stay in touch with her primal Amazon within. If there were wolves in those mountains, I'll bet she would run with them, howling. As for me, I'm not ready to sleep on the ground naked and wake up with bats in my hair and chiggers burrowing into my skin. Even if her land becomes part of a health resort with a double jacuzzi and an Olympic-size pool, I will continue to see her on Mondays at her ritzy Chevy Chase office with the complimentary bottled water. That reminds me, I just got a flyer in the mail for my shaman's group body-painting ritual for Beltane. She will be the maypole. Her clients are invited to dance around her and paint her body with edible primary colors. I think I have a dentist's appointment that day.

Right now I'm burning oregano in a tuna can, you know, to put the word out in the universe that I'm available again. My shaman says to burn sage in an abalone shell, but I'm out of sage because it's April, not Thanksgiving, and abalone shells are hard to come by on the East Coast. So the tuna can will have to do. I could take some time off and fly out to San Francisco, wrestle an abalone shell from an unsuspecting sea otter, and scramble to shore. Except I heard those cute, furry critters bite. Don't they all.

Of course, I could go to San Francisco anyway. Especially now, because my apartment smells like an Italian fishing boat. In the city by the bay I could walk the Embarcadero and have an ice cream sundae at Ghirardelli Square. Then, I could follow Route 1 down the coast past Monterey to Big Sur and see if Kim Novak is home. *Anywhere* but here. I'm desperate. The windows in my living room are wide open, but the odor lingers, morphs into old tuna socks with a twist.

I can change my reality. I will change. I remember my mantra and say it three times the way my shaman taught me. *Do-me Um Do-me Um do-me do-me do-me do.* This is supposed to open my throat chakra so I can ask for what I want. I am saying "um" a lot between sentences. This is progress. I'll meditate outside on the patio too. My mantra might work even better out there.

The patio cement is hard, like real cement. As I create my own reality, I must remember to ask for softer cement. Like tying my legs in knots, lotus pose is impossible for more than a minute or two. My ankles ache after that. My shaman says an alligator bit off my left foot in a past life when I lived in the Everglades. That's probably why I've always hated Florida.

The other problem with meditating is that I have to keep my eyes closed. Call me crazy, but I like to look around. Especially at night, stargazing. I'd rather watch the stars from out here on the patio than close my eyes and concentrate on world peace. My shaman made me take my VISUALIZE WHIRLED PEAS bumper sticker off my car. She says it's making fun of the wrong thing. But isn't that what humor is all about?

All winter long I watch Orion climb across the sky. Now that it's spring, I don't have a favorite constellation I can identify right away. Cassiopeia is a big "W." What fun is that? And the Big Dipper is for kids, even though I do like major bears. Light from these stars took millions of years to get here and shine in my eyes. On one hand, it's overwhelming and I am humbled by this idea. On the other hand, I really only care about the concept of time as it relates to my own existence and my personal happiness. I could become a cult leader.

Maybe five years isn't long in cosmic time, but it is for me. How would you feel if you spent more than half your lesbian life making love to one woman and then she up and left you for a tall, geeky ornithologist and relocated to Costa Rica?

My shaman wants me to change my name, reinvent myself. The problem is, "Xena" is taken. I liked "Io" for a while, one of the moons of Jupiter, where the Galileo space probe recently took some pictures and transmitted them back to Earth. Then I found out Io is a cow in Greek mythology. Forget it. That's all I need.

I wonder if Sappho ever broke up with anybody. At least they probably got a goodbye-forever poem out of it. Then they drank hemlock with Socrates's boys and jumped into the Aegean Sea or sailed for Crete to see if Icarus had any extra wings. I hear First-Dyke Cruises has a trip to Lesbos now. What an idea—the Mediterranean by boat. Perhaps a stop is planned for the oracle at Delphi, the ancient oak tree with the talking leaves and all the answers. What does the future hold for me? Will I be pretty? Will I be rich? *Que sera, sera.* Why am I channeling Doris Day? Well, I guess any friend of Rock Hudson's is a friend of mine.

To attract the woman of my reinvented dreams, my shaman tells me to build a tree house. I remind her I am not Tarzan's Jane. I am Edith, couch potato. She refuses to accept this as truth. Actually, rather than the tree house, I plan to dig a stupendous hole in the middle of the park down the street, cover it with branches and leaves, and then wait to see who falls in. This plan, if all goes well, will allow me to *catch* the woman of my dreams. No matter what, at least I know my brain stem is intact and my primal urges are reenergizing as we speak.

Wait. The phone is ringing. It's my shaman calling on her cell phone. The strangest thing just happened. She was walking in the park and fell *kerplunk* into an enormous hole. She doesn't know why she is calling. I am the only one she knows who actually picks up the phone when it rings. My entire life is about to change just because I don't believe in voice-mail. Cosmic.

I am thinking that maybe tomorrow I could take a drive with my shaman out to that cave of hers. It's time.

Ursula Roma

A Tiny Padded White Cell
Diana Eve Caplan

The first time I agreed to go with Ellen to see Lynn in a last-ditch attempt to save our failing relationship, I was suspicious. Lynn was Ellen's private therapist. I was skeptical about a therapist being able to do both private and couples counseling for the same person without bias, but we were near ready to break up every other week, and a leap of faith was better than a leap into nothing. I loved Ellen and knew I always *wanted* to love her, but I had been overwhelmed lately by moments of not loving her. So I went.

Lynn's office felt much more confrontational than Abby's. Abby was my private therapist. We'd decided to use Lynn for couples counseling instead of Abby because Ellen said she needed someone to tell her what to do and not just understand her.

"Abby works great for you, but I'm telling you right now if anyone asks how our fights make me feel, it won't do a thing for me. I need to fix our problems, not analyze them," she'd said.

I knew a therapist wasn't supposed to try to fix problems but rather help clients to fix them. Or maybe that was my own small view of the therapeutic world, based on my long and loyal experiences with Abby, who I thought of as the earth goddess of understanding. Ellen and I had fought once over Abby because Ellen was convinced I had a crush on her. Just because I always made references to "Well, Abby says…."

In addition to Ellen already having a grudge against Abby, it had happened one day in a session with her that Abby told me she thought she knew Ellen. She'd once lived in a little cottage with her partner, and behind their cottage was another in which lived another lesbian couple, Ellen and Lisa. She even remembered the name of the baby girl Lisa had while living there—little Julie. The details matched too much. She told me she didn't think her previous knowledge of Ellen would hinder my therapy, and I believed it.

It was agreed that Lynn, not Abby, was neutral territory since Ellen had yet to open up to Lynn in private counseling.

"She doesn't really know me at all," Ellen said.

"She's your therapist, Ellen."

"Yeah. She doesn't know me."

"What the heck do you talk about with her?"

"Work. And my schedule."

"Oh. You know you'd save a lot of money if you consulted a date book for that and not a therapist who charges $90 per hour. Why do you like her?"

"Because she doesn't take my bullshit."

It should have dawned on me that Lynn might not be the answer to our problems. In Lynn's office there was one window, a small one that looked out upon someone's laundry line. The room stank of fish and bacon, cooking one flight of stairs below us at Chez Pablo's, a stylish gourmet restaurant in Santa Monica. Ellen and I sat on the sofa, each taking an opposite end and hugging a small, exclusively decorative pillow. There was no jug of spring water or stack of Dixie cups like at Abby's office, nor were there cozy woven blankets or functional pillows to hide under. Actually, when I first looked at Lynn I understood hiding would be out of the question. Hiding would get me in trouble. There was a look on her face that told me there would be very little swapping of childhood trauma stories here and there was no excuse for our present dilemma.

Lynn sat posture-perfect across from us in a tall, black leather chair. It looked like a La-Z-Boy to me and made me wonder if her method was to use an imaginary remote control and stop us, make us rewind, zoom forward, or stand frozen in nerve-wracking pause, waiting for her next calculated interaction. Next to her was a small table with a date book on it and a pad of paper that Lynn picked up as soon as we started talking. She was going to take notes. I didn't know whether to be impressed or scared. I decided to watch what I said and try to come off as mature and experienced in the ways of compromise and listening.

"So, Delia. Nice to finally meet you." She smiled a wide, maternal smile that didn't fool me. There was something in her voice and demeanor that sparked recognition in my memory. I was suddenly positive I'd met her before. I was absolutely sure. But I couldn't place her. God, lesbian circles are sometimes excruciatingly small.

Lynn had a gray Caucasian version of an Afro hairdo that made her look like a lollipop because she was very tall and thin. She had thick-rimmed glasses and wore a big, flower-print blouse with gray slacks and white nurse-type sneakers. She didn't wear makeup as far as I could tell, but she did have on a string of gaudy red beads and bright plastic Earth sphere earrings. It unnerved me to see that she thought of herself as having the whole world dangle from her earlobes.

Ellen started talking about why we were there, and my mind wandered away. I panicked, wondering how I knew Lynn. If I really knew her, she might know me, and if she knew me, she had the advantage because if she remembered me but knew I didn't remember her, she could use it against me—or try to slowly wear me down. Maybe I'd met her under strange circumstances. Maybe she'd seen me drunk or stoned in public or, even worse, cavorting around with any one of the guys I used to date. Oh, God, maybe she'd try to prove I wasn't a lesbian. I prayed I'd remember meeting her before she remembered meeting me.

An image of her sitting in yet another reclining chair, this time with her feet up, flashed before me. When? Where? At a party? Whose party? Specifically, what kind of party? The kind of party could make all the difference. But she didn't look like the party type. Too old and out of style.

"Do you agree with that, Delia?"

Uh-oh. Fake shyness, Delia. Fake distress. I *was* in distress, dammit. I didn't need to fake.

"I…uh…it's hard to say."

"Why? Are you uncomfortable talking about it? It's important to talk about it, you know, or things won't improve. Open communication here is very important. Crucial, actually."

"Yes, I know that."

"Well, how do feel about Ellen thinking you don't help out enough with the kids or the house?"

Relieved to escape being caught not listening, I didn't want to incriminate myself with my feelings. I wished I knew where I'd met Lynn so I could better guess what she needed to hear to make her side with me, not Ellen. I wanted to help our relationship, but I believed firmly at the time that Ellen was the one who needed to adjust her attitude, not me, so I was determined to win Lynn's bias.

"You seem really young to be a mother, Delia. How old are you?"

"My kids already have two mothers," Ellen said. "They don't need a third. That's not what this is about."

Lynn acknowledged Ellen's comment with a nod and half a smile and turned back to me.

"How old are you?"

"Twenty-two."

"Wow. That's really quite young to be taking on motherhood." She spoke quickly, slipping over the would-be pauses. I couldn't get a word in. "There's a big age difference in life phases between 22 and 30. You just graduated from UCLA, right, Delia?"

"Yeah, but…"

"What did you study?"

"Theater."

"Oh. That must have been fun for you. So there's another big difference in your relationship. Ellen has an extremely stressful job in a male-dominated field, and you have a job as a, uh, what do you do in the theater?"

"I'm a massage therapist."

"Oh. I see. What about your theater degree?"

"Well, I still do theater. A friend of mine and I are codirectors of a women's improvisational theater group here in Santa Monica."

"So theater is a means of recreation for you, or does that bring in any money? I don't believe I've ever seen your group perform."

"Well, no, we don't do shows yet. But we're going to. But we won't really make much money."

"So Ellen is providing for you, right? Or do you make enough money doing massage?"

I wasn't stupid; I saw where this was going.

"I'm looking for a second job."

"I see. But until then?"

Damn. She was good.

"Yes, Ellen pays for most of the rent and groceries and stuff."

"And she pays all the expenses for the children too?"

"I don't expect Delia to pay for the kids," Ellen said. Again Lynn nodded and smiled vaguely with dismissal.

"Massage is a pretty peaceful occupation, yes? Quite different from being a police officer, huh?"

"Yes." I was hunted prey, cowering under a thin bush. Lynn had more arrows than I could escape.

"I'm sure you're much clearer about your boundaries and aware of your stress levels than is Ellen. See, Ellen really must not be able to afford that much introspection with a job like hers that is so focused on other people. It must be hard to leave work and the crisis level on the streets of the city and then transition into home. Is that right, Ellen?"

"Hell, yeah," Ellen said, laughing. "At work I'm surrounded by people screaming, bleeding, hurting each other, and stealing shit. I gotta decide when I need my gun, when I don't. Then I get flack for being a woman and for being a dyke. My partner is homophobic. I think he wants to shoot me. I'm grateful just to get home with my mind and my body intact. But then at home I have to change the kids into their pajamas and brush their teeth and feed them dinner. I gotta wipe the poop off my daughter's butt because she can't do it herself, but it tickles her and she wiggles around and runs away and touches her little ass and gets shit on the furniture and then I gotta clean that too. I gotta wash the dishes; I gotta plan the schedule with Lisa, which means I have to fight on the phone for three hours first. The kids mess around in their room because we don't even have real beds for them yet—Lisa kept all their furniture, and I'm too broke to buy new stuff now. By the time the kids are down and everything's done, I just want to sleep. It's impossible to unwind. I don't think I should even have to ask Delia for help."

OK, put that way, I was aware of the fact that my dilemma seemed trivial compared with Ellen's.

"Unwinding is something you must learn to do, for your own happiness and for your kids and your relationship. Of course, you'll need help. And Delia, maybe something good for you to start thinking about is how to take on your fair share of work involving the children. If you really want to be in this relationship, you'll have to learn to do that."

I swallowed hard and looked out the window. It was as if someone picked up the room and tilted it sideways, sliding all the benefit of bias over the sofa to Ellen's side. I could feel validation emanating in waves from her body.

"Don't you agree?"

"Well, I guess, partly, but I…"

"Do you think about what it's like to be in Ellen's shoes?"

"Yes."

"No, you don't," Ellen interjected. "You have no idea what my life is like. No idea. You have no responsibilities. You don't even know what the word means."

"That's not true. I have the dog."

When Ellen and I moved in together, she decided it was best if we had a dog to sort of be on guard when she was on duty. She'd been super excited about picking the puppy but wanted nothing to do with it after she realized it was covered with fleas and wanted attention at night.

"Sasha? It's a dog, for Christ's sake. A dog isn't a responsibility. You just feed it, that's all. That's nothing."

This could have gone two ways. If Lynn was an animal lover, she'd take a pet seriously and give it as much clout in the responsibility department as a kid. If she didn't love animals, I knew I'd come off even more as someone with no clue about life. The fact that I thought the dog was a real responsibility didn't seem to matter. I looked up to see if Lynn was going to intervene, but she looked interested in our fight, as if it might reveal some argument she could use to scrape out a compromise between us.

"You don't like animals, Ellen," I said. "You have to do a lot more than feed them. You don't understand what it's like to feel guilty that I should be walking the dog and playing with her, but I don't do it because our living space is so small and the kids require a lot of work. The dog has to stay outside all the time, alone, and I don't have time to take her for walks because we're always doing stuff for the kids."

"You mean, you're always watching me do stuff for the kids."

"Well, I've got an idea," Lynn said. "This weekend, why don't you take care of the kids, Delia? By yourself. To see what Ellen has to go through. And Ellen, you feed the dog."

I agreed to do it because I was determined to win back Lynn's bias. Obviously I missed the point, but what did I know? We left the office, Ellen feeling hopeful and me feeling full of dread. I wished I could remember where I'd met Lynn before.

I still partly assumed that since she was a professional and was being well paid (by Ellen) to help us be a couple, her idea was geared toward progress and mutual understanding.

On Sunday evening, after we got home from dropping the kids off at Lisa's house, Ellen and I broke up. I didn't care about winning Lynn's bias anymore. Nonetheless, I made the mistake of leaving a frantic message on Lynn's voice-mail, and she called back, demanding we come in for a visit ASAP.

We continued to see Lynn for about three months and continued to suffer through mini-breakup after mini-breakup. I almost forgot I'd known Lynn from somewhere before.

Miraculously Ellen and I started to get our act together, thanks, indirectly, to Lynn. Nothing had changed between Ellen and me but our perspective. We decided I needed a little bit more time to get used to being a mother-type person. Note *mother-type* person, not mother.

"So, what did you do this last week, Delia, to help Ellen with the kids?"

"I planned all the menus and made the grocery list and did most of the cooking."

"That's a start."

"I thought it was a big help, actually," Ellen said, squeezing my hand. I squeezed her hand back.

"Well, yes, I'm sure you did. Partners should help with all the duties in the house and with child rearing. I'm sure it felt natural to have this first little bit of help."

"No, really, it was a big help," Ellen said.

Thanks, sweetie. Chalk up a point for the girlfriend.

"How did you feel, helping like that, Delia? Was it stressful?"

I was supposed to say, "No, I enjoyed it. It felt so natural." But the words wouldn't come out. They weren't mine. They were foreign bodies, and I was gagging on them. Natural, shmatural—I wasn't ready to be a mom, and I knew it and Ellen knew it and Lynn knew it.

"That bad, huh?" Ellen laughed and smacked my back.

"Well, it's actually very important that we discuss how you felt, Delia, in the role of mother," said Lynn. "It will give you insight as to whether you think it's something you want to stick with or not. You need to be very clear about what you want now."

Now? I had to be clear *now*? I was beginning to resent that Lynn thought I could instantaneously deploy myself like Jiffy-Pop Mom. Dyke Jiffy-Pop Mom at that.

"Delia, do you know what you want? Do you know what you're looking for? It's important to know. We all need to know what we are looking for to get what we want."

As she said the words, I saw her again in a different reclining chair, feet up. Beside her was a woman who looked just like her but wore a skirt. She also sat, feet up, in a reclining chair. I heard her say, "No, we don't have meals together. We're looking to maintain a friendly but separate space. If you were to be the tenant in the downstairs studio, we'd ask that you cook your meals only after we're done with the kitchen ourselves. We are not interested in communal living, nor do we have the time to take in another member of our immediate living space. We'd say hello and how are you, but that's about it."

I'd been by their house twice. Once a friend came with me to check the basement studio they were subletting. The second visit was an "interview" to be tenant.

I only looked at the studio on the first visit. On the second visit

I came in and we all just sat in the living room. But I remembered enough what the studio looked like. To get to it you had to walk down a hallway in the house, down a narrow staircase, across a dark and smelly basement, past the washer and dryer, and under some cobwebby wooden beams. A little door creaked open, and there it was—an entire tiny studio, covered with white carpet, including the walls. It was a padded white room. Like in the loony bin. If I'd known then what Lynn's occupation was, I'd never even have thought of renting from them. Who would rent a tiny padded white room from a psychotherapist? Clearly, by the amount of money Lynn and her partner were asking poor Los Angeles students to pay as rent, they thought a tiny padded white room was chic and in high demand. There was a lamp but no ceiling fixture. There was a small excuse for a window that looked out at ground level onto an immaculate Japanese-style garden in the backyard. I couldn't picture anyone ever going out there, but Lynn had said it was off-limits if anyone was home. I could not plant anything. They liked the garden neat and tidy. There was a tiny rest room, toilet and sink only, outside the studio and across the dank basement floor. If I wanted to shower, I had to wait until their bathroom upstairs was free.

At that point in my life I was coming out of the closet. I was naïve, looking for older, experienced lesbians to guide me in the right direction of lesbianism. A lesbian tour guide, if you will. I'd asked about dining together because I wanted to establish a sort of lesbian household. I could have looked at a room in a communal house instead of a private studio in-law unit. I'd have found plenty of young dyke communes looking for fresh rookies, but no, I thought I was bypassing all frivolity and nonsense by seeking out wiser, more experienced lesbian role models.

I remembered sitting in their living room, watching their eight-year-old daughter take off her roller skates. I wondered which woman birthed her. I couldn't imagine either of them doing it. But I'd told them how cool it was they were a lesbian family and told them I'd just come out of the closet myself. I pathetically told them I was trying to learn more about the lesbian lifestyle and needed, in nonspecific terms, emotional support. Recalling my grand debut, embarrassment now flooded my cheeks pink. Lynn and her partner had made it clear they had no interest in a lesbian ingenue. They only wanted their studio filled so they could keep up with their mortgage payments. But they told me that they decided they had chosen me to be the tenant.

In retrospect, I realized that anyone in her right mind would have turned away someone pathetically asking for emotional support and guidance in addition to an extra room. The fact that they chose me, despite my life history and despite their desire for a civil-but-separate space, seemed proof now that I was probably the *only* person who had wanted to live with *them*.

After hearing their stubborn indifference to me, though, I wavered and told them I'd call back in a few days with my final decision.

"Make sure you do call us back," Lynn had said. "By Monday. Otherwise we'll have to give it to someone else."

I never called, feeling slightly irresponsible but reassured that I'd never see either one of them again. And here I was with Lynn, who was possibly retaining all this information, sitting across from me, holding the reins to my relationship. Maybe she wanted to teach me a lesson or two about responsibility. Maybe that's what this was all about. Or maybe she identified more with Ellen. I looked at Lynn and saw her in a new light. She was the butch in her relationship, if you could call her that. Really, she wore pants and her partner wore skirts. In her private life she was uncompromising and unsympathetic. That explained her tactics in the office.

Oddly enough, it was during my long remembrance of past

events that Ellen was able to say what she really wanted to without me interrupting to defend myself. Then she listened to my view of the relationship, and we discussed it almost as if Lynn wasn't in the room. She interrupted a few times, but we wouldn't let her dominate the conversation. I listened to Ellen with all my heart, truly wanting our relationship to work, partly to spite Lynn but mostly because Ellen was still here with me, tolerating Lynn's attitude because she loved me and wanted to be with me. I loved her. It was as if a cloud had lifted away. I stopped caring about what Lynn was saying. We spent the rest of the session defending each other, not ourselves, against Lynn—Lynn, the evil lesbian therapist.

When we left the office I told Ellen the story of how I'd met Lynn before but just hadn't remembered how until today, and we agreed suddenly that she was the worst therapist ever and a yucky person too.

"I wish we'd realized this before now," Ellen said. "It would have saved me a lot of money."

Thank Goddess for awful therapists. That was the first time I really felt Ellen was on my team and I was on hers.

Lynn called us numerous times, reminding us to reschedule. She even threatened that we might break up if we didn't come see her. We never did.

Four months later, Ellen and I were at the gym working out. I was sitting on a recumbent bicycle, pedaling lazily to warm up. I was listening to headphones. Someone tapped my shoulder. I looked up. There was Lynn, dressed in sweats with a towel around her neck and a red braided headband gathering sweat over her brow. I slid my headphones back to uncover my ears.

"Hello there, Delia," she said, beaming from ear to ear as if she'd proven something. "Are you getting Ellen's money's worth at the gym?"

I could not believe my ears. I looked around to see if anyone had heard. Who did she think she was? I decided she hadn't gotten over the loss of our business yet.

"Well," I said, smiling pure saccharine up at her and batting my eyelashes. "I'm getting her money's worth, but I guess you're not, Lynn, since we decided your therapy techniques really suck the big one. But I do hope at least that someone's renting that padded white hole of a studio you keep stashed under your house so you can make the payments on your mortgage. I wouldn't want the stress to put you and your partner into therapy. Lots of therapists are only in it for the money, you know. You have to be careful. Bye-bye now." I put my headphones back on and looked straight ahead.

Therapeutic Insurrection
Ivy Burrowes

Like most of the therapeutically unindoctrinated, I didn't know where to begin when I first decided to seek counseling. I had a specific problem for which I wanted a specific resolution. The problem was that the woman of my dreams was slipping away…yet again. In my youth I suffered a malady common to many lesbians that made me incredibly susceptible to a high fluctuation rate on the "woman of my dreams" continuum. The parameters of *dream woman* seemed to change every time a new dyke walked into my life, which made me a less-than-favorable candidate for long-term relationships, but this one was a keeper. I was nearing 40, and the fear of monogamy was replaced increasingly by terrifying thoughts of actually having to buy a U-Haul, and worse still, of being consigned to live in it. Alone. The prospect of how to arrange the furniture therein encouraged me to seek professional help.

Therapy. An interesting word. "The treatment of disease or of any physical or mental disorder by medical or physical means, usually excluding surgery." I liked that last part. I wasn't at all engaged by the notion of "going under the knife," though through the last breakup I'd felt like an appendage was being removed. And I, sadly, was the appendage.

I didn't know where to begin to look. I had left my home near San Francisco, left my job, and left my friends to try to make a go of it with this woman, and I didn't know anyone or anything but her. I decided against classified advertising or the Yellow Pages. I was a woman of the '90s, so I took a decisive '90s approach to the matter: I hopped onto the Internet. Little could I have guessed that there were so many different therapeutic avenues to choose from. Physical therapy. Occupational therapy. Hydrotherapy. (Take a hot bath and call me in the morning.) Chelation therapy—which involved the removal of heavy metals from the body. That sounded intriguing but I'd stopped listening to heavy metal back in the '80s. Of course, the heading of psychotherapy left me still in a quandary. Did I want social constructionist therapy, systemic therapy, narrative therapy? Gestalt, interpersonal, Freudian, Jungian, behavior modification? Couples? Duh. If I were a part of a couple, I wouldn't be looking for a therapist to begin with. The only thing I was certain of was that I wanted a therapist who, though not necessarily a lesbian, was amenable to and accepting of the existence and needs of lesbians. In other words, I wanted a lesbian therapist. I knew I was confused but I wasn't confused about *that*, and I definitely wasn't going to pay someone to tell me I was crazy!!!

I finally settled on group therapy. For one thing, I figured it was probably cheaper. Like renting a condo in Vail with a bunch of other people. And anything that brought forth images of a room filled with dykes and a couch sounded like something I could make the best of, no matter how bad it was!

And so I was delivered unto the Pink Practice—lesbian owned and operated. I figured that by having great health insurance I could, if nothing else, justify my participation by supporting the community. And I came out to them right away. (No, not about that.) I'd been out as a lesbian since way before it was in vogue or a political necessity, but about this I had to blast through a solid wall of closet. I was very up-front about the fact that I'd used drugs and alcohol for years on a regular basis. That in itself was very self-affirming. They kindly suggested that my honesty indicated that drug and alcohol use, as opposed to abuse, didn't seem to be my problem. They did however solicit a solemn vow that I wouldn't come to group fucked up, and I had to promise to stay with the group for six months. All members also had to agree not to date or see one another on a social basis. I agreed. The cost of each session was $85, all but $25 of which was covered by my insurance. The group was scheduled to meet on Monday nights from 6:30 to 8.

The first week I was anxious; thereafter I simply acclimated to hating Monday nights. There were eight of us in the group and two therapists. Actually some of the members of the group were also therapists, but the two Pink Practice therapists who administered the group cast themselves in "good therapist, bad therapist" roles that befitted Hollywood. The "good" therapist was young and attractive. Naturally I liked her the best. The other was a dyke who just sat there and looked around the room whenever an untoward silence ensued, her steely eyes gravitating from one of us to the next, indicating by posture and a practiced expression reminiscent of Nurse Ratched in *One Flew Over the Cuckoo's Nest* that we weren't doing our fucking jobs.

It wasn't so much what they said that started the ball rolling down a slope slick to the ridiculous, but what they didn't say. They never suggested anything vaguely resembling a "get-acquainted" session; introductions were limited to first names. They then expected us to open our respective veins and bleed all over one another, people who were virtual strangers, before we even knew what commonalities we shared.

In true lesbian fashion we resolved that problem ourselves. It wasn't long before a bunch of us began meeting in the parking lot after our Monday night sessions, where we would laugh and reassure ourselves that we weren't quite as crazy as we should've been. It was in the parking lot, far from the simpering, snide scrutiny of the rat patrol, that we became friends.

Granted, our problems weren't exceptional or unique…nothing that might require immediate or eventual hospitalization. Mostly lonely hearts and broken hearts. One gal was kind of crazy in general—or at least in a way that was very nonspecific. (Her name was Kitty, and she was the only straight member of the group—I think her therapist was trying to send her a message by delivering her unto us to begin with.) The therapists I think were there because they had a tendency to overanalyze everything…an occupational hazard. One woman was obsessive-compulsive about just about everything when she didn't take her medication. (Taking her meds seemed to be the only thing she wasn't obsessive-compulsive about.) But I liked her. One woman named Jasmine, who accentuated her wardrobe with cat hair and was cute enough to make that a viable fashion statement, was having trouble getting over her last lover. (Like all lesbians don't have *that* problem.) One woman had trouble coming out. (We told her to try the classifieds, and she did and never came back.)

Two months into six, a few of us happened to run into one another at a Club Skirt dyke function, or dysfunction. When that came out in group it created quite a stir. The group didn't mind so much—dyke drama had become a way of life for most of us—but the therapists were livid. In a way I felt sorry for them. There wasn't a thing in their alternating repertoire of *just let yourself go with that* versus *hands-on-top-of-the-car* approach to psychotherapy that could rake in 85 bucks an hour times eight. Strengthened by the friendship and camaraderie of the parking lot, we were out of control!

Inevitably one of us fell in lust with another. Occasionally inherent in the therapeutic situation is the danger of a patient/therapist liaison, but in this case the Dyke Ratched was untouchable, and her cohort took to painting her long fingernails bright red and digging them into whatever was handy whenever the good-therapist/bad-therapist scenario went awry—which was often, so projecting our emerging good feelings about ourselves (guffaw) on one or both of them was not even an option. And the therapists, with whom we all became so amused and amazed, further were in such a stew most of the time that the relationship that developed between Kitty and Jasmine was totally lost on them.

Certainly the rest of us knew, although the subject never came up, even in the parking lot. But when Kitty showed up wearing the residue of Jasmine's cat, sporting a box of Kleenex, and sniffling from allergies, we were immediately hip.

Jasmine dropped out of the group soon after; judging from Kitty's watery eyes and perpetually felined attire, we ascertained that, sans insurance, she'd opted for another kind of healing. Then one day Kitty came to group without her Kleenex or lint brush, and we all knew what had happened. Dyke Ratched honed in on the weak link in what had become a very formidable chain right away, and the other chewed her lipstick in anticipation. Of course Kitty broke immediately. She explained how she'd gone to a Chinese herbalist in the hope of getting something that might alleviate her allergy to a certain person's cat. She related the Chinese doctor's verbiage in the vernacular, which was quite amusing, mimicking perfectly his query, "Have you been…living…with cat?"

She admitted that she had. Then waited in vain to learn what remedy the oriental healing arts might provide.

We were all appropriately serious and supportive until she related his last statement to her, which was, "You must stay away from pussy."

I couldn't help it. I cracked up. And then everyone else laughed, even Kitty, who was salvaged from a full-blown crying jag and began chortling with the rest of us.

Someone whispered, "Here, Kitty, Kitty, Kitty," and that was that. The end of the group. We determined that night during our last session in the parking lot that our investment in psychotherapy had been wasted and that laughter is indeed the best medicine. Now we get together once a week for Indian food, which is considerably cheaper and infinitely more satisfying. And the bill is the same, whether one has insurance or not.

So Kitty came out, the patient therapists decided to merge their practices as well as their lives, and I was left to deal with my own problems, which seemed much more manageable with a small circle of friends to encourage me somehow. I bought a brand-new Harley—which made me feel better about my life than I have in years. And it really is the babe magnet I needed to simply reassure myself that my life could go on without my lover. Of course, as soon as I figured that out, so did she—she came to her senses immediately. Any more questions?

Neurotic in Relationships
Sara Cytron with Harriet Malinowitz

I go to therapy for a lot of reasons. One reason I go is that I'm extremely neurotic in relationships. I suffocate people. I mother them to death.

My lover, Harriet, and I have all these straight friends, and they're always complaining about the men they're involved with. They're cold, they're rejecting, they're uncommunicative. Harriet says to me, "Why can't you be like that?"

And I'm always afraid that she's going to leave me. Like the other day, Harriet goes to the refrigerator and says, "Shit! You forgot to get milk again?!"

I said, "Look, let's not make this messy. I'll move out."

Gwen explains why Lesbians have difficulty talking with straight women about female genitals in their self-help body image group.

It may be "down there" for them but it's "up here" for us.

GERMAIN ©88

Diane F. Germain

The Trouble With Women
G.L. Morrison

The trouble with women is I love them. The trouble with women is they drive me crazy. Literally. It was Fiona who first told me I needed a shrink. She ended every fight with that same catchall phrase: "You need professional help."

I finally realized she must be right. Why else would I keep ending up with two-faced, two-timing, two-dimensional women like Fiona?

To be fair, she had her good side. And she knew it. She flashed her "good side" at every passing man or woman. Like some Greek tragedy, she was in love with her own reflection. (We all were.) I'd catch her admiring herself in every reflective surface: store windows, the toaster, parking lots filled with side mirrors and shiny cars. It was impossible to drag her away from the three-way department store mirrors: Fiona in triplicate. Perfect. Perfect. Perfect.

She kept her good side turned toward the camera. In all the photographs of our years together she is flawless. It's only my mental image of her that's cracked.

But my therapist says that Fiona is only a symptom, not the cause of my problem.

Neither is Bette…who convinced me to move with her to Seattle without mentioning that her three ex-husbands lived there—without, in fact, mentioning that she had three ex-husbands or that she expected to spend "family" holidays with the three of them, individually or collectively. I hope the four of them are happy.

My therapist calls that defensive sarcasm. She says I use it to keep people at a distance. She says I'm afraid to let people get close enough to love me. It seems to me I've been pretty damn close to a lot of women! And I'm not sure how sarcasm helped manifest Bette's ex-husbands or Lori's compulsive gambling or Marlo's bail-jumping.

Marlo explained later that before she became a separatist she was into El Salvador. She explained that after I discovered that bounty hunters exist outside of Clint Eastwood movies.

My own politics tended to consist of feeling guilty whenever third-world children starve on television and sometimes giving money to vague environmental causes if the ringing of my doorbell coincides with my checkbook not being overdrawn.

So it was hard for me to understand how one might see gunrunning as the logical, moral course of action that Marlo explained it was. The FBI was even less understanding.

I learned a lot about the legal system. Did you know if the police (or some other officially uniformed men) knock down your door or shoot out your windows, they have no obligation to pay for them? My neighbors were also dismayed to discover this since, after months of surveillance, the SWAT team went to the wrong house and knocked down their door first.

My landlord's homeowner insurance wouldn't pay for it either. No matter how we tried to explain it as an act of God. So I got evicted. (I don't think my neighbors were sorry.)

Marlo still writes to me. (Actually her name turned out to be Clarice.) But 30 years is a long time to keep a pen-pal affair aflame. And her love letters are disturbingly political. I notice fewer men in black following me since I stopped answering her letters. I figure that ending that relationship saves taxpayers' money.

I tend to think the federal prison system is more likely to blame for putting distance between me and Marlo...uh, Clarice...than my defensive sarcasm. My therapist says I'm missing the point.

I suspect my therapist thinks my mother is somehow to blame. Or my low self-esteem. Or my mother's low self-esteem. Or some other therapist-y thing. She's probably right. She's usually right. The trouble with women is...me. I'm the common denominator. So what's the trouble with me?

I haven't talked about Jenny in therapy yet. Jenny. Just the word thrills me. I'm in love with Jenny. She's not like any of the women I'm usually attracted to. Flashy, self-absorbed, obsessive, psychotic or criminal, or polygamous women.

Jenny is sane, kind, and gorgeous. Who wouldn't love that? She has a good stable job. She's a great listener. I'm not sure any of my exes ever listened to me before. But could you blame them? Their lives are so much more colorful than mine. My most interesting stories are about the colorful lives of my exes. But Jenny listens. Really listens. She hangs on every word I say. No matter how dull.

I want to tell my therapist I'm in love again. But I'm afraid. Just saying the words out loud is like opening a cocoon too soon. What will I find inside? Will it be ready to fly? Maybe today. Yes, today. Today I'll tell her about what I see starting to happen between Jenny and me—what I want so much to happen.

"Dr. Robinson," I begin.

She smiles. "Please, call me Jenny."

Jenny. Just the word thrills me.

Robin K. Cohen

Straight Out
Pamela M. Smith

"Jesus Christ!" Mary swore as a movement on her right interrupted her thoughts and forced her to slam on her brakes to avoid
a collision. She fought to correct the fishtail as her car protested the
sudden reining in of all its horses. She lay on the horn, blaring at
the automotive derelict that had swerved into her path, narrowly
missing her front bumper.

She'd been ramming her sleek, ebon Corvette through the traffic with her customary reckless speed. It was a Thursday and the
end of yet another 12-hour day at her real estate office. Her mind
on the few hours of paperwork she still faced at home, she barely
noticed the warm air and brilliant sky of the July evening.

She'd pressed harder on the gas pedal and felt the 16 cylinders
hitting their mark. The engine's vibration pulsated through the
black leather upholstery and up into her body. It was a sensual
reminder that she'd been celibate for quite some time. There wasn't
any man she'd met that even remotely interested her, and besides,
her work kept her far too busy even to consider a relationship.

Her thoughts had shifted to the meeting she'd called for Monday
morning. Sales were down, she fumed, and she didn't want her
rivals making headway because of a problem in her office. As an
established leader in real estate sales, she kept her finger on the
market pulse. She grinned mentally as she thought of the finger she
held up to the rest of the pack. Yes, it was time to give her sales

team a little goose to get things back on track.

Her deliberation had been abruptly interrupted with the appearance of a multicolored Pinto ahead of her. Her 140 km speed was reduced to half that in a few hundred meters. Her heartbeat had accelerated to a triple rate in reaction to the sudden infusion of adrenalin. She couldn't believe the audacity of the driver.

In the rearview mirror of the heap ahead of her she could make out the shape of headphones on the unkempt long hair of the male driver. The car's motley color proclaimed that it had been assembled from an assortment of other Pintos. Undoubtedly a result of all the other concerts the driver had attended while operating his moving vehicle, Mary thought sourly. A passenger sat in the front seat, idly looking out the side window, oblivious to the near-accident. She also had headphones on, bopping to a different drummer than the driver. Mary saw her turn her head and casually look over her left shoulder, seemingly to read a sign on the other side of the highway. She started upright in her seat when she saw Mary's Corvette sitting almost on their trunk. Mary caught the widening of her eyes and her pert little mouth forming a surprisingly perfect circle.

She tapped the man on his arm in an attempt to gain his attention. He briefly glanced in his passenger's direction and irritably shook her hand off his shoulder, returning his attention to his music and the road ahead. She apologetically reached for his arm again, quickly tapped his arm, and hastily removed her hand.

He turned to her, ripping the headphones off his head, and appeared to demand what she wanted. She bowed her head meekly and spoke to him while she gestured toward Mary. Mary saw him glance in his rearview mirror and his eyes widening in surprise. He shrugged his shoulders and laughed toward his passenger.

Mary could tell from his body language what was in his misogynist mind. *She* was behind *him*, right where she belonged. He would show her that even though she had that big, flashy sports car, *he* was calling the shots. In a flash, Mary's vision narrowed to the car in front of her, and the rest of the landscape and other surrounding traffic disappeared. All memories of past injustices carried out against her by men welled up inside her, and she was consumed in a white-hot flame of rage. Slowly, purposefully, she depressed the accelerator and edged closer to the car in front.

The passenger ahead gaped back at her through the rear window, disbelief turning her face into a frozen mask of fear. Mary edged over to the left shoulder of her lane to get a clear picture of the pustule's face in the side mirror mounted on the rust bucket. It registered in her subconscious that he had a lovely shade of blue-gray eyes. Perspiration formed between his dark, wiry eyebrows and along his upper lip. She saw his face pop into an expression of disbelief. How could this be? This woman was actually retaliating and performing an act of aggression. This was not within the limited realm of his experience.

His passenger looked close to hysteria as Mary's bumper edged impossibly closer. Her fervent gesticulation distracted Mary, who turned her attention in the passenger's direction. She could decipher a few sentences by lip-reading.

"What the fuck do you think you're doing?" and "You're going to teach *her* a lesson?" The distraught woman flapped her hands around like the fins of an airborne salmon. The man reconsidered his attempt to teach this bitch who was boss as, this time, he checked over his right shoulder and hastily retreated to the slow lane. Mary tromped on the gas pedal and roared past the clunker as the man made a last ineffectual finger-flying gesture at her rapidly accelerating vehicle. Somewhere in her mind the rational Mary had been standing to one side with hands over eyes, questioning the intelligence of the road-raged Mary. Rational Mary had been speaking in muted tones since it took all of the road-raged Mary's concentration to terrorize the asshole in front of her.

As the offensive piece of junk cleared her path and she acceler-ated past, Mary's rational side unshielded her eyes and began ques-tioning her lack of judgment in handling the situation. As an aside, the rational Mary also pointed out that she heard somewhere that road rage was a symptom of sexual frustration. As quickly as she congratulated herself on the victory of the "war of the road" she gave herself a mental slap up the side of the head. What if the whole thing had turned out differently? Anything could have hap-pened. A third car could have attempted to gain control of the fast lane or the original offending car could just as easily have slammed on his brakes and forced her to take evasive action.

All this because she hadn't been dealing with her ever-increasing feeling of powerlessness over her world. Perhaps her assistant had been correct when she timidly suggested that Mary explore other avenues to deal with her anger issues. At the time, Mary had no idea what her peace-loving, granola assistant was talking about, but the road confrontation had helped jolt her into understanding.

*   *   *

Judith sat behind her desk, chin in hand and elbow resting on the desktop. She glanced wearily around her office. On the three walls facing her were floor-to-ceiling bookshelves jammed with books and various periodicals. Her desktop was buried beneath various reference books and papers. She hadn't been crazy about the idea of working another 12-hour day, but when Mary Anderson had tele-phoned to make an appointment late yesterday afternoon, explain-ing the urgency of her situation, Judith hadn't hesitated to book the appointment. With effort, she pushed herself to a standing position and looked longingly out the window. Beyond the once-white sheer curtains and grimy window shade that was torn along the seam was another fine afternoon that she would not be out to enjoy. She saw the sleek, raven sports car parked outside her office entrance. She thought it might be the newest model of Corvette but wasn't sure. She secretly hoped it wasn't her newest client's vehicle because choice of ride was usually a good indicator of the personality of the driver.

Judith didn't know if she had the energy this late in the day to deal with a type A personality. She turned away from the window and started to gather some papers into a file that was open on her desk before she saw the driver exit the car. After several moments she proceeded to take the file out to the long departed clerk's desk.

*   *   *

Mary checked the list of several names on the door to ensure that Judith Crenshaw was among them. When she confirmed it was, Mary grasped the doorknob with her usual determination. She walked into the room with the self-assured manner of someone used to getting her own way. She quickly surveyed the vacant reception area and with self-satisfaction noted she had correctly envisioned the decor. Striding across a tan Berber carpet that wasn't up to hiding a few coffee spills, she selected a magazine from several dated issues atop a large rectangular table. Mary sat in one of several off-white, overstuffed chintz armchairs that looked as if they had been purchased at a rummage sale at the end of the day. Scattered between the chairs were the prerequisite overgrown, somewhat dusty ferns, bulging from their pots. Flipping disinterestedly through the pages of her magazine, her attention drifted to the pictures hung on the walls. They were pastel depictions of women walking together along beaches, through forests and other cozy nature scenes. The pictures aggravated Mary's ill humor. They seemed to suggest that all women were interested in were ethereal activities. Airily, fairily meandering through life, heads conspiratorially close, strategizing about the best way to handle men, offspring, cooking, and all the other mundane things to which men decided women should devote their time.

The flaring of her temper reminded Mary why she was here. She simply could not live with her anger anymore. It was getting in the way of her ability to make sound decisions and was interfering with her efficiency. The incident of yesterday evening was the proverbial straw that broke her composure's back.

The opening of the door leading to the inner offices interrupted Mary's recollections. A tall, rather rumpled woman of indeterminate age entered the reception area.

"Oh!" the woman exclaimed, as she dropped a file on the receptionist desk, "I'm sorry, I didn't expect anyone to be out here." She tucked a strand of graying hair behind her ear in an attempt to appear less scattered than her plants. "Have you been waiting long?" she asked congenially.

"Not at all, I've only just arrived," Mary answered, taking in the woman's appearance. She was wearing an olive floor-length pleated skirt with a cream peasant blouse tucked into the elastic waistband. On her bare feet she wore black Birkenstocks. *Great!* Mary thought, *a natural woman*. She fully expected the long skirt to be concealing an abundance of leg hair. How could this person with the fashion sense of Charlie Brown's Pigpen possibly relate to any of her problems? She began, once again, to doubt her judgment in even entertaining the thought of seeking therapy. Just the sight of this woman set her teeth on edge and her little angry horde screaming for armaments.

"I'm Judith Crenshaw," the therapist said, moving forward with her hand outstretched. "Come on in." She motioned with her other hand for Mary to follow her into the inner office.

"Mary Anderson," she replied, taking the proffered hand in hers, perfunctorily shaking it. "Thank you for seeing me on such short notice." She followed Judith out of the waiting room.

They entered a dimly lighted hallway that had three opaque glass doors along the wall, presumably occupied by the other people listed on the main office door. They turned left to enter the last office at the end of the hall. The inner sanctum resembled the room they had just left. Strategically placed greenery similarly relieved the room's harsh fluorescent lighting.

Following Mary's glance to the disheveled desktop, Judith explained, "I'm doing research for a paper I'm working on. I'm developing a method of dealing with anger through an acute respiratory regulation technique. Some of my patients have been having great success with this method."

Mary found it hard to believe that this woman was seriously making any headway with a deep-breathing procedure, but at this point, she cautioned herself, she had to be open to any theory, no matter how half-baked it seemed. She couldn't risk another highway scenario, because it might not end as harmlessly as her recent experience.

Judith went past an antiquated oval table on the right side of the room and sat in an emerald green canvas chair. Atop the table was a floral tissue box standing sentry in anticipation of burst dams of emotion. Indicating a love seat at the opposite end of the table, Judith said, "Please, sit and we'll get started." Mary sat where she was directed, placing her briefcase beside her.

"Now," continued Judith, "you indicated on the phone that there was some urgency regarding your situation. First, I should ask how you got my name, and then we can go into detail as to what brought you here. From that, we can get a better idea of how we should proceed."

Mary was aware that Judith was scrutinizing her, much like a specimen under a magnifying glass. Mary was becoming uncomfortable with this whole thing. She was unused to being the object of scrutiny and was fairly certain that she hated it. This was different from being dissected for professionalism in business dealings. This was all about the intangibles of her personality. The first flutterings of uncertainty began to undermine her usual confident demeanor.

"Well, as I mentioned over the telephone," Mary began hesitantly, "I seem to be experiencing a certain lack of, well, control over my anger." *Shit, I have now actually started to stutter,* she thought. She was certain she hated this. "Harmony, my assistant, reads a magazine called *Serenity*. She came across your advertisement for anger management therapy and thought it might be something I could benefit from. She's worked for me for a number of years and says she has noticed increasing antagonistic behavior on my part when I'm dealing with certain situations. She suggested I make the appointment."

"Do you feel that you are losing control of your temper?" Judith questioned.

Why the fuck do you think I'm here, pencilhead? flashed through Mary's mind. Aloud, she explained that she was usually a rational individual but recently she was feeling overwhelmed by her workload and the stress of being a woman in the forefront of a predominantly male-regulated industry. She had begun to question how she handled situations that were beyond her power to control.

"OK," Judith responded after Mary had finished. "What I would like to establish is the event that precipitated you coming here. Could you tell me if there was anything specific that occurred?"

Squirming inwardly, Mary was reluctant to divulge the details of the traffic incident, but Harmony had been quite firm in emphasizing the importance of honesty on Mary's part. Frankly, if Mary hadn't found Harmony attractive, she might never have considered the idea of coming here at all. Now *there* was a confusing thought, but she mentally shrugged it off. Disassociating herself from any uncomfortable feelings, Mary dispassionately recounted her bumper tag story. She avoided looking at Judith, certain that the woman would be questioning her sanity. She finished the tale and looked across the table at Judith, fully expecting to see her wearing a look of disbelief. To her surprise she met a glazed expression.

*   *   *

Judith had been listening but found her attention starting to drift when Mary, caught up in the reenactment of the road experience, began to get agitated. Judith suddenly realized how little energy she herself had. She hadn't stopped for lunch—her appointments, crowded one after the other, hadn't left her any time to grab anything. Her lowering blood sugar was making her sleepy.

When she had entered the outer office, she found her presumption of the personality type of the sports car driver was accurate. The woman standing in the middle of the reception area appeared to be in her early 30s. She was attractive and slim-figured. Her stylish auburn hair was cropped short and coordinated well with the purple—excuse me, eggplant—Chanel power suit. Judith noted the gold Rolex on Mary's wrist and the black leather briefcase she held in that hand. The satchel probably cost more than what Judith paid for a month's lease. Mary's appearance brought back Judith's own mad dash to get to work this morning:

The flashing red numbers of the electric alarm clock on the night table beside Judith's bed had alerted her to the fact that there must have been a power outage overnight. She looked toward the window of the bedroom and thought the sky through the blinds seemed brighter than usual. *Shit!* She flung back the covers, jumped to the window, and pulled on the cord to open the blinds. They chose that moment to protest their constant up-and-down motion, let go of their brackets, and crash down on Judith's unsuspecting head. She was left standing in the window, stark naked, hand still held out with the cord from the blinds dangling from her fist.

She hurried toward the bathroom, where she always left her watch on the counter by the sink. Sure enough, the hands showed 8 o'clock, the time when she usually left the house.

Judith grabbed a spray bottle of mouthwash with one hand while she reached for her glasses on the counter with her other. She sprayed a generous stream of the liquid into her open mouth.

"Aagh!" She sputtered and jammed on her glasses. She looked at the canister in her hand and discovered she'd just ingested a fair amount of FDS feminine hygiene spray. *"Aagh!"* she exclaimed again and stuck her face under the running faucet, trying to rinse as much residue out of her mouth as she could.

Swishing water around in her mouth, Judith grabbed the hairbrush and tried to get her fine, graying, mousy-brown hair into some semblance of order. At the best of times her hair took about a half-hour of blow-drying before it all decided to behave and lie down in the same general direction. Unfortunately, this morning she didn't have that kind of time. She gave her hair a couple of swipes, patted it in place with wet fingers, then hairsprayed it down in a nice glue-type fashion.

Judith grabbed her contact lenses case and removed the first lens. She sprayed it with saline solution and placed it in her left eye. It stung a bit, as it always did, and she repeated the process with her right contact lens. The burning continued in her left eye and really started to sting in her right eye. Tears streamed down her cheeks as she lifted the bottle of what she thought was saline solution. Barely able to see, she could just make out the label that stated the solution was, in fact, a cleanser and should not be used directly in the eyes. *Oh, God.* She deftly removed both lenses, grabbed the correct bottle, and quickly dowsed the contacts before reinserting them in her eyes.

She looked in the mirror to check the results of her ministrations. Flat hair with a semigloss finish and majorly bloodshot eyes met her gaze. Well, that was all the beautification she could handle this morning.

Judith hurried to her closet and selected a suitable ensemble. Throwing on undergarments and silk hose, she pulled on her chosen outfit—a long, olive-green, pleated skirt with elasticized waistband, matching silk blouse and wide black leather belt. A pair of black Easy Spirit pumps completed her wardrobe. She took one last look in the mirror and admitted she'd looked better but would pass muster. She grabbed her keys as she rushed out the back door after setting the house alarm.

She rounded the corner of the house just as a stiff breeze twisted around a cedar shingle that finally gave up its hold on the side of the house. For the second time that morning, her head became the target of a frustrated inanimate object. After connecting with her head, the shingle slid down the front of her blouse, leaving a trail of wood splinters and black tarry residue. "Ouch!" she exclaimed in bewilderment at this second assault. She looked down the front of her blouse and realized she would have to go back and change clothes.

Judith pivoted on her heel, and it dug into the lawn. Her momentum carried her forward, and she lost her balance, pitching forward onto her hands and knees. *I've had just about enough of this,* she thought, and turned to see her heel stuck in the ground with no shoe attached. She hoped this past half hour wasn't indicative of how the rest of her day would continue. She caught movement out of the corner of her eye and turned to see a tabby cat strolling by on its morning mouse hunt. The cat looked away in disgust at her inability to land gracefully on all fours.

Judith pulled herself up and reentered the house, turned off the alarm, and headed for her closet. Naturally, she couldn't find anything similar to the blouse she had on, so she grabbed the nearest thing that would coordinate with her skirt—a flowing, cotton peasant blouse. Oh well, perhaps she could pass with a slightly bohemian look. She removed the black leather belt and shredded nylons, tossed her pumps back into the closet, and grabbed a pair of black Birkenstock sandals to complete the look. A hasty look in the mirror confirmed the oddness of the ensemble, but she'd run out of time and would have to go with it. Once again she set the alarm, departed the house, and managed to make it to her forest-green late-model Toyota Celica without further incident. She climbed in and sped to her office.

*   *   *

Judith became aware of the deafening silence that greeted her on her return to the present. *Oops!* she thought, as she returned behind her eyes to see Mary's puzzled expression at her lack of response to the obviously finished tale. The trick now would be to attempt to gloss over her mental lapse and appear attentive.

"Was this a deviation from your normal behavior in dealing with similar situations?" Judith asked, mustering every active listening technique she could recall. Leaning forward, ensuring her arms were uncrossed and feet on the floor, she looked directly into Mary's eyes.

"Well, I've experienced road rage before, but I've never acted on it. I mean, to think about ramming into the back of a car that cuts you off would be a normal kind of reaction, I guess, but to actually speed up and sit on that asshole's bumper the way I did...." Mary trailed off. She thought that Judith hadn't been paying attention to her and had mentally stepped out for a minute, but she must have been wrong. Never having been to a therapist before, Mary wasn't sure of their *modus operandi*. Maybe they didn't want to appear too observant when you were relating an event in case their intensity might make you uncomfortable. Well, it seemed to have worked for her. She couldn't imagine relating this incident to anyone if they had been staring at her. She began to feel good about Judith's obvious talent and relaxed into the cushions. She felt a weight had been removed and for the first time had a sense of hope that there might be a method to deal with her anger.

Phew! Judith mentally exhaled. That turned out OK. She had been having more and more of these mental lapses during sessions but so far had been able to disguise her inattention. She would have to try and focus. The puzzled look on Mary's face had dissolved when Judith had asked her a question, but what must she be thinking of her? Mary was obviously a success in her field and was probably used to judging character accurately on first impression.

Judith, still uncomfortable with what she surmised to be Mary's negative impression of her, continued. "Oftentimes we don't acknowledge our feelings of anger in situations that we have no control over. We tend to diminish the importance of our anger. We bury our feelings in our subconscious and explain them away as 'no big deal'—unaware that in burying them we really just put them aside to fester, one day to erupt in pustules over our consciousness." *Oh, gross,* Judith thought, *I'm glad I didn't have lunch.*

"Hmm," Mary said, "I see what you mean. I've put aside my hostilities using the excuse that I can handle them. To show others I can do just as well and even better than men. Makes sense. The additional tasks I've taken on recently must be piling on a little more than my subconscious can handle. This leads me to act out my anger inappropriately."

Hmm, probably, thought Judith, *sounds good to me.* "Exactly," she said. "That would seem to be the crux of the matter. Now we have to find a way that you can control your irrational behavior *before* you act on impulse. Initially, I'd like to suggest we try the acute respiratory regulation therapy I spoke of earlier."

"Oh, the deep-breathing exercises," Mary simplified.

"Er, yes, exactly," said Judith, a little unnerved that Mary had realized, hopefully inadvertently, that Judith's term for her therapy was actually coined after an already established technique of deep breathing to access suppressed feelings. "We need to find the source of your anger…past experiences that you may have buried that are in some way contributing to your feelings of rage. I've built a room to facilitate this process, and if you're willing, we can begin our first session."

Mary hesitated briefly but thought she might as well begin now. She needed to discover some way to deal with her anger before Monday morning's meeting. She suspected that some issues could come up that would make her lose her patience. She definitely didn't want her irrational behavior to seep into her workplace. She couldn't afford to have her employees think she had feet of clay with a rubber mind to match.

"OK. Yes. I think you're probably right. No time like the present. I really do need some immediate resolution," Mary said with staccato determination.

"Good. Follow me." Judith rose from her chair. "You might as well leave your briefcase here. The door to my office can't be opened from the outside, so it'll be safe."

Mary complied, leaving her briefcase on the love seat before she followed Judith through another door beside the bookcase on the far wall. She stepped into a room that was obviously constructed by an amateur. There was foam padding stapled to every surface. A waist-high platform took up four-fifths of the room's area. A large foam pad had been placed atop the platform and covered with several different-colored sleeping blankets. On the right side of the platform, near the ledge, was a large boom box. In the remaining floor space a folding chair stood by the portable sound system. None of the corners were quite square, and there was a definite sag in the platform.

It seemed to Mary she was expected to lie on this platform. She looked dubiously at the structure and wondered if it would collapse under her body weight. It didn't look like it could hold a thought, let alone anything of substance.

"Are you sure this is safe?" Mary asked apprehensively.

"Oh, certainly. Quite a few people heavier than you have been through two-hour sessions on this platform. The give in the surface is to ensure your comfort. If there wasn't any give, you'd find it uncomfortably hard even with the padding," assured Judith. "You might want to change into the robe that we provide so that you won't wrinkle your clothes." Judith took what looked like a hospital robe off a hook on the back of the door and handed it to Mary.

"That probably would be a good idea," Mary agreed, taking the garment from Judith somewhat reluctantly. She wondered what other person had worn this and if it had been cleaned after each use.

"Don't worry," Judith assured her, as if reading Mary's mind, "we provide freshly laundered robes for each visit. When you're ready, climb up on the platform and call me. I'll wait for you in the next room."

"Thanks," Mary said as Judith left.

Mary began to get undressed and reached for the hanger. *I can't believe I'm doing this*, she thought. *Stay focused*, she coached herself. *Try to forget that you are the owner of your own real estate office. Don't dwell on the thought that, should there be a fire and you get caught in this getup, your reputation might never recover.* She imagined a photograph showing her standing outside a therapist's office, half naked, with nothing between her and the elements but a threadbare hospital gown. *Thank God the robe doesn't leave your ass hanging out the back. Thank God for small favors.*

Mary hung her clothes on the door and climbed onto the platform. *Now what? I guess you lie down. Which way does your head go?* She lay down with her head at the same level as the boom box. She assumed the therapist would sit in the chair at the head of the platform and probably didn't want to look up her gown the entire session. "OK, I'm ready," she called out, not sure what it was that she was ready for.

"OK then, great," Judith said as she returned to the room. She sat down and selected a cassette from a pile on the floor beside the chair and inserted it into the cassette player. She set some dials and pulled the chair closer to the head of the platform.

"Now," Judith said as she finished preparing the sound system, "let me explain how this works. The shallower you breathe, the less you are in touch with your feelings. When we were in the office I was watching to see how deeply you breathed. I noticed that you don't breathe past your upper chest. After years of suppressing your anger, you're pretty much detached from your feelings. In this session, what we'll focus on is simply breathing right down into your lower stomach. Just imagine you're filling a balloon in your chest cavity and that you're trying to inflate it as much as possible. The music that you will hear is rhythmic drumming to help you match your heartbeat to the sound. Any questions?" she asked the top of Mary's head.

"Seems simple enough. The question I have is, how long will this last?" Mary addressed the ceiling. Once again she questioned her decision to come here.

"That depends on you, really. If you feel discomfort, we can stop at any time, but I would ask that you give it a chance for at least a few minutes before you call it quits. You might experience lightheadedness due to all the oxygen you'll be getting. You probably aren't used to deep breathing like this, so that would be expected."

"All right. Understood. I'll try to keep an open mind and give it a fair chance."

"Ready? Remember, inflate the balloon and relax," Judith said as she turned on the tape.

A deafening, deep, resonant bass of kettledrums filled the room, evoking primitive visualizations. Mary recalled a movie about a scientist performing sensory-deprivation experiments. He entered a flotation tank and remained inside for hours. His body began to metamorphose into that of a caveperson. She swore to God if that were to happen to her, she would hunt Harmony down and add her shrunken head to her collection.

Mary began to fill her lungs deeply with oxygen. She tried to match her breathing to the rhythm of the drums. Concentrating solely on this task, she began to feel dizzy. The extra oxygen was causing the predicted lightheadedness. If she hadn't been lying down already, Mary felt she would have fallen. She cleared her mind of all thoughts and just focused on her breathing. She wasn't aware how long she had been doing this when she felt as if she hit an emotional bubble. That was the only way she could describe the sudden feeling of wanting to sob uncontrollably. The unfamiliar sensation of tears rolling out of the corner of her eyes, down her cheeks, and into her ears was unpleasant.

She sat up abruptly, wiping away the liquid that had puddled in her ears. "Wait a minute," she said, momentarily panicked, "I just have to regroup for a second."

"That's all right," Judith answered, comfortingly, as she snapped off the cassette, "You're experiencing your buried feelings for the first time, and it's bound to be a little unsettling."

No shit, Sherlock, thought Mary. Without a doubt, she concluded, she hated this. Gone were her earlier feelings of optimism. She was about to gather herself up and terminate this "session" when she remembered the meeting Monday morning. Taking a deep breath, she unsteadily lay back down. *In for a penny, in for a pound*, she thought disjointedly.

"Whenever you're ready we can proceed. Take your time, we still have plenty left," Judith said, soothingly.

Mary took several shallow, quick breaths, exhaling sharply after each. "OK," she gestured with a raised hand, "Let the head games begin." Her attempt at humor didn't relieve her anxiety.

Judith, without speaking, leaned forward and pressed the play button on the cassette player.

Once again the sound of primitive drumming enveloped the room. Mary could almost feel the presence of the notes beating around her like wings of many small trapped birds. The brush of sound swept over her, and she was engulfed in its embrace. Breathing deeply into her aching chest, she was drawn further into the abyss of her emotions.

As unexpectedly as before, Mary felt a resistance within her consciousness. This time, however, she continued with her breathing. She felt as if she were physically pushing against a thickening mass of air that resisted her determined attempts to press through this barrier. At her sustained effort the obstruction gave way, shredding diaphanously, surrendering to her will.

Upon entering her psyche, which is what she thought it must be, Mary was surrounded by inky blackness. The absence of light was broken by trajectories of flashing, streaking, multicoloured orbs of light that left comet-like tails in their wake. Focusing with all her mettle, she concentrated on a slow-drifting orb floating lazily within her reach. Gazing into the center, she brought the image closer and held it there. She remembered herself as a small baby crawling across a crimson rug. A sense of wonder caused her to lose her concentration, and in a flash the orb broke free and whisked away, leaving her suspended in the black void.

Another globe, fleeter than the first, tried to elude her, but Mary, exercising her newfound power, gazed intently at her target. This effort created a gossamer thread that encircled the reluctant sphere. Now Mary willed the lassoed orb to yield the memory held within. She remembered tumbling down a snow-packed hill, out of control. She was wearing a blue one-piece ski suit, with metal skittering skis splayed out in opposite directions and aluminum ski poles windmilling in hopes she could right herself.

Ow! The gossamer thread snapped, releasing the orb as Mary's memory recoiled before she could remember the pain, and again she returned to the void. She became aware that the orbs that held the most significant memories were the ones that were the smallest and most elusive. She decided to concentrate her energies on the swiftest orbs, impatient to get to the source of her anger.

Her first few attempts were unsuccessful, but on the fourth try she managed to capture a wriggling, squirming globe. Looking within, she remembered chasing a nervous, giggling girl who had been a ten-year-old classmate. Before Mary captured her, the girl fell to the ground, holding her shirt down in a halfhearted attempt to keep Mary from pulling it up. Mary managed to wrestle the material from her friend's clutching fingers. The baring of her chest revealed the perfect symmetry of poached-egg–like, developing young breasts. The sight stirred an unfamiliar feeling in the pit of Mary's stomach. She became agitated and couldn't deduce why.

Snap! The thread released again as Mary lost her concentration just long enough for the orb to struggle free, careening among other quicksilver orbs. She recovered quickly and noted this last orb traveled with a group of a dozen similarly paced spheres. The cluster remained together in their movements through space. As one turned, the pack followed. This particular orb seemed to be the leader of the contingent, and Mary felt she should follow it. There was something unique and hypnotic about its opalescence. Of all the other globes she had seen in this kaleidoscope of her legacy, this was the most beautiful.

Mary sensed it held her truth. She couldn't convey exactly what she meant with the words, other than it felt like completeness. She willed herself to pursue the orb. She emulated the actions of the others and soon was frolicking amongst them. They didn't flee from her, just accepted that she had become one with them. Gradually she emerged beside the resplendent leader. Slowly, gracefully, timelessly, she looked into the orb and beheld the memory within…

It's the morning of her graduation day from a private, all-girls high school. She is in her dorm room and can see a pair of unmade single beds with matching scarlet bedspreads and fluff-deprived pillows tossed willy-nilly over the sparse frames. The beds squat below a tall, shuttered window that blocks the morning sun. A pair of scarred oak desks face opposite walls, corkboards mounted above each with various school notices tacked to the pockmarked surfaces with steel-tipped pushpins. The hideous concrete block walls are painted a baby-poo green. Posters of Marianne Faithfull, Joan Jett, and other female teen-pop heartthrobs cover them in an attempt to make the room feel less institutionalized.

She sees a young version of herself lying on one bed with another girl, whose face is a blur. Her arm is around the girl's waist. They are facing each other, embracing each other….

The orb started to fade and move away. For a moment Mary fought to regain her composure, then willed herself back to the memory. Again she peered within, remembering the feel of the other girl's mouth on hers. The hot breath, the warm wetness of their tongues seeking each other's. Tasting, suckling, mewling, pushing up against each other. She felt like never stopping, never letting go of this passion.

Mary now understood why this memory was so important for her. So many questions were answered in that instant, as Mary felt an acute sense of completeness. Clutching this recollection to her cognizance, she began to surface and reunite with her consciousness. She sensed herself emerging from the depths of the pool of her memories.

Resurfacing from the unctuous surroundings, her conscious

mind resisted this change in her, wanting things to remain as they had been, wanting her to leave this recollection behind. But Mary had waited too long to reclaim who she was and had no intention of forgetting ever again. Dimly she heard the drums pounding, throbbing, as she returned to her form lying rigidly on the padded platform. She sat up with a gasp and felt the greatest sense of inner peace she could ever recall.

She turned to Judith excitedly, wanting to relate her experience. "Judith," she began, then stopped abruptly.

Judith's day had finally caught up with and overcome her. Her head was tilted back awkwardly, her legs splayed out in front of her, folded hands upon her lap. Her mouth was agape, and the sound of her snores resonated in accompaniment with the percussion.

Mary smiled and nimbly slid off the platform, grabbing a sleeping bag with her as she rose. She draped the sleeping bag over Judith's slumbering form and removed her clothes from the back of the door. She slipped from the room, leaving the drums to harmonize with Judith's sleeping heartbeat. Hurriedly she dressed and crossed the room to retrieve her briefcase. She opened the bag and grabbed her checkbook. She didn't know how much to make out the check for. Any amount would not seem to be enough for this priceless reawakening. She decided on $200 and thought Judith could invoice her if this wasn't enough.

Mary felt incredibly buoyant as she passed through the reception area and closed the door after her. The Monday morning meeting no longer seemed important. She floated down the stairs and into her sports car.

She glanced in the rearview mirror. Perhaps she would let her hair grow out a bit, loosen up her blouse. She giggled, a sound she couldn't remember making for quite some time. Maybe she would buy a pair of jeans and a warm, fuzzy, flannel shirt to match. People were wearing Doc Martens now, weren't they? She smiled. Maybe she would call Harmony and see if she would join her for dinner.

She turned her key in the ignition and signaled her intention to return to the road. As she pulled out, she saw a cherry-red Mustang hurtling toward her. She braked momentarily and let the stampeding steel and chrome pass.

I Tell Her Everything, She Tells Me Nothing
Lorrie Sprecher

My therapist says to me, "When are you going to let down a few of your defenses and let me in?"

And I think, *Fuck you, what's your social security number?*

Contributors' Notes

Alison Bechdel's comic strip, *Dykes to Watch Out For*, has become a cultural institution for lesbians and discerning nonlesbians all over the planet. Nine collections of her cartoons, including the most recent, *Post-Dykes to Watch Out For*, have been published by Firebrand Books. She lives in Vermont.

Shari J. Berman decided in her 40s to be a lesbian fiction writer when she grew up. Her Internet serial, The Selena Stories (www.wowwomen.com/visibilities/fiction_1997/index.html), began as a 1,300-word story. Eighty thousand words later, the grammar-checker still rates the dialogue "grade four" and women read Selena in a dozen non–English-speaking countries. She penned the title piece in the Alyson parody anthology *Wilma Loves Betty*. Other short stories appear in German, Canadian, and British anthologies, and she has written four novels. "The Y Files" character Dr. Jude Felton (prebreakdown) originated in *Skipping Stones*, a her second novel.

Ivy Burrowes was born in Laramie, Wyo., long before the town gained a national and international reputation as a hotbed of homophobia. She graduated from Metropolitan State College in Denver in 1985 with a major in English. Ivy writes, makes candles, talks to strangers, and aspires to change the world. Although she has never actually endured therapy, this story is loosely based on absolute truth. (Thanks for sharing, Pede.) Ivy and her lover, Val, divide their time between their cabin in Conifer, Colo., and their home in Buffalo, Wyo. They have been together 22 years.

Jane Caminos is an illustrator, cartoonist, and painter of women; her work is known internationally. She grew up in Jersey and lived in Boston for many years, where she came out in the mid 1970s, a time of enforced androgyny, stringent feminist politics, and free-wheeling sexual occasions, sometimes celebratory, sometimes surprising, sometimes…oh no, now that was a lapse in judgment. Jane now lives in New York City with her lover of many years, her lab, and her old and creaky cat, and yes, she is very much in therapy.

Diana Eve Caplan completed her MFA in fiction writing at Mills College in Oakland, Calif., where she resides with her partner, two stepchildren, two dogs, and a cat. She vows they'll soon move out of the nasty hovel they live in beside a dangerous freeway off-ramp since it's fit to explode with all the books, toys, and clothes lying about. She is currently working on two novels and a lesbian step-parenting guide. She is the author of lesbian erotica pieces published under different personas, and she was the fiction editor of *580 Split,* Mills's graduate literary magazine.

C.C. Carter is a woman of size who doesn't let that stop her from squashing little attitudes. She is a graduate of Spelman College and has an MA in creative writing from Queens College. She is the winner of the Guild Complex's Fifth Annual Gwendolyn Brooks Poetry Competition. Her work appears in *Best Lesbian Erotica 2000,* and she has been published in many anthologies. C.C. just released a collection of poetry entitled *Body Language,* published by Wildheart Press. To contact her, E-mail LITEXC@aol.com.

Cato (pronounced kat-o, not like the philosopher or the institute) resides in Mt. Pleasant in Washington, D.C. You can find other Cato cartoons in *The Washington Peace Letter,* a free monthly newspaper published by the Washington Peace Center, a local, multi-issue, antiracist, nonprofit education and action organization based in D.C. You can also find Cato cartoons in other publications, many produced by peace and justice organizations and activists in D.C.

Robin K. Cohen draws cartoons and plays killer Scrabble while awaiting the dawn of the messianic age or a rich butch rescue—whichever materializes first. Meanwhile she works as a corprocomputer nerd. A former therapist herself, she believes mint Milanos, over-the-counter Rescue Remedy, and general licentiousness work wonders rarely achieved by weekly counseling sessions. Her piles of unsubmitted cartoons lampoon the conventions that lesbians hold most dear. Few know she authored an advice column under the pseudonym Aunt Sophie and a couple of novels under the pseudonym Jane Austen. She makes her home in Denver, Colo., and welcomes E-mail at robinkayla@juno.com.

Erin Cullerton is a poet, fiction writer, and freelance writer. She lives in San Francisco, where she spends her days peddling around on a bicycle searching for adventure and her evenings writing.

Sara Cytron left the world of lesbian stand-up comedy after 13 years to begin law school in her mid 40s. Now in her second year as an evening student at Brooklyn Law School, she also supervises the employee and labor relations department in a hospital.

Kelli S. Dunham is a two-time Vice Versa award winner for her humor column "Trippin' Out," which appears weekly in Philadelphia's *Au Courant* and has been reprinted nationally. She has been both a born-again Christian and a nun, although the current extent of her religious activity involves trying to seduce Amish women at the local supermarket. Kelli divides her time between working as a nurse, engaging in earnest dyke activism, and teaching her niece and nephew to insert french fries into their nostrils while making walrus sounds. You can send a message to Kelli at dolphodyke@aol.com or read more of her rantings at www.homestead.com/trippinout/bio.html.

Leslie Ewing has self-identified as an underachieving dyke cartoonist since 1981. Her work has appeared in *Gay Comix, Dyke Strippers, Wimmin's Comix,* and *Strip AIDS.* Her work often reflects the community work she has done with the NAMES Project, the 1993 march on Washington, and the AIDS Emergency Fund. She currently is the merchandise manager for Under One Roof, a nonprofit gift store benefitting 50 organizations supporting people with AIDS.

Diane F. Germain is a French-American lesbian-feminist psychiatric social worker who created and conducted a strength group for Women Survivors of Incest and/or Childhood Molest for five years. She was one of the founding mothers of Dykes on Hikes, The Lesbian Referral Service, Beautiful Lesbian Thespians (BLT), and California Women's Art Collective (CWAC); an early principal of the San Diego Lesbian Organization; and a collective member of Califia Community—a feminist education retreat. She was arrested and jailed for protesting the objectification of women in the "Myth CaliPORNia Kontest" in 1986. She creates humor as a hedge against the misogyny of heterosexist phallocentric patriarchy *and* to tickle the lesbians.

Jaime M. Grant is a lesbian writer/activist who can be accused of taking life too seriously at times. She lives in Washington, D.C., with her son, (The Life of) Reilly James Grant, and their village of beloveds.

Roberta Gregory has been creating her unique comics all her life and shows no signs of letting up anytime soon. Her first comic book was *Dynamite Damsels,* from 1976. She has appeared in lots of other comics and has also published three books—*Sheila and the Unicorn* and two volumes of *Winging It.* She is also known for her series, *Artistic Licentiousness,* but is best known for her notorious character Bitchy Bitch and her lesbian "cousin" Bitchy Butch, who appear regularly in her long-running solo comic book, *Naughty Bits* (and five trade paperback collections). Bitchy Bitch is also the star of the animated *Bitchy Bits* cartoons on the Oxygen network. All of the abovementioned books are still available! Check out www.robertagregory.com.

Mary Beth Hatem edits an international health care journal. In her off-hours, she's funny and poetic. She holds an MA in literature, never puts it down, and is regarded as a tennis legend in Harford County, Md. Proudly she hails now from that great lesbian capital, Takoma Park, Md., where she lives with her Brazilian partner of ten glorious years marked by continuous dance lessons and truly huge parties. You may recognize her distinctive voice from the humor anthology *Ex-Lover Weird Shit* (soon to be a documentary film).

Kris Kovick lives on medication.

Myra LaVenue, aka Arrow Matic, is currently in hiding in Portland, Ore. She used to write for a living but then decided that eating was important. So now she designs Web sites as a Human Factors Analyst, or HuFA, not to be confused with HeFA, the Web designer for cows. She plays soccer and has figured out that as goal-keeper, she can legally grab women. Her work can also be torn out of these anthologies: *Early Embraces, Awakening the Virgin,* and *Lip Service,* also by Alyson Publications. Read them at members.aol.com/mlavenue.

Harriet Malinowitz is an associate professor of English at Long Island University, Brooklyn. She is also a writer, scholar, and fea-tured speaker at academic conferences addressing issues of writing, rhetoric, women's studies, and gay and lesbian studies.

Renita Martin, one of Boston's most talented playwrights, blends poetic lyricism with great storytelling (Terry Byrne, *Boston Herald*). Her writings have most recently appeared in *Máka: Diasporic Jukes* and *Best of the Best Lesbian Erotica.* Martin's S*hotgun Wedding* appears in Baker's Plays' anthology of ten-minute plays from the 1998 Boston Theater Marathon. She has traveled nationally, per-forming most recently in Sharon Bridgforth's *Blood Pudding* and Martin's own latest one-woman-show, *Five Bottles in a Six Pack.* Her produced plays (*Peace in the Midst, Frisco's Cafe,* and *Lo She Comes*) have received critical acclaim in Boston and nationally. Martin earned her MFA in playwriting from Brandeis University, where she was an Annette B. Miller fellow, artist-in-residence in the women's studies department, and recipient of the Herbert and Nancy Beigel New Play Award. She combines her artistry and love for education to serve as artistic director of Rhythm Visions Production Company, Inc., a nonprofit (founded by her in 1996) devoted to teaching, pro-ducing, elevating, and celebrating artists of color.

G.L. Morrison is a white, working-poor, righteous, left-leaning, omnivorous, vitamin-deficient, professional poet, amateur mother, publitrix of the 'zine *Poetic Licentious,* editor, writing teacher, reluctant journalist, and sometimes scrawler of fiction, essays, and bathroom graffiti. Her muse is fueled by Dr. Pepper and social injustice. An über cyberdyke, she wrangles lesbian-writers@queernet.org and L-ink@queernet.org. Her work appears in numerous print and online magazines (www.erotasy.com) and the anthologies *Early Embraces 2, Pillow Talk 2, Burning Ambitions,* and *Mom.* An award-winning playwright and poet, she is a member of the Academy of American Poets, the National Writers' Union, the Fierce Pussy Posse Cabaret Theatre Co., and the performance-poetry band Nevertheless.

Lesléa Newman is an author and editor whose 30 books include *Out of the Closet and Nothing to Wear, The Little Butch Book, The Femme Mystique, Still Life With Buddy, My Lover Is a Woman,* and *Heather Has Two Mommies.* Her newest book, *Girls Will Be Girls,* contains a novella about a therapist whose girlfriend has an affair with one of her clients. Visit her Web site at www.lesleanewman.com.

Allison J. Nichol has been widely published in journals such as *The Pegasus Review, The Rockford Review, Common Lives/Lesbian Lives, The Evergreen Chronicles,* and *Folio* and most recently in the anthologies *Family Celebrations* (Andrews McMeel, 1999), *Reclaiming the Heartland: Gay and Lesbian Voices from the Midwest* (University of Minnesota Press, 1996), and *A Loving Testimony: Remembering Loved Ones Lost to AIDS* (Crossing Press, 1995). She resides with the girl of her dreams in Washington, D.C., a city she finds both steeped in irony and decidedly lacking in whimsy.

Ellen Orleans is a longtime writer of lesbian humor, a practice that has contributed greatly to her warped, skewed, and otherwise queer view of life. Ellen is the author of a two-act play, *God, Guilt, and Gefilte Fish,* and four books, including *Who Cares If It's a Choice?* and the Lammy-winning *The Butches of Madison County.* Her latest work, *The Inflatable Butch*, is due out from Alyson Publications in 2001. Ellen is currently working on an MFA in creative writing at Goddard College in Vermont. E-mail her at eorleans@aol.com.

Meredith Pond slept with the editor to get in this book. She is between therapists right now, but after writing these stories for *Dykes With Baggage* she is beginning to believe that writing fiction is the best therapy of all. By day she is a writer-editor for a woman-owned health communications firm. For fun, she teaches College Writing's Beat Generation seminar to first-year undergrads at American University in Washington, D.C., where she earned her MFA in creative writing in 1993 and won AU's Folio Award for Poetry in 1992. She is living happily ever after with her partner (you know who) and their pets in Takoma Park, Md. Her E-mail address is pondling@erols.com.

Gina "Little Miss Sunshine" Ranalli lives in Portland, Ore., with her pet iguana, Farrah. Period.

Claire Robson showed her story to her therapist. It's hard to say what this tells us about her. Perhaps she is brave. Perhaps she has unresolved feelings that she felt unable to communicate directly to her therapist, which will necessitate many more years in therapy. Perhaps she wanted to shock her therapist to win the attention she never had as a child. Perhaps she is just a sick masochist. You know what your shrink would say: "So…what do *you* think?"

Ursula Roma is a cartoonist, illustrator, and fine craftist doing her best to live freely in Cincinnati, Ohio. Her illustrations can be seen at www.UrsulaRoma.com or you can see more cartoons by requesting them by E-mail at Romabear@aol.com.

Anne Seale, creator of lesbian songs, fiction, and plays, used to drive around the eastern United States performing original songs from her tape, *Sex for Breakfast.* She has now retired to Arizona, where she sits in the sun and writes short stories, although the glare makes it difficult to see the monitor. Her short fiction can be found in many lesbian anthologies, including *Pillow Talk 1 and 2, Love Shook My Heart, Hot and Bothered, The Ghost of Carmen Miranda, Lip Service, Wilma Loves Betty,* and the hilarious *Ex-Lover Weird Shit* (also edited by Riggin Waugh). To buy her tape ($12) or say something nice, contact her at Anne Seale, P.O. Box 56, Webster NY 14580; E-mail SFBAS@aol.com.

Pamela M. Smith lives in New Westminster, a suburb of Vancouver, B.C., Canada. Pam has had a variety of careers, from letter carrier to financial administrator to commercial helicopter pilot and currently earns her living as a flight service specialist. From her life experiences she concludes life should not be taken too seriously but with large doses of humor. She lives her credo "Don't dream it...be it." She is working on a collection of stories.

Lorrie Sprecher is the author of the novel *Sister Safety Pin* (Firebrand, 1994). She lives in Santa Barbara in the land of California, where she is writing and rehearsing with her band, The Daydream Believers. For more information about their upcoming CD or to get on their E-mail list, contact Lorrie at kurtrat@aol.com. Also, visit The Daydream Believers on the Web at www.onlinerock.com/musicians/lorrie/index.html.

T.O. Sylvester is a pseudonym for Sylvia Mollick, artist, and Terry Ryan, writer, who have been a cartooning team for more than two decades. Their literary cartoons ran weekly in the *San Francisco Chronicle* for 16 years (1983-1999). Their single-panel cartoons have also appeared in other sections of the *Chronicle* and in the pages of *Ms., Mother Jones, Saturday Evening Post, Saturday Review, Boy's Life, Datamation, Vegetarian Times, The Bay Guardian, San Francisco Magazine, The Advocate, Gay Comics, Women's Glib* cartoon calendars, and a number of textbooks and anthologies. In 1993, their cartoons were featured in a three-month exhibit at the Cartoon Art Museum in San Francisco.

Laura A. Vess is better known to various people as "Alex" the leather-clad bar goddess, "AlexiV" the Internet junkie, and "Housedyke" the laundry-doer. She keeps trying to convince her latest therapist that she does not suffer from "multiples"; she is just weird. This is her third piece published with Alyson, and she is much better now, really. Though if you visit her Web site, StrangeGirl.cjb.net, you might disagree.

Riggin Waugh was born in Washington, D.C., during the Eisenhower administration. Her work has been widely anthologized. She has spent the past few years rewriting Dr. Seuss for lesbians and getting her MFA in creative writing at American University in Washington, D.C. She makes her home with her beloved and their pets in Takoma Park, Md. The first anthology Riggin edited—*Ex-Lover Weird Shit: A Collection of Short Fiction, Poetry, and Cartoons by Lesbians and Gay Men*—is available at better bookstores or by contacting LezTherapy@aol.com.

Sue Weaver was born in Waco, Tex., which explains a lot. She graduated from the University of Texas at Austin in 1987 and has been on the move ever since. Sue taught English in Japan for five years, then went to England and married the woman of her dreams to live out the rest of her days in domestic bliss. She now lives alone in Madison, Wis., where she writes short stories and overwaters her houseplants. Sue is also working on a novel.

Julia Willis is the author of four books, including the comic novel *Reel Time* (Alyson, 1998). She's been in therapy twice, and she often wonders if her sessions might have gone better had she been carrying a sword, like Xena.

Judith K. Witherow was born in 1944 in the Pennsylvania Appalachians. A mixed-blood Cherokee, Seminole, and Irish lesbian, she was raised in rural poverty. Judith has many illnesses, including multiple sclerosis and systemic lupus. Judith is a storyteller, writer, and poet, and the winner of the first annual Audre Lorde Memorial Prose Contest for Non-Fiction, April 1994. To date no one has approached her about her trapping and relocating squirrels as a means of therapy, but she remains optimistic.

Cassendre Xavier (Aquarian Sun, Libra Moon, Cancer Rising) is a Haitian-American multimedia "artivist" (which combines "artist" and "activist." Isn't that clever?!) and events promoter. She's a deeply spiritual member of the BDSM community working on increasing a vegan sensibility among leatherfolk. She collects books, exotic soaps, and candles. A chyk with a wicked goatee, Cassendre considers her ideal therapy these days to be getting horizontal with cats Dylan, Perseus, and Misha with as many books as can fit in their single bed. She has never had a cavity. E-mail: cx321@hotmail.com; Web site: www.cassendrexavier.com.

Yvonne Zipter is the author of the essay collection *Ransacking the Closet;* the nonfiction study *Diamonds Are a Dyke's Best Friend;* the poetry collection *The Patience of Metal,* which was a Lambda Literary Award finalist and runner-up for the Poetry Society of America's Melville Cane Award; and the nationally syndicated column "Inside Out." Her poems and essays have been published in numerous periodicals and anthologies. She is the recipient of a Sprague/Todes Literary Award and holds an MFA in writing from Vermont College. She lives in Chicago with her longtime partner Kathy Forde, who is her best therapy ever.

Zonna is 39, bisexual, and living in New York. Can you tell from her accent? She's had stories published in anthologies by Alyson (*Skin Deep*) and Arsenal Press (*Hot & Bothered II*). You can also find her work on the Web. When she isn't writing—lesbian vampire stories, erotica, novels, and dyke dramas—she performs as an out musician, as she's done for the past ten years. Never one to keep a low profile, she believes in visibility and refuses to write the story of her life in invisible ink.

Credits

Grateful acknowledgment is made for permission to use the following previously published material.

Alison Bechdel—#73, "The Session," first appeared in *New, Improved! Dykes to Watch Out For* by Alison Bechdel (Ithaca, NY: Firebrand Books), 1990. #97, "Emotional Energy," and #112, "50 Minutes," first appeared in *Dykes to Watch Out For: The Sequel*, by Alison Bechdel (Ithaca, NY: Firebrand Books), 1992.

Jane Caminos's "We've covered why I can't and why I can…" first appeared in *That's Ms. Bulldyke to You, Charlie*, cartoons by Jane Caminos (Northboro, Mass.: Madwoman Press), 1992.

Kelli S. Dunham's "Crazy Is as Crazy Does" first appeared in *Au Courant* (newspaper), October 26, 1998.

Diane F. Germain's "Lesbian Intellectuals Anonymous" first appeared in *HOT WIRE: The Journal of Women's Music and Culture*, July 1988. "Gwen explains…" first appeared in *Yoni* (newsletter), August 1988.

Kris Kovick's "Leather Jacket," "Transference," "Tomboy," and "My Shrink" first appeared in *What I Love About Lesbian Politics Is Arguing With People I Agree With*, cartoons and essays by Kris Kovick (Boston: Alyson Publications), 1991.

Ellen Orleans's "Affirmations in Action" first appeared in *Can't Keep a Straight Face*, by Ellen Orleans (Bala Cynwyd, Penn.: Laugh Lines Press), 1993.

Renita Martin's "Five Bottles in a Six-Pack" is an excerpt from a one-woman show, which Renita first performed at the Boston Center for the Arts in 1999.

Claire Robson's "Art Cannot Hurt You" first appeared in *Silver Web*, Issue 14, 1997.

Ursula Roma's "She Decided to Leave Her Baggage Behind" first appeared as a postcard.

Lorrie Sprecher's "Therapy Pride," "Beyond the Pleasure Principle," "The Interpretation of Dreams," and "I Tell Her Everything, She Tells Me Nothing" first appeared in *Anxiety Attack*, by Lorrie Sprecher (Ithaca, NY: Violet Ink), 1992.

T.O. Sylvester's "Gertrude Stein After Therapy" and "Interview With Mary's Little Lamb in Therapy" first appeared in the *San Francisco Chronicle*, June 8, 1997, and December 10, 1995, respectively.

Yvonne Zipter's "Adventures in TherapyLand" first appeared in *Ransacking the Closet*, by Yvonne Zipter (Duluth, Minn.: Spinsters Ink), 1995.

Mary Beth O'Connor

About the Editor

Riggin Waugh is the author of the audio collection *Homo Neurotica and Other Short Stories* and the editor of the Lambda Literary Award-nominated *Ex-Lover Weird Shit: A Collection of Short Fiction, Poetry, and Cartoons by Lesbians and Gay Men*. She lives in Takoma Park, Md.